continued . . .

MURDER ON SISTERS' ROW

A Gaslight Mystery

Victoria Thompson

BERKLEY PRIME CRIME, NEW YORK

THE BERKLEY PUBLISHING GROUP
Published by the Penguin Group
Penguin Group (USA) LLC
375 Hudson Street, New York, New York 10014

USA • Canada • UK • Ireland • Australia • New Zealand • India • South Africa • China

penguin.com

A Penguin Random House Company

MURDER ON SISTERS' ROW

A Berkley Prime Crime Book / published by arrangement with the author

Berkley Prime Crime Books are published by The Berkley Publishing Group.
BERKLEY® PRIME CRIME and the PRIME CRIME logo are
trademarks of Penguin Group (USA) LLC.

For information, address: The Berkley Publishing Group,
a division of Penguin Group (USA) LLC,
375 Hudson Street, New York, New York 10014.

ISBN: 978-0-425-24800-3

PUBLISHING HISTORY
Berkley Prime Crime hardcover edition / June 2011
Berkley Prime Crime mass-market edition / May 2012

PRINTED IN THE UNITED STATES OF AMERICA

15 14 13 12 11 10 9 8 7 6 5 4

Cover illustration by Karen Chandler.
Cover design by Rita Frangie.

To Roselyn and Rosanna,
who taught me the true meaning of charity

I

SARAH AND THE GIRLS WERE STROLLING BACK FROM THE Gansevoort Market, thoroughly enjoying the crisp fall morning and chatting happily about the purchases piled high in the large baskets Sarah and Maeve carried over their arms.

"Oh, no," Maeve said when they'd turned the corner onto Bank Street and saw the carriage parked in front of Sarah's house. "Looks like you won't be helping us bake any pies this afternoon."

The carriage most likely meant that someone had come to fetch Sarah to deliver a baby.

"I'm sure you and Catherine will do just fine without me," Sarah said, looking down at the small girl who clung to her free hand. Her foster daughter looked up, her eyes full of disappointment.

"I'll miss you," Catherine said in her whispery voice.

When Sarah had first found her at the Prodigal Son Mission, Catherine had been completely mute. She'd only started speaking a few months ago, and she still spoke softly, as if afraid of startling herself with the sound of her own voice.

"I'll miss you, too. You know I'd much rather spend my days with you and Maeve, but I have to help ladies have their babies. That's how I earn the money we need to buy things with."

"I know," Catherine said, but she stuck her lip out in an unmistakable pout.

"We'll ask Mrs. Ellsworth to help us with the pies," Maeve said, naming their next-door neighbor. Mrs. Ellsworth was always available to help the girls do anything at all.

Mention of Mrs. Ellsworth banished Catherine's pout. Maeve knew just how to cheer her up. Sarah thought for at least the thousandth time how fortunate she was to have Maeve as Catherine's nursemaid. The girl had also come from the Mission, and the three of them had formed a real family in the months they'd been together.

A young man stood beside the carriage, and he straightened as they approached. He'd been smoking a cigarette, and he tossed it away. He wore a uniform of some kind, and he looked quite dignified when he put his mind to it, although Sarah noticed that he gave Maeve a very efficient once-over. He managed not to be offensive about it, though.

"Can I help you?" Sarah asked when they were close enough for conversation.

"Are you Mrs. Brandt, the midwife?"

"Yes, I am."

"I been sent to get you. Mrs. Walker, the lady I work for, she said to come quick. If you'd be so kind," he added awkwardly, remembering his manners.

"Is Mrs. Walker having a baby?"

Something about that question amused the young man, although he controlled his expression almost instantly. "No, ma'am. One of her guests is."

Sarah glanced at the carriage and the horses. The horses were well fed and groomed, the carriage clean and in good repair. Not a rented outfit but one owned by someone who had the means to care for it. "I'll be right with you. I just need to get my things. Would you like to wait inside?"

He looked at Maeve again, as if weighing her attractions against his own responsibilities. "I'd better stay with the horses," he decided.

They went into Sarah's house, and a few minutes later, Sarah came out carrying her black bag, the medical bag that had belonged to her husband, Dr. Tom Brandt, dead now for well over four years.

The young man hurried to carry the bag for her, but Sarah didn't release it when he reached for it. "It's usually faster if I walk," she said. "Because of the traffic. Unless it's too far."

"Mrs. Walker said you was to come in the carriage. She's very particular, and I wouldn't want to make her mad."

And Sarah wouldn't want to get him in trouble. "All right, but if we get stuck, I'll get out and walk the rest of the way. Where are we going?"

The question seemed to alarm him, but he recovered quickly. "We won't get stuck. We don't have far to go. Just a few blocks north."

He helped her into the carriage, and she placed the medical bag on the floor at her feet. Then he closed the door and hurried to climb up to the driver's perch. Only when the door was closed did Sarah notice the curtains had all been drawn over the windows. She pulled back the one at the window beside her to let in some light to relieve the gloom. Then she leaned back on the cushioned seat and tried to relax. This would probably be the last time she got a moment's peace for at least twenty-four hours. She closed her eyes, hoping to catch a brief nap before she reached her destination, or at least to rest a bit.

Sarah was surprised to be awakened when the carriage rattled to a stop. She really had dozed off for a little while. Disoriented, she looked out the window she had uncovered and saw she was in an alley behind some large houses. The carriage shifted on its springs as the driver climbed down. A moment later, he opened the door and helped her out, taking her bag from her.

"This way," he said and directed her to precede him down the walkway that bisected the small patch of weedy ground that formed a backyard of sorts for one of the houses. It led to a porch and a kitchen door. A large Negro woman stood in the open doorway. She wore a bright red bandanna tied around her head, and her enormous apron was stained. Her hands were planted firmly on her broad hips, and her expression said she was furious.

"Took you long enough," she said to the young man.

"She was out. I had to wait for her to get back, didn't I?" he said.

The woman made a rude sound and stood back so Sarah could enter the kitchen. It was a large, untidy room. The wooden table in the middle of the floor was covered with flour and mounds of dough, where she had been working on some pastries.

The cook looked Sarah up and down, withholding her approval. "You the midwife?"

"Yes, I am," Sarah said. "Can you show me where to go?"

"Take her upstairs, Jake, and show her Amy's room. Mrs. Walker's up there with her."

"I gotta take care of the horses. Take her up yourself," Jake said. He thrust Sarah's bag at the cook and stomped out again.

Sarah smiled apologetically at the woman. "If you'll just direct me . . ." she began, but the woman was already marching through the kitchen, muttering to herself.

"Miz Walker'd have my hide if I let you be wandering around by yourself. I don't know what's got into that boy. He knows my rheumatism been bad lately. I can't hardly walk, and now he expects me to go upstairs." The cook pulled open a door on the other side of the kitchen and revealed the narrow back stairs that the servants would use. "Watch yourself on these stairs," she warned. "Miz Walker'll have my hide if you falls down and hurts yourself. Come on now. Miss Amy'll be getting anxious, I expect. Don't know what got into that girl to go and have a baby for anyways. Foolishness, it is, but you can't tell young people anything nowadays."

For all her complaining, the cook made short work of the stairs. Sarah had to hurry to keep up with her. The door at the top opened into a hallway lined with about half a dozen doors, all of them closed.

"Be quiet now," the cook warned. "All the other ladies is still sleeping, though I don't expect they'll be sleeping long once Miss Amy gets started good. I reckon she'll shout the house down, don't you?"

Sarah didn't offer an opinion, although she felt reasonably certain the woman was correct. She had a moment of confusion at the thought of the "other ladies" still being asleep until she recalled that when she'd still lived in her parents' house as a member of one of the wealthiest families in New York City, she'd always slept late, too. It was a natural consequence of late-night social gatherings.

They moved quickly down the hallway to the third door. The cook knocked once and then opened it without waiting for a response. "This here's the midwife," she announced, plunked down Sarah's bag, and stood back for Sarah to enter before making her escape back down the hall.

The curtains were drawn, so Sarah needed a moment to get her bearings in the dimness. She found herself in a lavishly furnished bedroom. An enormous four-poster bed draped with netting, piled high with bedclothes, and skirted with royal blue satin flounces dominated the room. She saw an elaborate dressing table covered with all sorts of bottles and jars, and a wardrobe with one door ajar and a riot of petticoats hanging out of it. At the far end of the room stood a chaise and a pair of upholstered chairs in a grouping, as if for conversation. A woman had been sitting in one of the chairs, and now she was up and walking to greet Sarah.

"Mrs. Brandt?" she said. "I'm Rowena Walker. I'm so grateful you could come." She looked to be about forty, but Sarah couldn't judge accurately in the dim light. Her voice was well modulated and cultured, and she wore a housedress of rose pique, something Sarah's mother might have worn to breakfast except for the excess of lace trimmings at the throat and cuffs.

"I'm glad I was available." Sarah heard a moan and turned toward the bed, where she could now see a woman lay amid the confusion of satin coverlet, pillows, and sheets. "Is this my patient?"

"Yes, young Amy. This is her first."

Sarah went over to the bed and greeted the young woman

with a smile. Amy looked as if she might be about twenty and quite attractive under other circumstances. At the moment, she was moaning, her face twisted in pain, and her golden blond hair ratty and tangled. Her nightdress was silk, Sarah saw with surprise, and cut unusually low in the front. It was stretched taut over her rounded belly.

"Help me," the girl begged, grabbing Sarah's hand. "Please, get it out of me!"

"We'll have to wait for the baby to come out on his own, I'm afraid, but I can help you be more comfortable while it's happening."

"Just tell me what you need," Mrs. Walker said, "and I'll have Beulah get it for you."

Sarah requested a rubber undersheet and clean sheets to start. In a few minutes Beulah, the cook, brought them. Sarah got Amy out of bed and helped Beulah change it. Although this took only a few minutes, Amy began complaining almost immediately.

"I have to lay down. I can't stand this pain! Give me some laudanum or something!"

Sarah left Beulah to finish the bed and hurried over to where Amy was reclining on the chaise. "You shouldn't take any laudanum," she cautioned. "It can affect the baby."

"I don't care about the baby," Amy insisted. "I can't stand this any longer!"

"What an awful thing to say, Amy," Mrs. Walker said, glancing at Sarah with an embarrassed shrug. "You don't mean that, and of course you can stand it. Thousands of women before you have stood it, and you will, too."

"I promised I could make you more comfortable," Sarah said. "The first thing we need to do is get you up and walking around."

"Walking around?" Amy fairly screeched. "How can that make me more comfortable?"

"It will make your labor go faster. And do you have a . . . a *plainer* nightdress? One that's looser? This one is so pretty, it's a pity to get it stained," Sarah added tactfully.

The young woman looked at Sarah for a long moment, as if she were seeing her for the first time. Then she threw back her head and started laughing hysterically.

Sarah's mind was racing, frantically trying to decide what to do, but before she could, Mrs. Walker drew back her arm and slapped the girl smartly across the face. Sarah cried out in protest, but neither of the other women appeared to notice. Amy's laughter ceased abruptly, and she stared at Mrs. Walker with mingled surprise and . . . Sarah needed a moment to identify the other emotion she saw in Amy's clear blue eyes: fear.

The girl reached up and cradled her cheek and whispered, "I'm sorry."

"You should be. Now stop acting like a child. Mrs. Brandt will lose patience with you and leave, and then what will you do? You can't have this baby on your own, you know."

Amy turned to Sarah in alarm. "I'm sorry," she repeated, more fervently this time. "Don't leave."

"I'm not going to leave," Sarah assured her. "But you need to do what I tell you. I've delivered hundreds of babies, and you have to trust that I know what I'm doing."

The girl glanced at Mrs. Walker, who was still glaring at her. Amy turned back to Sarah. "I'll do what you say. I don't have another nightdress, though. A plainer one, I mean."

"That's all right. I meant what I said about walking. It will make the baby come faster. Your mother and I can take turns walking with you."

"My *mother?*" she echoed in surprise, looking at Mrs. Walker.

Mrs. Walker smiled rather stiffly. "I think she means me," she said, an odd expression on her face. "I'm not her mother," she told Sarah, "just her . . . hostess. She boards here, you see."

"I'm sorry," Sarah said. "I misunderstood." Now she recalled that Jake had said one of Mrs. Walker's *guests* was having a baby. She should have remembered that.

"That's quite all right," Mrs. Walker said.

"I don't think I've ever seen a boardinghouse this . . ." Sarah groped for the right word, not certain how to say what she was thinking without giving offense.

"Fancy?" Amy offered, earning a disapproving glare from Mrs. Walker.

"Yes," Sarah agreed.

"Mrs. Walker does run a *fancy house*," Amy said with mock innocence.

Some silent communication passed between Mrs. Walker and Amy, a warning of sorts, and then Amy clutched her stomach and moaned again.

"Let's get you up and walking," Sarah said when the contraction had passed.

For at least an hour, Sarah and Mrs. Walker took turns holding Amy's arm as she paced around the room. During that time Sarah asked her questions about her health and the progress of the pregnancy and the details of her labor thus far. One thing she didn't learn about was the baby's father. No one had mentioned him at all. Beulah had remarked that the other *ladies* were still sleeping, indicating the other boarders were all female. Sarah began to wonder if Mrs. Walker was actually running a refuge for other girls like

Amy, unmarried girls from good families who had gotten with child and needed a place to have their babies secretly. She'd heard of such places, but she'd never been called to one before. She had always assumed they had arrangements with midwives whom they knew and trusted. She wondered why she'd been chosen today.

Beulah brought them some luncheon, an elegant arrangement of sandwiches and tea cakes. Amy could manage only a few bites, but Sarah ate heartily, not sure when she'd have another chance. Mrs. Walker nibbled a bit, but she seemed preoccupied.

When Beulah came to remove the tray, a young woman appeared in the open doorway. She was about Amy's age, barefoot, and clad only in a silk nightdress like Amy's, her dark hair tied up in rags, the way girls did to make it curl. Her eyes were still heavy with sleep as she peered into the room.

"Is the baby coming?" she asked of no one in particular.

Amy paused in her pacing and groaned, clutching her stomach as another contraction seized her.

"What does it look like?" Mrs. Walker snapped. "Go on and mind your own business, Dolly."

The girl sniffed, offended. "I was just trying to be friendly."

"Be friendly someplace else," Mrs. Walker said.

The girl turned with a toss of her head, but the flopping rags spoiled the effect. Only when she was gone did Sarah realize that she didn't look as if she were with child. Of course, she might not be showing yet. Some women didn't begin to show until late in the pregnancy, especially with their first baby. Perhaps even more curious was Mrs. Walker's rudeness to the girl. Somehow Sarah would have expected a "hostess" to be kinder to the unfortunate girls in her care.

After an hour of walking, Amy wanted to rest for a while. Sarah helped her lie down on the chaise lounge.

"I could brush your hair out for you, if you like," Sarah offered. "We should probably braid it so it's easier to manage."

"I'm not going to braid my hair," Amy snapped. "It'll look like a washboard!"

"Don't be rude," Mrs. Walker warned her. "Mrs. Brandt is only trying to help. It won't matter anyway. No one will see you for a while. Let her braid it."

Once again Amy's gaze glinted with what could have been fear, but only for a moment. Then she turned to Sarah. "All right," she said grudgingly, then grimaced as another contraction claimed her.

Sarah got a brush from the dressing table, and when the contraction was over, she began to brush the tangles out of Amy's hair. Unlike the other girl, Dolly, Amy had natural curls that needed only a little encouragement to appear out of the rat's nest her hair had become. Sarah found some stray hairpins in the mess and set them aside. Amy had obviously not used any care when she took her hair down the last time.

"Oh, that feels so good," Amy said after a few minutes. "My mother always made me cry when she brushed out the rats."

"You have beautiful hair. I can see why you don't want to braid it," Sarah said, remembering her childhood and the way her braided hair would hold the crinkly waves for days after being undone. "If you have a hairnet or something, we can tie it up instead of braiding it."

"I think there's one in the top drawer in the dressing table," Amy said.

Sarah found it jumbled in with the various odds and ends Amy had stuffed into the drawer. She worked it free and found it reasonably intact. In another minute, she'd gathered Amy's fall of hair securely into it and out of the way.

"How much longer is it going to take?" Amy asked as she relaxed again after another contraction.

"Hours yet, I'm afraid."

"Hours?" Amy said, her voice rising until she caught the warning look from Mrs. Walker. She clamped her mouth shut. "I guess I better walk some more then."

She and Sarah began the circuit around the room again. Mrs. Walker sat and observed them, her patience apparently endless. Didn't she have anything better to do than watch over Amy? If Sarah hadn't seen the way Amy reacted to her, she'd think Mrs. Walker genuinely cared for the girl or at least felt a responsibility for her. But no, she gave no indication of any tender emotion at all. She just sat, more like a reluctant chaperone than a concerned friend.

When Amy tired again, Sarah rubbed her feet and legs, using a lavender-scented lotion she found on the dressing table.

"Have you decided on names yet?" Sarah asked as she massaged Amy's swollen ankles.

Oddly, Amy glanced at Mrs. Walker before answering, almost as if she were silently asking approval or perhaps checking to make sure she didn't *disapprove*. Whatever the reason, her expression was guarded when she looked back at Sarah.

"No, I . . . I haven't."

"She wants to wait until she sees if it's a boy or a girl," Mrs. Walker said. "Don't you, dear?"

"Yes, that's it," Amy agreed quickly. Too quickly.

Sarah knew she was lying, but she couldn't imagine why she would lie about such an ordinary thing. Unless . . .

Of course. If Amy was an unwed mother, she wouldn't be able to keep her baby. The whole point of coming to a place like this to give birth in secret was so no one would know about her transgression. Bringing a baby home with her would defeat the whole purpose. Her friends probably thought she was on a trip someplace far away. When she returned, she'd tell stories about the wonderful adventure she'd had, but she couldn't bring a baby back as a souvenir.

No, her family had probably already made some kind of arrangements. Perhaps a distant relative would adopt the child. Then Amy might see it from time to time and know it was all right and loved and cared for properly. Or maybe they intended to send it to a foundling home, where its future was more uncertain. Perhaps a loving couple would adopt the baby and give it a good home. Or maybe it would grow up in an orphanage, unwanted and unloved. Or maybe it wouldn't grow up at all. Abandoned infants sometimes died of disease or neglect.

All these possibilities went through Sarah's mind in a matter of seconds as she finished up the foot massage. A wave of pity for the girl washed over Sarah.

"Why don't you try to get some sleep before the contractions get worse," she suggested.

"Worse! Are you saying they're going to get *worse*!" Amy cried, tears springing to her eyes.

Mrs. Walker was on her feet in an instant. "Of course they are, you silly girl. Don't you know anything? Now do as Mrs. Brandt said and get some rest. You won't do anybody any good if you wear yourself out."

Amy's full lips tightened into a thin, white line, as if she were biting back words she didn't dare say. She let Sarah help her up from the chaise and lead her over to the bed and tuck her in. Sarah had her roll over onto her side, and Sarah gently rubbed the small of her back until she dozed off.

Sarah went back to the chaise and took this opportunity to get some rest herself. She stretched out, glad to be off her feet for a few minutes. Mrs. Walker still sat perfectly straight in one of the chairs, her gaze wandering to Amy every few minutes, as if to make sure she hadn't disappeared.

"You really don't have to wait here," Sarah said softly, so as not to wake Amy. "You probably have things to do, and the baby won't be here for hours, maybe not until morning. I can send for you when it's getting close."

Mrs. Walker folded her well-tended hands in her lap and gave Sarah a long, steady stare. "I couldn't leave Amy at a time like this. Beulah can take care of things for me."

"Suit yourself, but if you don't mind, I'll try to rest a bit while Amy's asleep."

"Suit yourself," Mrs. Walker echoed sarcastically.

What an odd woman, Sarah thought, but she didn't think about it for long. She closed her eyes and emptied her mind, a trick she'd used many times to force a catnap.

She was at a concert. A musicale at her mother's house. Some of her old friends were there, and someone was playing the piano. She couldn't hear it very well. She needed to get closer so she could hear the music, but every time she tried, someone stopped her and wanted to talk. They wanted to know the name of Amy's baby and where her husband was. Sarah didn't know, but they kept asking her anyway. They seemed angry when she couldn't tell them, but she didn't care. She wanted to hear the music. She could see the piano now and the man playing. His back was to her, but she knew him just the same. She didn't even know he could play the piano. She reached out to touch his shoulder and called his name.

"Frank."

Sarah awoke with a start, disoriented and aware that she'd spoken aloud. She needed a moment to remember where she was. Then she quickly sat up and looked around to get her bearings. Amy was moaning softly. Mrs. Walker was sitting exactly where she'd been, and she was looking at Sarah curiously. She probably wondered who Frank was. Sarah had no intention of enlightening her.

"I should check on Amy." Sarah got up and saw that the girl was awake.

"I think I wet the bed," she said in alarm.

"Don't worry. It's just your water breaking," Sarah said with relief. "That's why we put the rubber sheet on the bed. Things should go faster now."

Mrs. Walker rang for Beulah to change the sheets again, and Sarah helped Amy get up and change her nightdress. The new one was just as impractical as the old one. While they were waiting for Beulah, Sarah realized the piano music from her dream was real. "Who's that playing the piano?" she asked.

"One of the girls," Mrs. Walker said quickly. "They have some guests this evening."

How odd that they'd be entertaining in a place like this. But perhaps family members came to visit the girls. Sarah imagined they would get lonely, being confined here for months.

Beulah arrived and helped Sarah change the sheets again.

"How are things going?" Sarah heard Mrs. Walker ask the cook while she was helping Amy get settled again.

"Just fine. The girls is taking care of everything."

"If there's any trouble, come get me."

"Won't be no trouble. I'll see to that. You want some supper now?"

Mrs. Walker said they did, and a few minutes later, Beulah brought up some roast beef with rich gravy, potatoes baked in their skins, apple dumplings, and coffee. The roast beef was remarkably tender. Her neighbor Mrs. Ellsworth would want to speak to the cook about how she'd managed it.

Sarah encouraged Amy to eat, but she said the smell was making her sick, and she didn't even try.

The piano stopped for a while, then started again. The hours slipped by. Amy walked for a while, then rested and walked some more. Sarah thought she heard voices in the hall, a man and woman laughing, but the sound was probably coming up from downstairs. Sarah thought it odd that the young ladies were permitted to have visitors so late, but Mrs. Walker didn't seem concerned.

Amy paused and grabbed hold of one of the bedposts as a contraction seized her, and Sarah glanced over at Mrs. Walker. The older woman had finally nodded off. Her chin rested on her chest, and she was snoring softly.

As Amy straightened, Sarah nodded at where Mrs. Walker was dozing in the chair. To Sarah's surprise, Amy grabbed her arm.

"You have to get me out of here," she whispered urgently.

"You can't go anywhere right now," Sarah said in surprise. "You're going to have a baby any time."

"No, no, not now!" she said, her fingers digging painfully into Sarah's arm and her blue eyes filled with anguish. "After the baby's born. I have to get out of here! You have to help me."

Sarah couldn't understand her distress. "But won't they let you go home after the baby is born?"

Amy's eyes widened in surprise. "No, they'll never let me leave here, not ever. They'll kill me if I try!"

"*What?*" This made no sense. Why would they kill her?

Amy's anxious gaze kept darting to Mrs. Walker, checking to make sure she was still asleep. "They're going to take the baby away and then——" Her words twisted into a cry as an especially strong contraction claimed her, and she doubled over with the pain.

The cry woke Mrs. Walker, who snorted in surprise and jumped to her feet. "What is it?"

"Something's wrong!" Amy said, her eyes wild with fear.

"Do you feel like you need to bear down?" Sarah asked.

"Yes, yes, that's it! What's happening?"

Sarah smiled. "Your baby is coming, that's what's happening. It's time to start pushing. Come on, I'll show you just what to do."

Sarah got Amy back into the bed and gave her the necessary instructions. Sarah had fashioned fabric loops attached to the headboard that the girl could hold on to as she bore down. In a few minutes she was laboring in earnest, falling back against the pillows propped against the headboard and gasping between contractions.

"It won't be long now," Sarah said, and lifted Amy's nightdress to check on her progress. "Look, Mrs. Walker, you can see the top of the baby's head."

The unflappable Mrs. Walker looked, and all the color drained from her face. Sarah hurried to grab her in case she fainted, but she turned away, both hands clamped over her mouth.

"Are you all right?" Sarah asked.

"Yes, I . . . I just . . . I'll go and get Beulah. She can help you." She hurried to the door and in another second she was gone.

"Close the door, quick, before Beulah comes," Amy whispered. "I have to tell you what to do!"

Sarah hurried to close the door, and Amy was already instructing her before she started back to the bed.

"You have to help me get away from this place. You have to contact Mrs. Van Orner."

The name was familiar, but Sarah couldn't place it. "Is she a relative?"

"No, no!" Amy said desperately. Then a contraction started, and she couldn't talk.

Sarah supported her through it, and as soon as she could speak again, she said, "Mrs. Van Orner helps girls like me. Tell her I want to be rescued. She'll know what to do."

"If you want to leave here, I'll help you," Sarah said. "As soon as the baby is born, I can take you to my house for a few days and—"

"No, no! You can't help me. They'd never let you take me. They'd kill you!"

"Who'd kill me?" Sarah asked in confusion, wondering if Amy had lost her senses.

"Jake will. Mrs. Walker will tell him to. They never let any of us leave, and I hate it here! I hate what I have to do, and after they take the baby, they're going to make me do the most disgusting things!"

"Amy, what are you talking about? What kinds of things do they make you do?"

"With the men," she gasped, going into another contraction. "With the customers!"

Customers? Sarah's head was spinning. Suddenly, all the

little things that hadn't made sense before came together. The piano music. The company that stayed very late. The man's voice. The large, fancy house full of young women. The hostess wasn't a hostess at all. She was a *madam*!

"Is this a brothel?" Sarah asked, feeling incredibly stupid.

"Of course!" Amy panted, falling back against the headboard again. "What did you think?"

"I thought it was a refuge for unwed mothers."

Amy gave a bark of bitter laughter.

The door opened. Beulah came in and looked around. "Miz Walker said you was about to pop that baby out."

"Yes, she is," Sarah said, managing to regain her composure.

"What do you need me to do?"

"You don't have to do anything," Sarah said quickly, wondering if she'd be as weak stomached as Mrs. Walker. "And don't watch if you don't want to."

"Ain't nothing I ain't seen before," she said, stepping to the foot of the bed as Sarah checked Amy's progress again. "Oh, look there. You'll have that baby out in a couple more tries."

"Really?" Amy asked desperately.

"Yes, really," Sarah said. "Push really hard this next time."

Amy did, and just as Beulah had predicted, she pushed out her son just a few minutes later.

Sarah held him upside down by his ankles and cleared his mouth with her finger. She didn't even need to slap him. He started screaming bloody murder all on his own. "Listen to that, Amy," she said. "A healthy boy!" Sarah turned him upright and held him out for his mother to see.

Amy stared at him from where she lay against the headboard. Her hair was matted with sweat, and her face was red from exertion, but her eyes glowed with some inner fire. Not the pride or the joy Sarah usually saw from new mothers, but something primal and raw, something almost angry.

"Cut that cord so I can take care of the baby," Beulah said.

Sarah looked up in alarm. "You're not going to take him away, are you?"

"Lord, no, whatever give you an idea like that?" she asked in genuine surprise. "I just wanna get him cleaned up for his mama."

Sarah turned to Amy, who nodded almost imperceptibly. Sarah took care of the cord and placed him in the blanket Beulah held out. The cook took him over and laid him on the chaise, where she started to clean him up. Meanwhile, Sarah helped Amy deliver the afterbirth and got her cleaned up and comfortable again.

"Here now," Beulah said, bringing the swaddled infant back over to the bed. "You wanna put him to the breast right away. We wanna get your milk started real good."

Amy's face looked as if it had been carved in stone. She took the baby, but she didn't look at him. She was glaring at Beulah.

"Don't look at me like that, girl," the cook said. "Ain't my fault you got yourself in trouble. Now you gotta do what you gotta do."

"Why don't you go tell Mrs. Walker that the baby is born?" Sarah suggested, wanting a few more minutes with Amy. "I'm sure she'll want to see for herself."

Beulah sniffed, aware that Sarah was trying to get rid of her, but she left, closing the door behind her.

Sarah turned back to Amy, who still wasn't looking at her baby.

"Do you know how to find Mrs. Van Orner?" the girl

asked. "Mrs. Gregory Van Orner. She helps prostitutes get out of the life. The girls all talk about her."

"I told you, I can help you."

"No, you can't. It's too dangerous. Mrs. Van Orner has people who help her, though. She knows how to do it. Can you find her?"

"Yes, I think I can." Sarah had heard about the women who did that kind of work. "But what about the baby? You said they were going to take him away."

"They'll let me keep it for a few days. They want my milk to come in. Some of the customers like that," she said, her lip curling in distaste.

Sarah felt nauseated, but she swallowed it down. "I'll do whatever I can to help you get out of here."

2

WHEN THE DOOR OPENED AGAIN, MRS. WALKER STEPPED into the room. She'd recovered somewhat from her earlier unease. She glanced at Amy, who, after instruction from Sarah, had started nursing her baby. Then she looked at Sarah, who made no effort to hide her anger.

"I see you finally figured it out," Mrs. Walker said.

"I don't appreciate being tricked."

"I needed a midwife, and you wouldn't have come to a whorehouse," Mrs. Walker said with a shrug.

"I've never refused to help any woman."

Mrs. Walker didn't seem to care if that was true or not. "I guess you want to leave now."

"I'll stay until I'm sure Amy is all right. And I'll need to come back again to check on her in a day or so."

"If you're willing to come, you're welcome. I don't want anything to happen to her."

"You're very kind," Sarah said sarcastically.

"No, I'm not," Mrs. Walker said. "I'm practical. Amy is very valuable to me. I take good care of all my girls." She gave Amy a meaningful look. "Even when they lie to me."

Amy simply glared back at her.

"Ring for Beulah when you're ready to leave," Mrs. Walker told Sarah. "She'll pay you and have Jake bring the carriage around to take you home."

When Mrs. Walker was gone, Sarah realized she hadn't bothered to even notice the baby. Obviously, he meant nothing to her.

"Amy, they can't keep you here against your will," Sarah said. "You have the right to leave."

Amy looked at her as if she'd lost her mind. "Of course they can keep me here. You should see what they do to girls who try to leave on their own. You can't get far, not alone with no money, and they never let us have any of the money we earn. So they always catch you and bring you back. They only have to beat up one girl and let the others see it. Then nobody ever tries to get away again."

Sarah swallowed down her outrage. She needed to be practical, like Mrs. Walker. "Do you have any idea how long they'll let you keep your baby?"

"No. I heard Mrs. Walker telling Beulah the other day to watch for when my milk came in. I don't know how long that takes, though."

"A few days, maybe a week. Do you know where they'll take the baby?"

"No, I don't know anything. And if they take it before Mrs. Van Orner can get me out of here, how will I find it again?" She looked down in dismay at the baby nursing hungrily at her breast. So far, Sarah hadn't seen her show any tenderness toward the boy, so Sarah was glad to see her showing some concern at last.

"I could offer to take him," Sarah realized. "I know a place where he'd be safe. It's a mission, a refuge for young girls. They'd take good care of him."

"A mission? They're church people then?"

"Yes, they're Christians. They think it's their duty to take care of the poor."

Amy didn't like it, but she really had few options. "Do you think they'll keep him until I come for him?"

"I'll make sure they do. Now tell me everything you know about this Mrs. Van Orner. You said all the girls know about her?"

"Yes, they talk about her. She has a group of friends, and they go into a house like this and rescue the girls who want to leave. The trouble is, nobody knows how to get a message to her."

"I'll do that for you. I'm sure I can find out how to get in touch with her."

"I think she has an office in a building someplace with a lot of other do-gooders. That's what I've heard anyway."

"Oh, I know the building you mean. The Charity Organization Society."

"I don't know. I've only heard it called by some letters."

"The COS, that's what they call it for short."

"Yes, that's it! Oh, Mrs. Brandt, can you find it? Can you go there and tell Mrs. Van Orner about me?"

"Of course I can. I won't leave you here, Amy. You can trust me."

Amy sighed and closed her eyes. Her shoulders sagged, as if she'd been bearing the weight of the world and someone had suddenly lifted it for her. "You don't know what this means to me," she whispered, and a tear slid down her cheek.

"I think I do," Sarah said.

"ARE YOU SURE THIS IS WHERE YOU WANT TO GO?" JAKE asked with a frown when he'd opened the carriage door for Sarah. They were on Mulberry Street, in one of the poorest sections of the city. Decrepit buildings loomed on both sides of the filthy street, and hordes of ragged children played disorganized games of tag and kick the can, shrieking wildly as they raced past.

"Yes, I do volunteer work at the Mission here," Sarah said. She indicated the Old Dutch Colonial house with the newly painted sign that said, DAUGHTERS OF HOPE. The women whom Sarah had recruited to take over the management of the Prodigal Son Mission had decided to change the name to something more appropriate.

"If you're sure," Jake said doubtfully, lunging to scare away a filthy boy who looked as if he wanted to pick his pocket. "Do you want me to get you tomorrow at your house?"

"No, I'll find my own way," Sarah said.

"Best come around noontime," he said. "Everybody sleeps all morning, and I guess you want to get there before the customers start coming."

"Yes, I do," Sarah said, trying not to let her disgust show. "Thank you for your help."

"Glad to be of service, Mrs. Brandt," he said with a small bow and an insolent smile.

Sarah couldn't help recalling how Amy had said he would kill her if she tried to help the girl get away. She managed not to shudder. He handed out her black medical bag and waited until she was safely inside before climbing up onto the carriage and driving away.

The girl who answered the door at the Mission greeted her warmly and scurried away to find the matron, Mrs. Keller.

Sarah set her bag down in the front hallway and glanced around. She'd come to know the place well since first discovering it a little over a year ago. In spite of its shabby furnishings and worn carpets, this truly was a refuge for girls. How could she have mistaken the house she'd visited last night for anything other than it was? No one would decorate a refuge for wayward girls the way Mrs. Walker's house was furnished.

Mrs. Keller was walking toward her from the back of the house, drying her hands on her apron as she came. "Mrs. Brandt, we're so glad to see you. How are Catherine and Maeve doing?" she added.

"Catherine is growing like a weed, and Maeve has blossomed into quite a young lady. I'll bring them for a visit very soon."

"Please do. Have you come to see me about something? I've got bread in the oven, and I was just cleaning up the kitchen, so I have a few minutes if you need me."

"No, I don't need to see you, but I do need to ask you a favor. I was wondering if one of the girls would take a message to Police Headquarters for me." Police Headquarters was located just a block down Mulberry Street.

Mrs. Keller smiled. "I'm sure any one of them would. Is the message by any chance for Detective Sergeant Malloy?"

Sarah smiled back. The residents at the Mission had

many reasons to be grateful to Malloy. "Yes, it is, and if his fellow officers find out I sent him a message, he'll never hear the end of it."

Sarah and Malloy had worked together on quite a few murder cases in the past year and a half since they'd first met, and their relationship had made Malloy the butt of many jokes, not all of them good-natured. Sarah didn't want to cause him any unnecessary embarrassment, but she desperately needed to speak to him about what she'd learned from Amy last night.

"Come back to my office and write your note. We'll say it's from me, that I need to see Malloy right away. They'll think I've got a troublesome girl here."

A few minutes later, one of the girls had been dispatched with Sarah's note and her instructions to say it was from Mrs. Keller. Sarah didn't really expect Malloy to be available, but she'd wait until the girl got back, just in case they knew when to expect him. She was too tired to wait long, however. She'd either have to go home soon or ask Mrs. Keller if she had a spare bed.

To her surprise, however, the girl returned in short order with Malloy on her heels. He pulled off his hat as he entered the foyer, looking around for her. She'd been waiting in the parlor, and she went to meet him.

"Malloy," she said, absurdly glad to see him, and she felt her fatigue falling away. His solid figure seemed to dominate the foyer.

"Mrs. Brandt," he replied, as he always did. His dark eyes examined her critically.

She touched her hair self-consciously. She must look a fright after being up all night.

"Your note said you needed to see me," he said, mindful of the girl still standing there, hanging on every word, and Mrs. Keller, who'd followed Sarah out of the parlor.

"Yes, I have some questions I need to ask you, if you have a few minutes."

"Hilda and I will get you some coffee," Mrs. Keller said tactfully, ushering the reluctant girl down the hallway toward the kitchen and leaving them alone.

Sarah led him into the parlor and closed the pocket doors behind them.

When she turned toward him, he was frowning in apparent disapproval. "And where have you been all night?"

"In a whorehouse," Sarah replied baldly, in no mood to be disapproved of.

If she'd hoped to shock him, she'd more than succeeded. "My God, are you serious?"

"Perfectly. I was called to a birth yesterday, and the mother happens to live in a brothel." She took a seat on the horsehair sofa that someone had donated to the Mission long after its usefulness was over.

Malloy plopped down beside her as if his knees had suddenly come unhinged. "Where?"

"In the Tenderloin," she said, naming the triangular neighborhood north of Twenty-third Street between Ninth Avenue and Broadway whose northern portion was Longacre Square.

"My God," he said again, looking at her in utter amazement. "Why did you let them take you there?" Now he sounded outraged.

"The young man picked me up in a carriage. All the curtains were drawn, and I enjoyed the privacy and didn't pay much attention to where we were going. We stopped in the alley behind the house, and they took me in through the kitchen and up the servants' stairs to the girl's bedroom. I thought it was a boardinghouse."

He rubbed a hand over his face and muttered something that was either a prayer or a curse.

She pretended not to hear. "As you can see, I emerged unscathed, but I do have something I want to ask you about."

His dark eyes were nearly black when he turned to her. "You're not going back there. And you're going to start paying attention to where people are taking you when you go to deliver babies. And furthermore—"

"Stop it, Malloy," she snapped. "I already have a father whose opinions I have to ignore. I don't need another one. Now stop lecturing me and listen. I'm very tired and my patience is wearing thin."

He didn't like it, but he pressed his lips together into a thin line and just glared.

"Good," she said, seeing his compliance. "The girl whose baby I delivered asked me to help her escape."

This time he did curse, making Sarah jump. "Are you *crazy?*" he almost roared. "Do you know what happens to people who try to get girls out of places like that?"

"Yes, they get killed."

He'd already opened his mouth to continue, but her reply stopped him dead. "What?"

"You were going to tell me that I could get killed. I know that. Amy told me."

"Who's Amy?"

"The girl who had the baby. It's a little boy, Malloy, and they're going to take him from her."

"Of course they are. A brothel is no place for a baby."

"I'm sure it isn't," Sarah agreed. "It would be awfully bad for business, I imagine."

Malloy glared at her again. "If you're going to ask me to rescue this girl or something—"

"No, I wouldn't ask you that. If they'd kill me, they'd probably kill you, too."

"They wouldn't kill me, but I'd lose my job. Places like that pay the police to protect them, not kidnap their girls."

"I hadn't thought of that."

"I'm sure there's a lot of things you hadn't thought of, like not going to a brothel in the first place."

"You don't have any reason to be angry with me. I already told you, it wasn't my fault."

He rubbed his face again. "I'm not angry with you. I'm just . . . angry."

Sarah bit back a smile. She knew he wouldn't be so mad if he didn't care about her. "You don't need to be. I'm not going to do anything foolish."

He frowned, obviously not believing her for a minute.

"I know I don't stand a chance of helping Amy, and so does she. She asked me to contact a Mrs. Van Orner for her."

His eyes narrowed in suspicion. "Who's that?"

"She has a charity that takes care of girls like Amy. She helps them get away and—"

He groaned. "One of those rich do-gooders. I thought the name sounded familiar. She's going to get herself killed one of these days, too."

"She has people who help her, I understand."

"Other rich do-gooders," Malloy said in disgust.

"I'm going to ask her to help Amy."

Malloy half turned on the sofa so he was facing her, his dark eyes nearly glowing with the strength of his emotion.

"Sarah, leave it alone. I'm warning you, you don't know what you're getting yourself into."

"But that poor girl and her baby! She's obviously from a good family, and she hates it there, hates the things she has to do. I can't even imagine what it must be like for her."

"She's not what you think, Sarah. Those girls are all liars. They'll say anything to get what they want."

"But you didn't see her. She's terrified of Mrs. Walker—"

"Who?" he asked sharply.

"Mrs. Walker. She's the . . ." Sarah tried to think of a nice word and failed.

"The *madam*," Malloy supplied, rolling his eyes. "Of all the madams in New York, you had to pick one of the Sisters, didn't you?"

"The Sisters?"

"Yeah. Maybe you didn't notice, but the house you were in is one of seven that are just alike. They say seven sisters came to the city from New England years ago and each one set up her own house of ill repute . . . Well, I don't think the madams at the houses next door are really Mrs. Walker's sisters, but they call that street Sisters' Row."

"I have to admit, I was surprised at how well appointed the house was."

"It has to be," Malloy said. "They cater to the wealthiest men in the city, which means they pay lots of protection money to the police. If you get in trouble there, no one will help you, Sarah."

She heard the fear underlying the harshness in his tone. "I told you, I'm not going to do anything foolish."

"You're going to help that girl. That's foolish."

"I can't turn my back on her, Malloy. How could I live with myself?"

Malloy sighed. "You don't know what those women are like. She's not an innocent country girl who got kidnapped and forced into a life of shame—and even if she was once, she's not innocent anymore," he added when she would have protested.

"What about her baby?" Sarah argued. "She can't bear the thought of being separated from him."

"So she said, but she probably figured that was the easiest way to get you to help her. Look, do I have to lock you up to keep you from getting involved in this?"

Sarah couldn't help smiling at the idle threat. "Just try, Malloy," she taunted. "And no, you don't. I told you, I'm going to find this Mrs. Van Orner and turn the matter over to her. I'm not going to put myself in danger. I've got a family to think about now, you know."

"Don't forget it either. How are the girls doing?"

Sarah gave him a report on Catherine and Maeve, then asked, "How is Brian getting along in school?"

"Almost as well as his grandmother." Malloy's young son was deaf, and he attended a special school. Malloy's mother escorted him there and back and helped out in the classroom.

"Is she learning to sign, too?" Sarah asked, delighted.

"She says somebody needs to be able to talk to the boy."

A knock at the door announced Mrs. Keller's return with a tray of coffee and some freshly baked cookies. Malloy begged off, saying he had to get back to Police Headquarters, but he took a handful of cookies with him.

He stopped in the doorway on his way out and turned back to Sarah one last time. "Don't forget what you promised."

Sarah couldn't remember exactly what she'd promised.

* * *

THE NEXT MORNING, SARAH AWOKE EARLY AND PUT ON the suit she wore when she wanted people to take her seriously. She'd had it for a long time, since she'd left her parents' mansion to marry Dr. Tom Brandt, but since she hardly ever wore it, it was still presentable, if a bit out of style.

"You're pretty dressed up to be going to see a new mother," Maeve observed over breakfast. She knew Sarah's routines after living in her house for so many months.

"I have an errand to run first."

"You look pretty, Mama," Catherine said softly, looking up at her with shining eyes.

"So do you, my darling," Sarah said, bending down to give her a peck on the forehead.

"Will that boy be fetching you in the carriage again?" Maeve asked.

Sarah looked at her, trying to judge the reason for the question. Jake was a handsome young man, after all, and Sarah didn't want Maeve getting ideas about him. "Are you hoping to see him again?"

Maeve looked genuinely shocked. "No! And I don't think you should see him again either."

"Why?" Sarah asked in surprise.

"He's a bad one. You can always tell. He's too cocky and full of himself. He's mean, too. You can see by the way he treats the horses."

"You're right," Sarah said, impressed. "He's a bad one. If he ever comes here again, don't let him in the house."

"But you're going to that house where he works again, aren't you?"

Sarah hadn't said a thing about her experiences on Sisters' Row, not wanting to frighten Maeve. But she tended to forget what kind of life the girl had lived before going to the Mission and then coming here to live. Maeve knew more about the world than Sarah ever would.

"I'll be fine."

Maeve didn't argue, but she didn't smile either.

SARAH TOOK THE NINTH AVENUE ELEVATED TRAIN UP TO the Twenty-third Street Station, then walked across town to Fourth Avenue and back down one block to Twenty-second Street. A check of the City Directory that morning had revealed the address of the Charity Organization Society. The United Charities Building, she knew, had been built with donations from the wealthiest families in the city, with an eye to organizing the charitable relief of the poor and solving the problem of poverty once and for all. Many charities were housed here, offering a variety of services. Sarah's socially elite parents had doubtless contributed to the construction.

The building was modest but impressive, and Sarah discovered a beehive of activity inside. A young man sat at a reception desk, greeting visitors and directing them to the correct office. For some reason, Sarah had expected to see the needy lined up here to receive assistance, but she saw no trace of the needy. Everyone was well dressed and moving with purpose.

"Good morning," the young man said cautiously, as if afraid she was going to make some demand of him. He looked to be about twenty and hadn't yet filled out. He stared up at her with large, watery eyes. "May I help you?"

"Yes, I'd like to see Mrs. Van Orner."

Sarah saw the slightest flicker of emotion passing over his young face, but she couldn't identify it. He hesitated another second as he examined her more closely, his gaze darting over her as if to form some sort of judgment. She couldn't tell if he was satisfied or not, but he said, "Mrs. Van Orner isn't in today, but you may speak with her secretary, Miss Yingling." He directed her to an office on the third floor.

As she made her way up, Sarah passed several young women and another young man on the stairs. They all carried papers or folders and seemed bent on a mission of some importance. They did not greet her or even meet her eye, Sarah noticed. Such behavior was typical in the city, but somehow she'd expected the people here to be friendlier.

She found the office easily, but the words painted on the door stopped her: "Rahab's Daughters." Sarah had learned the story of Rahab the Harlot in Sunday school, although she hadn't known exactly what a harlot was back then. Rahab had hidden the Israelite spies whom Joshua had sent to Jericho. In exchange for protecting them from her own people, she asked them to spare her and her family when they took the city. Rahab had done well for herself afterward, Sarah recalled, although she couldn't remember the details.

She supposed the name was appropriate, considering the work Mrs. Van Orner did, but Sarah couldn't help thinking that "Daughters of Hope" was a bit more inspiring. She opened the door. A young woman looked up from her typewriter.

Like the fellow in the lobby and the people on the stairs, she was young, probably in her early twenties. Sarah could tell that she could be a beauty if she took some pains with her hair and her clothing, but apparently, she cared nothing for that. She wore her dark hair scraped back into a severe and unflattering bun, and her suit was ill-fitting and a sickly shade of olive green that turned her skin sallow. "May I help you?"

"Yes, I need to see Mrs. Van Orner."

"Mrs. Van Orner isn't in today, but I will be happy to give her a message."

"I'm afraid this is a rather urgent matter."

The girl smiled slightly, or at least her lips curved upward. Nothing else of her expression changed though. "It's always an urgent matter."

"A young woman's life is at stake," Sarah tried.

"Then perhaps you will tell me what you need so I can give that information to Mrs. Van Orner."

Sarah could see that she had no choice. "All right."

"Please, sit down," Miss Yingling said, indicating the wooden chair placed beside her desk.

Sarah did so.

The girl had taken a piece of paper and a pencil out of her desk, and she looked up expectantly. "What is your name?"

Sarah told her. The girl then asked for her address.

"Is all this really necessary?" Sarah asked impatiently.

Miss Yingling looked up, her eyes calm, completely unaffected by Sarah's urgency.

"I'm afraid it's very necessary. All of the charities in this building cooperate with each other very closely. We keep careful records of everyone we help and share that information with each other, so that people can't just go from one charity to another every time they get into difficulty. That would encourage them to be dependent and weak instead of forcing them to take responsibility for their own lives."

This seemed so unfair, Sarah hardly knew where to begin asking questions. "You mean people can't get assistance from more than one of the charities in this building?"

"With some rare exceptions, yes. As I said, our resources are limited, and we can't waste them on people who are too lazy to improve themselves. Not everyone agrees with these rules, of course," she added, "but we must abide by them nevertheless. So yes, I do need this information. What is your address?"

Still stinging with outrage, Sarah provided it.

Miss Yingling took down the information in neat handwriting. Then she looked up again. "This girl you want us to help, what is her relation to you?"

"She's no relation to me at all. I'm a midwife, and two days ago, a young man came to take me to a birth at what I thought was a boardinghouse. I eventually realized I was in a house of ill repute. The young woman whose baby I delivered begged me to help her get away."

"Did you try?" Miss Yingling asked with interest.

"No, she warned me not to. She said . . . Well, she said it wasn't safe. She asked me to find Mrs. Van Orner and ask her for help."

Miss Yingling was intrigued. "How did she know about Mrs. Van Orner?"

"She said all the . . . the girls who worked there knew about her."

Miss Yingling nodded. "That's good. Word of our work is spreading."

"Can you help her?"

"Do you know where the house is?"

"Yes, it's on Sisters' Row."

Her blue eyes widened. "Oh, my."

"Is something wrong?"

"Oh, no, it's just . . . The police protect these places, you know, and Sisters' Row . . ."

"I've been told it serves very wealthy clients."

"And that's another problem."

"In what way?"

Miss Yingling seemed surprised by the question. "I . . . Oh, I mean . . . Well, because the place earns a tremendous amount of money, and they can bribe just about anyone they want."

Sarah didn't believe her. "Are you afraid of offending someone wealthy?"

"No, no, not at all. Mrs. Van Orner isn't afraid of anything," the girl insisted. "We'll just need to be more careful than usual."

"We also have to rescue the baby," Sarah said.

"Baby?"

"The baby I delivered," Sarah reminded her. "Mrs. Walker, the woman who runs the place, is going to take him away from his mother in a few days, and the mother is very concerned that she won't be able to find him again."

Miss Yingling frowned. "That's very odd. They don't usually allow the girls to have babies."

"What do you mean?"

Miss Yingling shrugged. "Interestingly enough, very few of these women conceive at all, but when they do, they see an abortionist."

Sarah remembered a remark Mrs. Walker had made about Amy lying to her. Had she managed to keep her pregnancy a secret until it was too late to end it? But none of that really mattered now. "Can you help this girl and her baby or not?"

"I'll have to discuss the case with Mrs. Van Orner, of course—"

"I'm going to see the girl today. It may be my last chance to visit with her, and I'd like to tell her some good news."

"I can't promise anything without Mrs. Van Orner's approval."

Sarah seldom used her family's power to her own advantage, but this time she saw it was necessary. "Perhaps Mrs. Van Orner knows my mother, Mrs. Felix Decker."

Miss Yingling's eyes widened again. "Mrs. Decker is your mother?" Like the fellow downstairs, she looked Sarah over and found nothing to impress her. "But you're a . . ."

"A midwife. Yes, I earn my own living. Do you know if my parents are donors to your cause? They're very generous, and I could certainly put in a good word with them about the work you do."

Miss Yingling carefully wrote, "Mrs. Felix Decker," on the paper beneath her notes about Amy's case. When she looked up again, she seemed much more eager to help. "Did you say this girl had a baby two days ago?"

"Early yesterday morning."

"How soon will it be safe to move her?"

Sarah knew that most doctors wouldn't even allow a woman out of bed for two weeks after she delivered, but she also knew few women could afford such a lengthy time of idleness. Most of her clients were up doing housework after a week, some even sooner. "I'd like to say a week, but if you need to get her sooner . . . I'd say the day after tomorrow at the earliest, and she'll need a safe place to go where she can finish recovering."

"We have a house in the city where the women can stay until they find honest work."

"This is a wonderful thing you're doing," Sarah said, feeling absurdly grateful even though Miss Yingling hadn't even agreed to anything yet.

"Yes, it is," the younger woman said, but for some reason,

she didn't look as if she believed it. "Now tell me everything you know about this girl and the house where she lives."

SARAH REACHED SISTERS' ROW JUST BEFORE NOON. SHE went to the back door again so she wouldn't be seen. Few respectable women would want her to attend them if they knew she'd been in a place like this, and she couldn't risk her livelihood.

Beulah let her in. "Didn't expect to see you again," she remarked.

"I wanted to make sure Amy and the baby are all right. I always visit new mothers the next day."

Beulah sniffed. "I'll tell Miz Walker you's here."

"I'll just go on up to see Amy," Sarah said, hoping she could get some time alone with the girl before the madam joined them. "I know the way."

Before Beulah could object, if she really was going to object, Sarah found the back stairway and went up. The house was eerily quiet, and she recalled Jake's reminder about the girls sleeping late. She saw no sign of anyone stirring on the second floor. All the doors were shut. Sarah tapped lightly on Amy's door, then entered without waiting for an invitation.

Amy lay in bed, supported by pillows, and she looked up in alarm when Sarah entered.

"Oh, it's you," she said with a sigh. "I'm as nervous as a cat. I'm afraid they're going to come get the baby."

Sarah hurried over to the bed. She saw that the baby lay beside her, wrapped tightly in a blanket and sound asleep. "I spoke with Mrs. Van Orner's secretary this morning."

"Why didn't you see *her*?" Amy cried. "I told you to see Mrs. Van Orner!"

"Shhh," Sarah cautioned, aware that Mrs. Walker could appear at any moment. "She wasn't in, but the secretary was going to tell her your story today. You can't be moved for at least a few more days yet, and they need some time to make plans. But they're coming for you, Amy. I promise you they are."

"What if they take the baby before they get here? I'll never find him!"

"I told you, I'll take him. I'll speak to Mrs. Walker today about it."

"What if she won't let you? What if I lose him!" Tears flooded her eyes, and Sarah was afraid she would get hysterical. She'd have a difficult time explaining that to Mrs. Walker.

"You have to be strong, Amy," Sarah told her. "Trust me. I'll take care of everything."

Amy didn't look willing to trust anyone, but Sarah heard the door opening.

"How often is the baby feeding?" she asked in a normal voice.

Amy looked at her stupidly for a second before she noticed Mrs. Walker had come in. "He kept me up half the night," she said. "He's a greedy little thing."

"That's good." Sarah put her hand on the girl's forehead. "You don't have a fever. I'll need to—"

"So you came back," Mrs. Walker said.

Sarah turned, feigning surprise. "I told you I would."

This morning Mrs. Walker wore a red silk kimono. She looked weary, as if she hadn't slept well since the last time Sarah saw her. "I always assume people are lying to me, Mrs. Brandt, and I'm usually right." She nodded at Amy. "How's she doing?"

"I haven't had a chance to examine her yet, but I'll be happy to give you a full report when I'm finished."

"You do that. I want her healthy so she can get back to work real soon."

Sarah flinched and Amy made a small sound of protest, but if Mrs. Walker noticed, she gave no sign. She just turned and left the room, closing the door softly behind her.

"I hate her!" Amy whispered.

"You won't have to be here much longer," Sarah promised. "Now let me examine you and the baby."

"And tell me everything that secretary person said."

Half an hour later, Sarah could delay her departure no longer. She left Amy with a promise to return as soon as possible. When she reached the kitchen, Beulah led her down a hallway to what she discovered was Mrs. Walker's office, a modestly decorated room in stark contrast to the rest of the house.

The woman sat at an elaborately carved desk, still wearing her kimono. She'd been making a list of some sort, and she looked up when Beulah brought Sarah in. When the cook had closed the door behind her, Mrs. Walker said, "Don't believe anything that little whore told you."

3

"PARDON ME?" SARAH SAID IN SURPRISE.

"I already told you, I always assume people are lying to me, and I'm usually right. That's because I spend so much time with whores, Mrs. Brandt. They'll say anything to get what they want."

"Amy wants her baby to be safe."

Mrs. Walker raised her eyebrows. "Nobody's going to hurt it."

"She's afraid you're going to take it away."

She sighed impatiently. "Of course I'm going to take it away. This is no place for a baby. If men wanted to hear babies crying, they'd stay at home."

"Where are you going to take him?"

"What business is it of yours?"

Sarah clenched her fists until the fingernails bit into the skin of her palms, but somehow she managed not to scream at this horrible woman. "None, but I know what happens to abandoned babies in the city. I'd like to take him someplace where he'll be taken care of and perhaps even adopted."

"You have high hopes for the little brat, don't you?"

"I just think he deserves a chance to survive. He didn't choose to be born here."

"Nobody chooses where they're born," Mrs. Walker said. "A midwife should know that. How is Amy?"

"She's doing well. She should stay in bed for at least two weeks." Sarah hoped the girl would be gone long before then.

"Since she works on her back, that's not a hardship," Mrs. Walker said.

Sarah felt the heat rising in her face, but she refused to let Mrs. Walker make her angry. "She shouldn't have relations for at least two months."

"Two months?" Mrs. Walker echoed in outrage.

"She could get childbed fever and die. You told me yourself she's valuable to you."

"She's not valuable if she can't work for two months." Mrs. Walker sighed again, this time in disgust. "All right. If you're finished with Amy, you can go." She turned back to her list making, but Sarah didn't move.

"Will you let me take the baby?"

Mrs. Walker looked up, annoyed. "What on earth do you want him for?"

"I told you, I want to make sure he has a chance. I know an orphanage where they'll take good care of him."

"I'm not giving you any money to take him," she warned.

"I haven't asked for any."

"Are you going to sell him?"

"Whom would I sell him to?" Sarah asked in surprise.

Mrs. Walker smiled unpleasantly. "Lots of people would pay to get their hands on a little baby boy."

"Even if that's true, I don't know any of them."

"You aren't going to give up, are you?" Mrs. Walker asked.

"No."

"All right then, you can have him. You'll save me the trouble." She turned back to her desk again.

"When should I come for him?"

Mrs. Walker's expression turned cunning. "How long until Amy's milk comes in good?"

Sarah remembered what Amy had said about that and managed not to flinch. "A week."

"Come back when he's a week old then."

"Thank you, Mrs. Walker. That's very kind of you," Sarah said sincerely.

Her eyes widened in surprise, and the color rose in her pale cheeks. "I don't mean the child any harm," she said gruffly. "And I don't know what she told you, but Amy has a good life here. I take care of all my girls. They get the best of everything."

Unless they try to leave, Sarah thought, but she said, "I'm sure they do. Will you tell Amy you've agreed to let me take her baby?"

"Of course I will. It'll keep her from crying and carrying on. Men don't like to hear women crying either. You can go now, Mrs. Brandt. I've given you everything you're going to get."

WHEN SARAH GOT HOME, SHE FOUND A MESSAGE FROM Mrs. Van Orner, asking Sarah to meet her at the Rahab's Daughters' office the next morning. Miss Yingling hadn't wasted any time in contacting her. As much as Sarah hated using her family's name, the ploy had worked very well this time. Now she supposed she'd have to ask her mother to make a donation. Sarah would make one herself if Mrs. Van Orner and her people could get Amy out of that place.

Sarah spent the rest of the day with her family, enjoying Catherine's antics and the relief of knowing there was hope for Amy's predicament. The next morning, she put on her good suit again and made her way to the United Charities Building.

The young man at the front desk remembered her and greeted her by name with much more warmth than she had expected. Miss Yingling must have told him about Sarah's family connections. Even Miss Yingling welcomed her, although Sarah suspected she was never warm to anyone.

"I'm so glad you could come, Mrs. Brandt," she said. Her lips curved upward without really forming a smile in the odd way Sarah had noted before. "I'll announce you."

She went to a door on the side of the room and knocked, then opened it and told someone Sarah had arrived. She turned back to Sarah and said, "Mrs. Van Orner will see you now."

She stepped aside so Sarah could enter the adjoining office, and then she closed the door behind Sarah. Mrs. Van Orner had risen from her chair and came around from behind her desk to greet her. Sarah caught a whiff of something clean and minty. Mrs. Van Orner offered her hand, and Sarah took it.

"I'm very pleased to meet you, Mrs. Brandt. Thank you so much for coming on such short notice." Mrs. Van Orner was nearing forty, but she was still a lovely woman and had maintained her youthful figure. She wore a blue serge walking skirt and a matching bolero jacket over a fashionable Gibson girl shirtwaist, but her light brown hair had been pulled into a simple bun. Her hand was smooth, befitting her status in life as the wife of a wealthy man. The line of her jaw had just begun to soften with age, but grief had carved deep lines into the otherwise fine skin of her face. She had known disappointment in her life. Even wealth could not prevent that, as Sarah knew.

"Thank you for seeing me," Sarah said when she'd taken a seat in one of the straight-backed chairs that had been placed in front of Mrs. Van Orner's desk. This room was also simply furnished. A plain wooden cross hung on the wall behind Mrs. Van Orner, the only decoration. The desk and chairs had probably been purchased new but were cheaply made. Mrs. Van Orner wasted nothing on appearances.

Mrs. Van Orner sat down behind her desk again. "Tamar—Miss Yingling—told me about the young woman whose baby you delivered. She's in one of the houses on Sisters' Row, I believe?"

"That's right. I had no idea where I was going that day. I thought it was a boardinghouse."

"So Miss Yingling said. I'm surprised you stayed once you realized the truth."

Did Mrs. Van Orner disapprove? Sarah thought perhaps she did, but she didn't particularly care. "I'm a midwife, Mrs. Van Orner. I couldn't leave until I knew the young woman and her baby were all right."

"That's commendable," she said, although she didn't sound as if she really thought so. She'd reached into a desk drawer and she drew out a small tin. "Would you like a peppermint?" She removed the lid and offered the tin to Sarah, who took one.

"Thank you."

Mrs. Van Orner popped one in her mouth and replaced the lid on the tin. Sarah thought she must suffer from digestive troubles.

"How did this young woman know to send you to me?" Mrs. Van Orner asked.

"She said the other women who work in the house talk about you all the time, about how you rescue girls from brothels."

"I wish we did," she said with a sigh, "but we seldom have an opportunity to do so. The women are watched so closely, it's difficult for them to ask for help, and it's even more difficult for us to get inside, so we mostly work with streetwalkers. They may have a man who protects them, but it's still much easier to approach them and get them to safety than to break into a brothel."

"How will you get into this house?"

"We'll figure out a plan. We'll probably go in the morning, when everyone is still sleeping, and catch them by surprise. We'll have to have a carriage waiting to take the girl away, I suppose."

"Yes, she won't be able to walk very far. What about the other women in the house?"

"What about them?"

"Will you rescue them, too?"

Mrs. Van Orner folded her hands on the desktop and leaned forward slightly, her expression solemn as she stared right into Sarah's eyes. "Mrs. Brandt, this is very difficult work, made more so by the fact that few of the women in these places truly want to be rescued."

"I can't believe that!"

"I couldn't believe it either, when I first started. I assumed that all of them longed to live respectable lives and would gratefully accept my help to free them from their bondage. What I have learned, however, is that even those who do accept my help in escaping will very often return to their lives of shame. They find they prefer that to earning their bread through honest labor."

"But Miss Yingling said you have a house where they can stay," Sarah remembered.

"We do, but we can't keep them forever. Gratuitous charity works evil rather than good, you see. If we continue to support these women, they will learn the dreadful lesson that it's easy to get a day's living without working for it."

Sarah didn't know where to begin to argue with that philosophy. "What about a woman like Amy, who has a baby? Surely, you can't expect her to go out and earn her living."

"The Salvation Army has a crèche where women can leave their children while they work. We wouldn't expect her to go to work immediately, of course, but eventually she would have to. You earn your own living, do you not?"

"Yes, but—"

"You do have advantages these women do not, however," Mrs. Van Orner continued. "You could have returned to your parents' house when you were widowed. You might even eventually remarry and have a husband to support you. If these women do have families—and they usually do not—the families don't want them back. And I assure you, Mrs. Brandt, there are few men in the world who would knowingly marry a woman who has been a prostitute."

She was right, of course, as difficult as it was to accept. "But you will try to rescue Amy."

"Of course. This is a wonderful opportunity. Her story would bring all sorts of attention to the cause."

Sarah would have preferred her to want to rescue Amy

for the girl's sake, but she would take what she could get. "What can I do to help?"

"As I said, we have to make a plan. First we'll have to decide when the girl can safely be moved."

"I've arranged with Mrs. Walker, the madam, to take the baby next Tuesday."

"She's going to let you have the child?" Mrs. Van Orner asked in surprise.

"Yes, I made a nuisance of myself until she agreed. Amy was terrified that they would take the baby and she'd never see him again, so I wanted to be able to keep him safe."

Mrs. Van Orner seemed to be seeing Sarah in an entirely new light. "That was very clever of you."

"I don't feel very clever. I feel helpless."

"You won't feel helpless when this is over, Mrs. Brandt. You are going to be of tremendous assistance to us. You will need to meet with the people who work with me and tell them everything you remember about the house and the people in it."

"I'll be happy to do that. When can we meet?"

"Would you be available on Monday?"

"I'll make a point of it."

"I'll gather my associates, and we'll meet here at ten o'clock. That will give us adequate time to arrange for the carriage and whatever else we will need."

"Is this going to be dangerous?"

"Extremely."

Sarah looked at Mrs. Van Orner and wondered what had motivated her to take up such a mission. "I must admit, I admire you very much."

"Please don't. We all do our duty. 'Faith without works is dead,'" she added, quoting a scripture verse.

"Yes, but a woman of your position in life could be considered a 'faithful servant' by just rolling bandages for a leper colony or filling barrels of old clothes for foreign missionaries."

"A woman of your position could do the same, yet you've chosen to be a midwife."

Sarah had to smile. "You're right. I didn't think of it that way."

"There's no need to think of it at all. I do what I must. Don't admire me for it, Mrs. Brandt. It is my cross to bear."

SARAH WAS STILL TRYING TO FIGURE OUT WHAT MRS. VAN Orner had meant by that odd comment as she walked to the United Charities Building on Monday morning. She'd been worried that a birth might prevent her from keeping the appointment, but she'd delivered a baby on Saturday and found herself free when the time came.

Several people were already at the Rahab's Daughters' office when Sarah entered. A tall, muscular gentleman and a shorter, plump man appeared to be in their thirties. The taller man wore a tailor-made suit and had the well-tended look of the very rich. She'd known no other type of men when she was growing up. The other man seemed less affluent, but perhaps that was just because his suit was rumpled and his hair a little disheveled. A lady, dressed in a deceptively simple but hideously expensive gown and a hat with a large white bird perched on it, had been chatting with them, but they all stopped and turned to her as she closed the office door. Miss Yingling, Sarah noticed, sat behind her desk, apparently absorbed in some papers lying on its top.

"You must be Mrs. Brandt," the lady said. "I'm Mrs.

Spratt-Williams. This is Mr. Porter." She indicated the tall man. "And Mr. Quimby."

Both gentlemen bowed.

"I'm very pleased to meet you," Sarah said.

Miss Yingling rose from her chair and went to the door of Mrs. Van Orner's office. She tapped lightly, then opened it. "Mrs. Brandt is here." She turned to the people gathered in the outer office. "Please go in."

Mrs. Spratt-Williams went ahead, and Sarah followed. The two men came up behind, and Miss Yingling also came in and closed the door. Someone had gathered additional chairs and placed them in a semicircle around the desk.

As everyone took a seat, Mrs. Van Orner greeted them and thanked them for coming. Miss Yingling, Sarah noticed, pulled her chair slightly away from the desk. She sat down and balanced a small notebook on her knee, apparently prepared to take notes of some kind.

"Mrs. Brandt, have you met everyone?"

Sarah could smell the peppermint on her breath. "Yes, I have."

"Then let's begin by asking you to tell your story once again, so Mrs. Spratt-Williams and the gentlemen know the situation."

Sarah started at the beginning, when Jake had come to fetch her. Mrs. Van Orner and the others stopped her occasionally to ask a clarifying question. They wanted to know every detail, including her impressions of each of the people she had encountered at the house. Mrs. Van Orner produced paper and a pencil and asked Sarah to sketch out the floor plan of the house showing the location of outside doors, Amy's room, and Mrs. Walker's office.

When she was finally finished and had answered all of

their questions, Sarah sat back and studied the faces of each person gathered around the desk. Miss Yingling continued to scribble in her notebook. The others exchanged glances, silently communicating as good friends often do.

After a long moment, Mrs. Van Orner said, "I believe this Jake person will present the greatest obstacle."

"Yes," Mr. Porter agreed. "If we can get rid of him, we shouldn't have too much difficulty."

Mrs. Spratt-Williams turned to Sarah. "You're going to get the baby tomorrow, is that correct?"

"Yes."

Mrs. Spratt-Williams turned back to Mrs. Van Orner. "She could ask this Jake to drive her home in the carriage. She'll be carrying the baby, so this would seem like a logical request."

"I wasn't going to take the baby to my home," Sarah said. "There's a mission on—"

"Your destination doesn't matter," Mrs. Van Orner said, "so long as you make sure he takes you in the carriage and is gone at least an hour."

"That's an excellent plan. As soon as they are out of sight, we can act," Mr. Porter said.

"I'm sure the cook, Beulah, will offer resistance," Sarah said.

"I'll go to the front door and ring the bell, the way I did the last time we tried a rescue," Mr. Quimby said. "She'll go to answer it, and while she's doing that, Mr. Porter and Mrs. Van Orner will enter through the back door and go up the stairs to Amy's room."

"What shall I do?" Mrs. Spratt-Williams asked almost eagerly.

"You'll wait in the carriage and be ready to cause a distraction if anyone takes notice of what we're doing," Mrs. Van Orner said.

This assignment didn't please Mrs. Spratt-Williams. "But I could help you in the house. If some of the other women wake up—"

"You'll be a tremendous help to us out in the carriage, Tonya," Mrs. Van Orner said a little too sharply. She saw Mrs. Spratt-Williams's hand tighten into a fist, the only outward sign of her true reaction.

"What about the other women in the house?" Sarah asked quickly to distract them.

"We'll go early in the morning, while the household is still asleep," Mrs. Spratt-Williams said. "If all goes well, they may never know we were there."

"I mean, what if some of them want to be rescued, too?"

Sarah felt their resistance to this like a physical force. They exchanged glances again, their expressions grim.

Mrs. Van Orner cleared her throat. "Then they will have to make themselves known to us."

"But if they're asleep and they don't even know you're coming or why you're there—"

"Mrs. Brandt," Mr. Porter said kindly, "the truth is that it's unlikely any of these women will want to be rescued, even if they know why we have come."

"And they're *very* likely to stop us from taking Amy if they have the chance," Mr. Quimby said. "The last time we attempted a rescue in a brothel, the women themselves drove us away before we could locate the one we'd come for."

"Good heavens!"

"So you see," Mrs. Van Orner said, "if we hope to rescue this Amy, we can't risk alarming the other women or we may not even be able to get her out."

"I know it's disappointing," Mrs. Spratt-Williams said, reaching over to pat Sarah's hand. She'd obviously forgotten her own earlier frustration. "We'd like to save them all, but we must be content to do what we can."

Sarah knew that feeling only too well from her volunteer work at the Daughters of Hope Mission. "Shall I tell Amy you're coming when I get the baby?"

"I don't think that's a good idea," Mrs. Van Orner said. "She might say or do something to give it away."

"They may not even allow you to see her again, in any case," Mrs. Spratt-Williams added. "They might be afraid she'll get hysterical if she sees you taking the baby away."

"You must be prepared for anything," Mr. Porter added. "One never knows how these people will behave. They might not give you the baby after all, or the girl might change her mind at the last minute and refuse to go at all."

Mr. Quimby nodded vigorously. "Yes, indeed, we've seen that happen, haven't we?"

Sarah gazed at them in dismay. "Then I suppose I should ask what I should do if Jake won't take me in the carriage?"

"You should do nothing," Mrs. Van Orner said. "Simply take the baby away, if they do give him to you. Let us worry about Jake."

SARAH FELT DISTRACTED AND IRRITABLE THE REST OF the day. Even spending time with Catherine and Maeve couldn't keep her mind off what was going to happen the next morning. Maeve asked her several times if she was all right, and she'd lied and said yes, she was fine. She went to bed early, wanting to get a good night's sleep, and then lay awake most of the night, too tense to rest.

"What's going on?" Maeve asked her after breakfast, when Catherine had gone upstairs to play.

"Nothing you need to worry about."

"Well, I *am* worried, and whatever it is can't be worse than I'm imagining, so just tell me so I'll know!"

"I'm so sorry! I was just trying to spare you, but I see I've done just the opposite. I'm going to a brothel this morning to take the baby I delivered last week from his mother."

Maeve's mouth dropped open. "Dear heaven! What were you doing delivering a baby in a brothel? And why are you taking it away?"

Sarah quickly explained what had happened and how Mrs. Van Orner and her friends were going to help Amy escape.

"Does Mr. Malloy know about this?" Maeve asked with a frown.

Sarah hated the heat that rose in her face. "Of course not, and he won't ever hear about it either."

"Do you know how dangerous this is?"

"Not for me. The madam expects me to come and take the baby this morning. I'll be perfectly safe, and nothing else is going to happen until after I'm gone."

"Will you bring the baby here?"

"No, I don't want you and Catherine involved in this at all. I'll take him to the Mission, but only for a few hours. Mrs. Van Orner has a house in the city where these women can stay, and as soon as Amy is safely there, I'll take the baby to her."

"You'd better get him away faster than that. Jake will know where the baby is because he took you there, and they'll probably try to get the baby to force Amy to go back to the brothel."

"Oh, my, I never thought of that."

Maeve gave her a pitying glance. "Of course you didn't, because you're a good person. As soon as Jake drops you off, you need to go right back out again. Go straight to this house where they're taking the girl. That's the safest thing."

"You're right. I'll do that."

"And don't say a word to Amy about them coming to get her. She'll never be able to keep it a secret. She's probably told half the girls in the house already anyway."

"They warned me not to tell her, but how can I just leave her there without any hope?"

"It's only for a little while. Better she doesn't have any hope than Catherine doesn't have any mother."

Sarah scowled at her, but Maeve ignored it.

"You know I'm right."

"Yes, I do. Thank you, Maeve, for giving me very good advice."

Maeve rolled her eyes. "Just be sure you take it."

SARAH WALKED ALL THE WAY TO SISTERS' ROW, HOPING the exercise would help her burn off some of the tension she'd been feeling all night. By the time she reached the house on Twenty-fifth Street, she felt calm enough to carry out her mission. At least she hoped she was.

As she had before, she approached the house from the rear. She looked around, but saw no sign that she was observed or that the rescue party was anywhere nearby.

Beulah answered her knock. The cook looked her up and down. "I told Mrs. Walker you'd come. She didn't think you would."

Sarah stepped into the kitchen. "I hope she hasn't changed her mind about letting me take the baby."

"He's still here. That's all I know. You stay right here. I'll get Mrs. Walker."

"I'd like to check on Amy."

Beulah glared at her through narrowed eyes. "You stay right here," she repeated sternly.

Sarah decided she'd best obey. She didn't want to antagonize anyone and fail to get the baby away. While she waited, she listened for any sounds of activity, but she heard nothing. The stillness was almost eerie, as if the very house itself was sleeping.

In a few moments, Beulah returned and told her Mrs. Walker wanted to see her.

This morning, Mrs. Walker was in her nightdress and robe, with her hair still braided for sleep. Her heavy eyelids and creased face told Sarah that Beulah had awakened her.

"I'm sorry to disturb you, but I thought I should come before the other girls were awake."

"I wish you'd waited until *I* was awake," Mrs. Walker said, "but you're right. There's no sense in getting everybody stirred up."

"I'd like to see Amy, to make sure she's doing well."

"She's doing fine, and if she sees you, she'll know why you're here. I don't want her upset."

"She'll be upset when she finds out the baby is gone."

"Yes, but it'll be too late then, and she'll get over it quick enough."

Sarah wondered if a woman could ever get over the loss of her baby, but she didn't dare express her doubt to Mrs. Walker. She had to avoid antagonizing her at all costs. "I'll make sure he's taken care of. You can tell Amy that."

"I'll tell her what I please," Mrs. Walker said. "And I hope never to see your face again."

Sarah hoped the same thing.

The office door opened, and Beulah came in, carrying a small bundle. "He's sleeping like a lamb."

"What did you tell Amy?" Mrs. Walker asked.

"Nothing. She's sound asleep, too."

"Good."

Beulah handed the infant to Sarah. A wave of tenderness swept over her as she gazed down into his sweet face.

"You can go now," Mrs. Walker said. "And be quick."

Sarah had almost forgotten the most important part of her task. "Oh, dear, I was wondering, could your man Jake take me in the carriage? It's a long walk to where I'm taking him, you see, and—"

Mrs. Walker muttered something under her breath, but she said, "Beulah, go wake Jake up and have him take her wherever she wants to go. But take her with you. She can wait in the stable. I don't want Amy to wake up and have the baby still in the house."

"Thank you very much, Mrs. Walker," Sarah began, but the woman waved her off.

"Get out of here."

Sarah obediently followed Beulah out, onto the back porch, through the yard, across the alley, and into the stable. She waited just inside the door, holding the tiny, almost weightless bundle, while Beulah went up the stairs to what was apparently Jake's quarters over the stable. She heard some loud grumbling and a lot of thumping around, but in a few minutes, Beulah came down the stairs with a groggy and furious Jake behind her. He was still buttoning the jacket of his uniform, and he glared at Sarah.

"I'm very sorry," Sarah said, trying to sound sincere, "but you were the one who told me to come early in the day."

He made a rude noise, and silently went about the task of harnessing the matching horses to the carriage.

Beulah came over to Sarah and, using one finger, pushed the blanket back from the baby's face so she could take one last look. "Good luck to you, boy. You'll need it." She stepped back. "You really think somebody'll adopt him?"

"It's possible."

Beulah shook her head. "But not likely. You're doing a good thing, though, getting him away from here. That's a start."

Sarah tried to think of an appropriate response, but before she could, Beulah turned and walked away. She didn't look back.

Jake wasted no time getting the horses hitched, moving with practiced ease in spite of his groggy state. When he was finished, he moved to the carriage door and held it open for Sarah, indicating with a wave of his hand that she could enter. He made no effort to assist her, though, crossing his arms in silent rebellion against good manners.

Sarah struggled a bit climbing in with the babe in her arms, but she managed. When she was settled, he said, "Where do you want to go?"

"To the Mission, the same place you took me last time."

His expression told her he thought this was crazy, but he slammed the door shut and climbed up to the driver's seat. Sarah hastily opened the curtains at the windows in hopes of seeing some indication that the rescuers were nearby and waiting. At least they would see her and know she'd gotten away. She even held the baby high against her chest, so the bundle he made would be visible. As they turned onto Seventh Street, she saw a shabby carriage stopped on the next block, its driver slumped over as if drunk or sleeping. Could that be them?

Her carriage started down the street, and she caught a glimpse of a gentleman strolling leisurely on the opposite sidewalk, a walking stick in his hand. She recognized him. Mr. Quimby. She held the baby up even higher, so he'd know she had him. He didn't seem to take any notice, and then they were gone, rattling away. Sarah lowered the baby to her lap and sank back against the cushions and started to pray.

NEARLY TWO HOURS LATER, SARAH ARRIVED AT THE house where Mrs. Van Orner had provided a refuge for the women she rescued. Mrs. Keller, at the Daughters of Hope, had loaned her a market basket in which to carry the baby. She'd be less noticeable, they'd decided, if Jake did return and started asking if anyone in the neighborhood had seen a woman carrying an infant. By the time she arrived at the modest clapboard house in the Lower East Side, however, she was extremely noticeable. The baby was screaming bloody murder, drawing looks varying from pity to outrage from the people passing her in the street.

Having only the address and seeing nothing about the house to distinguish it from its neighbors, Sarah breathed a silent prayer that she was at the right place and pounded on the door. A young woman opened it, her astonished gaze taking in Sarah and the screaming baby in the basket with one glance, then sticking her head out to hastily check the street before drawing Sarah inside and closing the door securely behind them.

"Are you Mrs. Brandt?" the girl asked.

"Yes, I—"

"Thank heaven you've come. That girl Amy, she's half out of her mind worrying about what happened to you and the baby." She reached into the basket and snatched up the squalling child. "He's soaking wet!"

"I was in such a hurry to get him away, I didn't even think to ask them for spare diapers," Sarah said by way of apology, but the girl was gone, hurrying toward the stairs at the end of the front hallway.

Sarah stood there stupidly, watching her disappear up the stairs. Then she looked around. The place reminded her of the Daughters of Hope Mission, an old house furnished with threadbare rugs and castoff furniture. Faded wallpaper covered the walls, unrelieved by a single picture. A far cry from the house on Sisters' Row.

She heard a door open upstairs and a woman's voice raised in anguish, the words indistinguishable. The door closed, muffling the baby's cries, and then they ceased altogether. Sarah sighed with relief.

"Not exactly what you expected, was it?" a familiar voice asked.

4

Being summoned by the chief of detectives was never a good thing, Frank observed as he made his way upstairs to Stephen O'Brien's office. When he saw a woman was already in O'Brien's office, he knew it was even worse than he'd thought.

"Close the door, Malloy," O'Brien said. He didn't sound happy to see him.

Frank closed the door and took a few steps closer to O'Brien's desk. The chief didn't invite him to sit down.

The woman glared up at him from where she sat, as if she held him personally responsible for whatever she was so angry about. He thought she looked familiar, but maybe she just looked like every other madam in the city—a bit past her prime, more than a bit plump, and wearing expensive clothes that still looked cheap. Her hat had probably cost more than Frank made in a month, but the bird perched on it and staring at him with beady glass eyes was orange. Not a color found in nature.

"Mrs. Walker, this is the detective sergeant I told you about," O'Brien was saying.

"The one who knows this Mrs. Brandt?" she asked sharply.

Frank's stomach knotted, and he managed not to swear aloud, although the curses were roaring in his head. In the one second that ticked by, he saw in his mind's eye exactly what had happened. Sarah had ignored his advice and done a very stupid thing. He wasn't going to let on that he knew, though. Things were already bad enough. Frank just clamped his teeth shut and waited, knowing anything he said would be wrong.

"You do know Mrs. Brandt, don't you, Malloy? The midwife?" O'Brien prompted.

What had happened to Sarah? Was she all right? "We've met," he allowed.

O'Brien wasn't amused. "Met? Hasn't she been involved in some of your cases?"

"A few."

"*Involved in your cases?*" Mrs. Walker echoed. "Does she work for the police?"

"Of course not," O'Brien assured her. Frank noticed his face was a dangerous shade of scarlet. "Don't be ridiculous."

"I'm not being ridiculous," Mrs. Walker informed him. If possible, she was even more furious than O'Brien. "I've been robbed, and I want you to do something about it."

"Did Mrs. Brandt rob you?" Frank asked before he could stop himself.

Mrs. Walker hadn't missed the sarcasm in his voice, but she squared her shoulders righteously. "As a matter of fact, she did. She kidnapped a baby."

Frank wanted to groan. He could easily imagine Sarah kidnapping a baby if she thought that was the right thing to do. He wasn't going to admit that, though. "What were you doing with a baby? What kind of a place do you run anyway?" he asked, pretending to be shocked.

Now *her* face was a dangerous shade of scarlet, but she turned to O'Brien. "I don't have to sit here and be insulted. I pay good money for the police to protect me, and I expect you to earn it!"

"Malloy, what do you know about this?" O'Brien demanded.

"I know Mrs. Brandt isn't a kidnapper. She's a respectable lady, and she never would've gone into a brothel voluntarily. Maybe she was the one who was kidnapped."

"Nobody did anything to her," Mrs. Walker said indignantly. "She got away scot-free."

The knot in Frank's stomach loosened a bit. At least she was all right. For now. "With this baby?"

"Yes, with the baby, and his mother, too."

Frank gaped at her. "She took a woman and a baby out of your house, and nobody stopped her?"

Mrs. Walker made an exasperated noise. "Of course not! I told you, she took the baby. Then some other people came and took the woman. Kidnapped her! Carried her out of there against her will."

Frank remembered what Sarah had told her about those rich do-gooders who rescued prostitutes. Apparently, they'd succeeded. "Don't you have a bouncer in the place?"

"Of course I do, but your Mrs. Brandt asked him to take her and the baby in the carriage, so he wasn't there when the rest of them showed up."

"She's not *my* Mrs. Brandt," was all Frank could think to say to that.

"Do you know anything about this, Malloy?" O'Brien asked.

"No," Frank lied. "And if I did, Mrs. Brandt wouldn't be involved in it."

"Well, she is involved in it, and I want you to get her in here so she can tell us where they've taken this woman."

Fury welled up in Frank, almost choking him, but he knew anger wouldn't get him anywhere with O'Brien. Fortunately, he had another weapon he could use. "Do you know who she is, Chief?"

"Mrs. Brandt? Of course I know who she is."

"No, I mean do you know who her father is?"

"Her father? No, why should I?"

"Because he's Felix Decker, that's why. I don't think he'd be happy to hear you hauled his daughter down to Police Headquarters to ask her questions about something that happened in a brothel."

"Who's Felix Decker?" Mrs. Walker asked.

"One of the richest men in the city," O'Brien said sourly. "And not one of your clients, I take it."

Mrs. Walker glared at him. "I just want my girl back. I don't care who took her. I pay you to protect me, O'Brien. I expect to get my money's worth."

"Malloy, go see this Mrs. Brandt and find out what happened to the girl," O'Brien said.

"She'd have to be crazy to tell me that, knowing I'd have to tell you," Malloy said. "And she's not crazy."

"I don't care about any of that. Just find out what happened to the girl and get her back to Mrs. Walker."

Why, Frank wondered as he let himself out of O'Brien's office, couldn't Sarah ever take his advice?

* * *

"**N**OT EXACTLY WHAT YOU EXPECTED, WAS IT?"

Sarah looked up in surprise to see Miss Yingling standing in the doorway of what must be the front parlor. She wore the same drab olive green suit she'd worn the first day Sarah had met her, but she seemed much more animated today than she had then. Her eyes were actually sparkling.

"No, it wasn't," Sarah admitted. "I didn't expect to get away with the baby so easily."

"Mrs. Van Orner had a bit more trouble, I'm afraid."

"But she did get Amy out, didn't she?"

"Oh, yes, but the stupid girl wanted to get dressed and pack up all her clothes. Mrs. Van Orner tried to reason with her—how much use will those clothes be to her outside of a brothel, after all?—but she kept arguing. Finally, Mr. Porter just picked her up bodily and carried her out of the house in her nightdress."

"Oh, dear! I knew I should have warned her they were coming. She could have been ready."

"Oh, yes, waiting at the door with her grip," Miss Yingling scoffed. "That would be a pretty picture."

"She could have at least gotten dressed," Sarah said.

"It's just as well. They never want to part with the fancy clothes, and they even want to wear them. A woman can't walk down the street dressed like that without attracting the wrong kind of attention, so we end up having to burn the clothes."

"Did Mrs. Walker try to interfere?"

"A little, but she was late to the party. Mr. Quimby kept the cook busy at the front door for quite a while, long enough for Mrs. Van Orner and Mr. Porter to get back downstairs with the girl. The girl was making a fuss by then, and the cook heard it and started shouting for the madam. She and Mrs. Walker came running, but Mr. Quimby and Mrs. Van Orner were able to hold them off until they got Amy into the carriage."

"Were you with them?"

"Oh, no, I was here, helping Lisa get everything ready. Mrs. Spratt-Williams told me all about it."

"Lisa?"

"Lisa Biafore, the Italian girl who let you in just now. She's really Analise, but she's trying to be more American, so she changed it to Lisa."

Sarah heard a door open and close upstairs. "I'd like to examine Amy, to make sure she's all right after the carriage ride and all the excitement."

"I'm sure Mrs. Van Orner will see the wisdom of that. Should I ask her?"

"Yes, please."

She left Sarah standing in the front hall as she hurried off toward the rear of the house. In a few minutes, Mrs. Van Orner came into the front parlor, where Sarah had found a seat on a battered sofa. Miss Yingling came trailing along behind.

"Mrs. Brandt, we can't thank you enough," Mrs. Van Orner said as Sarah rose. "Your information was invaluable."

"Not as invaluable as your courage," Sarah replied. "If you and your friends hadn't been willing to go in there . . ."

Mrs. Van Orner waved Sarah's praise away. "Not at all. We simply do God's work. Tamar said you wanted to examine the girl. I think that's a good idea. She was extremely agitated during the entire event. I'm so glad you brought the baby over, though. Perhaps she'll calm down now. If not, we can give her some laudanum."

"I'd rather not, since it can go through the milk and make the baby too groggy to feed well. Let me see how she's doing first."

"Certainly. Tamar, will you take Mrs. Brandt upstairs?"

Miss Yingling seemed only too glad to oblige. She led the way and Sarah followed.

"How many women live in the house?" Sarah asked as they climbed the stairs.

"Just two others right now. We have room for more, but the women don't do well if they have to share a room with someone, I'm afraid. They have a difficult time adjusting to normal life, so we try to give them privacy when we can."

"Is it unusual for a woman to be as agitated as Amy was?"

"Not at all. They're frightened and excited at the prospect of freedom. Some of them become hysterical while others just huddle in a corner and shake."

Miss Yingling stopped in front of one of the doors that lined the upstairs hallway. Sarah could hear the murmur of voices from inside. Miss Yingling tapped lightly, then opened the door without waiting for an invitation.

"Mrs. Brandt would like to see Amy," she announced.

The room was already crowded. Furnished with a plain iron bedstead, a wardrobe, and a washstand, the place felt more utilitarian than comfortable. Plain muslin curtains hung at the window, and the walls were painted an ugly shade of brown. Amy lay propped in the bed, the baby at her breast, and Mrs. Spratt-Williams and the girl Tamar had told her about, Lisa Biafore, stood by, ready to help in any way. Miss Yingling and Sarah took up the remaining floor space.

"Mrs. Brandt," Amy said, brightening. "I got out!"

"Yes, you did. I'm very happy for you."

"You should be. You have no idea how horrible that place was. Of course, my room there was a lot nicer than this," she said, looking with disfavor around her current accommodations.

"You should be grateful you've got a roof over your head and a bed to sleep in," Lisa Biafore chided.

Amy ignored her. "I'm hungry. I have to keep up my strength to feed the baby."

Lisa sniffed in disapproval. "It's not mealtime yet, but I'll see what we have in the kitchen."

"I'd like some bread and jam," Amy said. "Strawberry is my favorite."

Lisa rolled her eyes as she passed Sarah on the way out of the room.

"You missed all the excitement, Mrs. Brandt," Mrs. Spratt-Williams said.

"Miss Yingling told me. Amy, how are you feeling?"

If Miss Yingling's eyes were sparkling, Amy's were glittering. "I'm as happy as I can be."

Sarah smiled. "No, I mean are you having any discomfort? Any bleeding?"

"Oh, I don't know. I haven't had a chance to even think about it." But now that she did, she apparently decided she needed to complain. "That man was very rough with me, you know. Carried me out of the house and practically threw me into the carriage. Didn't give me a chance to get dressed or anything!"

"They didn't have time," Mrs. Spratt-Williams said. "They had to get you out before someone raised the alarm."

"And the carriage was so old, I don't think it even had

any springs left. I'm probably black-and-blue from bounc-
ing around."

"Would you mind if I examined you? I want to make sure
you're still doing all right."

"Oh, yes, of course." She unceremoniously removed the
baby from her breast and held him out to Mrs. Spratt-
Williams. "Would you take care of him for me? That girl
who was here said she was going to get something to use
for a diaper."

Mrs. Spratt-Williams took the damp baby gingerly,
holding him away from her so as not to soil her gown. "I'll
just . . . I'll take him downstairs." She hurried out.

Miss Yingling closed the door.

"I don't have my medical bag with me, but if I need
something, I can always come back later," Sarah said.

Amy cooperated completely as Sarah examined her, making sure she was none the worse for the excitements of the
day.

"I'm awfully tired," Amy said when Sarah had finished.

"That's to be expected. I would never advise a new mother
to go for a carriage ride on her first day out of bed, but you
seem to be just fine otherwise. Get some rest now, and you'll
be your old self in another week or so."

"Who's going to help me with the baby? I can't take care
of him all by myself, you know."

"The other women will help you, I'm sure," Miss Yingling said. "Having a baby in the house will probably be
something of a novelty."

"What other women?" Amy asked.

"Other women like you," Sarah said. "Women who es-
caped from prostitution."

"I wasn't a prostitute," Amy said, a bit indignantly. "I

was only in that house for my safety, until the baby was born."

"Is that so?" Miss Yingling asked with interest. "How did you get there?"

"My baby's father took me there."

"A brothel seems an odd place to take a woman who's expecting a baby," Miss Yingling said.

Amy glared at her for a moment, and then she said to Sarah, "I want to see Mrs. Van Orner."

"She's too busy to see you," Miss Yingling said.

"I want to thank her for saving me and my baby," Amy said to Sarah, totally ignoring Miss Yingling.

"Saving you from what?" Miss Yingling scoffed. "If you weren't a prostitute—"

"Miss Yingling, would you ask Mrs. Van Orner if she can see Amy?" Sarah asked to make peace.

Miss Yingling shook her head in dismay, but she went out in search of her employer.

"How long do you think I'll have to stay here?" Amy asked, glancing around the room with obvious disdain.

"Miss Biafore was right, you should be grateful you have a place to live."

"Oh, I am, but I didn't realize it would be so . . ." She shrugged, unable to think of a word to describe it.

Sarah didn't help her. "I'm very glad you're in a place where you have someone to look after you until you get your strength back."

"If everybody here is a whore, it's not much different than the place where I was."

"I doubt you'll see any men here," Sarah said.

Amy widened her eyes in appreciation of Sarah's observation. "Oh, no, I won't! Do you know they don't allow men

in here at all? They can't even come through the front door.
Those men who helped rescue me? One of them carried me
to the door and set me down. I had to walk inside myself."

"I'm sure they're trying to avoid any appearance of evil."

Amy shrugged one shoulder carelessly. "I can't imagine
how boring it must be here. I'll bet they don't even allow
music or anything."

Sarah was becoming annoyed at Amy's lack of appreciation. "I'm sure they manage to amuse themselves somehow."

"Those prigs? Not likely."

"Do you have any idea what you'll do when you're recovered?" Sarah asked.

Amy looked up in surprise. "What do you mean?"

"I mean, you'll have to make your own way in the world,
and now you have a baby to support. Do you have any family
who can help you?"

"My family couldn't take care of themselves, much less
me."

"Friends, perhaps?"

Amy considered the question for a long moment. "Yes, I
do have friends."

"I'll be happy to get in touch with them for you."

Amy smiled mysteriously. "You've already done enough,
Mrs. Brandt. I'll take care of that myself."

Before Sarah could reply, the bedroom door opened, and
Mrs. Van Orner and Miss Yingling came in.

"How are you feeling, Amy?" Mrs. Van Orner asked.

"Much better, although I'm starving. That Italian girl
said she'd get me something to eat, but she hasn't come back
yet."

"I'm sure she'll take care of you. We're very glad to have
you here."

"I'm very glad to be here. I wanted to thank you for all your help, Mrs. Van Orner. I don't think I thanked you before."

"You were upset," Mrs. Van Orner said. "That's understandable."

"I couldn't believe you made me leave all my things behind," Amy said, still aggrieved. "I don't have a stitch to wear."

"We'll make sure you have everything you need, including new clothes that are more appropriate to your new life." Mrs. Van Orner glanced meaningfully at Amy's frilly dressing gown.

Miss Yingling had left the door open, and Mrs. Spratt-Williams walked in carrying the baby in her arms. He was wrapped in what looked like part of an old sheet.

"Here he is," she announced to all, as proudly as if she'd just given birth to him herself. "All clean and dry. Miss Biafore tore up an old towel to make a diaper. We'll need to get a layette for him, Vivian," she said to Mrs. Van Orner.

"We certainly will," she agreed, admiring the baby as Mrs. Spratt-Williams held him out for all of them to see.

"What's the baby's name?" Miss Yingling asked. Sarah had the oddest impression she wasn't so much interested as she was goading Amy, although that couldn't possibly be true.

"I haven't named him yet," Amy said. "I was afraid to, in case they took him away from me, you see."

"Oh, how awful for you," Mrs. Spratt-Williams said. "But you don't have to worry about that anymore." She leaned over and placed the baby in Amy's arms. "No one's going to take him away now."

"No, they aren't," Mrs. Van Orner said.

"So you can name him now," Miss Yingling said, her lips

stretching into a mirthless smile. "Maybe you want to name him after your father."

"That no-good bum? Not likely," Amy said. "He lost all our money and left us to starve."

Mrs. Spratt-Williams tut-tutted. "That's all too common, I'm afraid. Yes, indeed, a very familiar story."

"Perhaps there's a man you admire," Mrs. Van Orner suggested. "Someone you'd like your son to be like when he grows up."

"Oh, yes, there is," Amy agreed, admiring the boy as she spoke. "I know exactly who I want to name him for."

"Who is that, my dear?" Mrs. Spratt-Williams asked.

"I want to name him Gregory, for his father."

All the other women gasped, Sarah included. She couldn't imagine why Amy would want to name the boy for the man who had seduced and betrayed her. If she could even be sure who the baby's father was, that is.

If Amy was aware how she had shocked her audience, she gave no indication. She just continued to admire the baby, giving him her finger to grasp, and when Sarah turned her gaze to the other women, she realized that Amy's remark had disturbed them even more than it had her.

Mrs. Van Orner had gone white. "Excuse me," she murmured and hurried out of the room. Mrs. Spratt-Williams followed her immediately, leaving Miss Yingling, who stared at Amy with the oddest expression on her face. Sarah could have sworn it was grudging admiration, although she couldn't imagine what she saw in Amy to admire. Then she, too, was gone.

"Yes," Amy said to no one in particular, "I think I'll call him Gregory. It's such a dignified name, don't you think?" She looked up and seemed surprised to notice that most of her company had gone.

"Do you know where your baby's father is?" Sarah asked.

"I can find him."

"Does he know about the baby?"

"Oh, yes. I told you, he sent me to Mrs. Walker's so I'd be safe until the baby came."

Sarah had indeed heard her say that, but she hadn't believed it for a moment. And if he had, why had she needed Mrs. Van Orner's help to escape? "You told me that they made you . . . uh . . . entertain customers there."

She gave Sarah what could have passed for an apologetic look if Amy had actually been sincere. "I had to tell you something so you'd help me get away. I could see what that old bitty was planning. She really was going to take the baby and put me to work."

"But if your baby's father . . . ?"

"Once she made me a whore, he wouldn't want me anymore, would he? That's what she was thinking. That's why I had to get away."

Sarah had to admit, this made a tiny bit of sense, and if there was any truth in it at all . . . "Your baby's father, will he . . . help you?"

Amy stared at Sarah, considering her question, or perhaps considering her answer. "He will now," she finally said.

Sarah wanted to ask what she meant by that, but she wasn't sure she wanted to know. If it was true, Amy and her baby would be taken care of. Such a scenario seemed too good to be true. Much too good to be true, in Sarah's experience. Perhaps Amy didn't have the same experience.

"You should try to get some rest now," Sarah said, deciding this wasn't the time for a discussion on the subject. "And if you have any discomfort or anything seems not quite right, send for me."

"Oh, I will," Amy promised. "I'm going to take very good care of myself, Mrs. Brandt."

Sarah was still mulling over Amy's words when she reached the bottom of the stairs. Lisa Biafore came from the rear of the house carrying a tray and muttering imprecations under her breath. She passed Sarah on her way up the stairs. Amy was getting her strawberry jam, Sarah noted.

"Mrs. Brandt?"

Sarah looked up to see Mrs. Spratt-Williams coming out of the parlor, a worried frown creasing her brow.

"Would you have a few minutes? Mrs. Van Orner would like to speak with you."

"Of course." Sarah followed her into the parlor.

Mrs. Van Orner sat on the sofa where Sarah had waited earlier, her face still chalk white, and her hands clasped tightly in her lap. Miss Yingling stood across the room, by the fireplace, her back ramrod stiff, her expression pinched. Two spots of color burned in her cheeks.

Mrs. Spratt-Williams closed the parlor doors behind them and turned to face Sarah. "I told Vivian that it's just a coincidence, that she couldn't possibly have known."

"Known what?"

Mrs. Spratt-Williams pressed her lips together and took a step back. She didn't want to say. Sarah turned to Miss Yingling for an explanation, but she simply stared back, looking miserable. Finally, Mrs. Van Orner said, "My husband's name is Gregory."

Oh! Of course! Sarah remembered now. No wonder they'd gasped and looked so horrified.

"I know it's just a coincidence," Mrs. Spratt-Williams repeated. "Please, Mrs. Brandt, tell her."

Sarah wasn't sure what she was supposed to tell her. She

looked at Mrs. Van Orner helplessly. Mrs. Van Orner managed to smile. "I was shocked, of course, to hear his name, but I don't believe it's a coincidence."

Sarah managed not to gasp again. "Mrs. Van Orner, you can't possibly think . . ."

"That my husband fathered that child?" Mrs. Van Orner asked archly. "Of course not. I am, however, concerned that the girl will make the claim in order to . . ." She waved her hand vaguely.

"To get money from you," Miss Yingling said baldly.

Mrs. Van Orner did not acknowledge the accusation. "Mrs. Brandt, would you be so kind as to sit down here and tell me everything you know about this girl?"

"Of course!" Sarah took a seat on the sofa beside her and proceeded to recount every conversation she'd ever had with Amy, including the last one. Not surprisingly, she knew very little about the girl's background, and what few facts she'd been told seemed to contradict each other.

"So she told you how much she hated the things she had to do with the customers, and just now she claimed she'd never actually been a prostitute," Mrs. Van Orner mused.

"That's easy enough to explain," Miss Yingling said. "Now that she's out of the brothel, she doesn't want people to think she was a whore."

"Tamar's right," Mrs. Spratt-Williams said. "Men don't put women in brothels for safekeeping, and madams don't rent rooms to young women who are waiting to deliver a baby."

"That's true," Mrs. Van Orner said, "but madams don't allow their girls to carry babies either."

"I remember Mrs. Walker made a remark about how

Amy had lied to her," Sarah said. "She could have concealed her pregnancy until it was too late to do anything about it."

"I suppose that's possible," Mrs. Van Orner said. "You would know better than I. I'm afraid I have little experience with such things."

Sarah saw the sadness in her eyes, the disappointment of a woman whose purpose in life had not been fulfilled. Sarah recognized it because she bore that same disappointment. "I've known women who were able to conceal their condition for many months, especially with a first baby."

"But why would she do that? Why would she want to keep the child?" Miss Yingling asked.

The other three women just gaped at her. Finally, Mrs. Spratt-Williams said, "Perhaps she wanted it, my dear."

"And that would also explain her desperation to escape that awful place," Mrs. Van Orner added. "She must have known they'd take her child from her."

"Could Amy have known Gregory is Mr. Van Orner's name?" Miss Yingling asked in a naked effort to turn the subject back to their original concern.

"I suppose we could ask her," Mrs. Van Orner said with a sigh.

"She'd lie about that just like she lies about everything else," Miss Yingling said, reminding Sarah of what Frank Malloy had told her about prostitutes. Plainly, Amy had lied about many things. The problem was figuring out which ones.

"Mrs. Brandt," Mrs. Spratt-Williams said. "When Amy asked you to help her, did she know Mrs. Van Orner's name or did she just ask you to find someone who does this sort of work?"

"She knew Mrs. Van Orner's name," Sarah said. "In

fact . . ." She closed her eyes, replaying that desperate conversation in her mind. What had Amy said exactly? "She told me to contact Mrs. *Gregory* Van Orner."

Mrs. Van Orner made a tiny sound, as if she'd felt a sudden, sharp pain, but Mrs. Spratt-Williams said, "There you are, she knew Gregory's name. She was trying to shock you and frighten you. She wants money, that's all."

"Or maybe . . ." Miss Yingling said, drawing everyone's attention. When they were all looking at her, she said, "Or maybe the baby's father really is named Gregory."

ALL THE WAY HOME, SARAH KEPT TRYING TO MAKE SENSE of it all. Miss Yingling had quickly explained that she meant the baby's father could be some other man named Gregory, not Mr. Van Orner at all. What an innocent explanation that would be.

Why had they only pretended to believe it?

Oh, they had all insisted that they did, but Sarah could see that they didn't. They all thought Amy had some sinister reason for choosing Mr. Van Orner's name for her child, even if none of them had said so aloud. Sarah was already beginning to regret helping the girl, although how she could have refused, she didn't know.

Sarah felt unutterably weary when she finally arrived at her house. She let herself in the front door and called out to tell Maeve and Catherine she was home. As always, Catherine came running to meet her, emerging from the kitchen and racing through the front room, which served as Sarah's office, and straight into her arms. Sarah hugged her tightly, inhaling her sweet scent and silently vowing never to let anything bad happen to this precious little girl.

When Catherine had given and received the proper number of hugs and kisses, she leaned away so she could see Sarah's face and said, "We have company."

"We do?" Sarah asked, playing along. "Is Mrs. Ellsworth here?" Sarah's elderly neighbor spent most of her free time with the girls.

Catherine shook her head, smiling smugly. "Guess again."

Sarah scrunched up her face, pretending to think very hard. "Mrs. Decker?" she asked. Sarah's mother also enjoyed visiting the girls.

Catherine shook her head vigorously, grinning broadly now.

"Oh, dear, I don't know," Sarah said. "Can you give me a hint?"

Catherine pursed her lips as she considered. After a moment, she said, "He's mad at you."

"He's *very* mad at you," a familiar voice said.

Sarah looked up to see Frank Malloy standing in the kitchen doorway. He obviously knew what she'd been up to this morning, although how he could have heard about it already, she had no idea. He must be ready to throttle her, but even still, she found herself embarrassingly happy to see him.

"Malloy," she said by way of greeting.

He didn't return her smile. He really was angry.

Maeve was hovering behind him, plainly at a loss as to how to act. "Girls, could you go upstairs while Mr. Malloy and I talk?"

"I told him he shouldn't be mad at you," Catherine informed her importantly.

"Then I'm sure he won't be for very long," Sarah said, setting the girl down on her feet.

Maeve came over and took her hand. "Come on, we'll play with your dollhouse."

They started for the stairs, but Catherine stopped and looked back over her shoulder. "You'll call us when he's not mad anymore?"

"Oh, yes," Sarah promised, not daring to look at Malloy for confirmation.

She waited until the girls were out of sight, then took her time removing her hat and gloves. When she looked up again, he hadn't moved, and he was still glaring at her. She tried another smile. "At least no one's dead," she pointed out.

"Not yet," he replied grimly.

5

"Did the girls feed you?" she asked, walking toward him.

"They made me a sandwich."

"Is there anything left? I'm starving."

He stood aside and let her precede him into the kitchen. She saw the loaf of bread still on the cutting board. She sliced herself two pieces and found the cheese in the icebox and cut some. Malloy had found a cup and poured her some coffee from the pot on the stove and refilled his own cup. He waited until she was seated and halfway through her sandwich before he started in on her.

"I warned you not to get involved with that madam."

Sarah sighed with resignation. "I told you, I couldn't refuse to help that girl. Besides, all I did was take the baby, and the madam had already given me her permission to do that."

"You also made sure the bouncer wasn't there when those rich do-gooders got there to take the girl away."

Sarah tried not to show him how surprised she was. "How did you know that?"

"Mrs. Walker told me."

Sarah gaped at him, giving up all semblance of dignity. "When did you see Mrs. Walker?"

"When she came to Police Headquarters to complain to the chief of detectives that someone had kidnapped one of her girls."

"Oh, dear!"

"Yes, oh, dear. She made sure to complain about you by name, so of course O'Brien sent for me right off."

"I'm so sorry."

He gave her a look that said she shouldn't lie to him, so she took another bite of her sandwich.

"She told me what happened. Whose idea was it to get the bouncer away?"

"Theirs," Sarah said when she'd swallowed. "Mrs. Van Orner and her friends at Rahab's Daughters."

"Whose daughters?"

"Rahab's. You remember the Bible story about Joshua and Jericho and how they sent in the spies and she was a harlot and—"

Malloy was waving his hand. "Never mind. So you went to this Mrs. Van-what's-her-name—"

"Van Orner."

"Van Orner," he repeated patiently. "And she and her friends came up with this plan?"

"Yes, they told me exactly what to do. They knew Mrs. Walker would have a man there to keep order when necessary, and if they could just get him away from the house, they thought they could get Amy out without too much trouble."

"Mrs. Walker has accused you of kidnapping one of her girls."

"I wasn't even there."

"You organized it."

"No, I didn't. I told Mrs. Van Orner that a young woman needed help, and she did the rest. All I did was take the baby, and Mrs. Walker had told me I could."

Malloy looked around meaningfully. "If you took the baby, where is it?"

"He's with his mother."

"And where is that?"

Sarah opened her mouth to reply and caught herself just in time. "Why do you want to know?"

Malloy sighed. "Because the chief of detectives has ordered me to find her and take her back to Mrs. Walker."

"You can't be serious!" Sarah cried, nearly choking on the last bite of her sandwich.

"I'm perfectly serious. The girl is Mrs. Walker's property, and she wants her back."

"The girl isn't anyone's property," Sarah insisted. "We abolished slavery in the United States thirty years ago!"

"That's the rumor," Malloy said blandly.

"And I can't believe the police are helping a madam force a young woman back into prostitution!"

"Mrs. Walker pays a lot of money to make sure the police do whatever she wants, and they usually oblige her."

"Well, I have no intention of telling you where she is."

"I know you don't."

"You do?"

"Of course I do," he said with some exasperation.

"Then why are you here?"

"Because if I didn't come and ask you, I'd lose my job. I've got a mother and a son and a very expensive school to support, if you'll recall, so I need my job."

Malloy's son Brian was deaf and attended a special school. Sarah tried not to feel guilty. "I don't want you to lose your job, but I can't let you take Amy back to that place."

"Where is she now?" Malloy held up his hand when she would have protested. "You don't have to tell me the address. I just need to know if she's someplace safe. Good God, she's not here, is she?" He looked around in alarm.

"No, of course not! I wouldn't put Catherine and Maeve in jeopardy."

"Thank God you thought of that. So where is she?"

"Mrs. Van Orner has a house where she takes the girls. They stay there until they can make their own way in the world."

"If they could make their own way in the world, they wouldn't have ended up in a brothel in the first place."

"Mrs. Van Orner did say that many of the women end up back on the streets. It's very difficult for them to find honest work."

"Honest work that will keep them from starving."

They both knew how little women got paid in factories and sweatshops.

"Yes, a woman needs a husband to support her, but as Mrs. Van Orner pointed out, few men are willing to marry a woman who has been a prostitute."

"Sounds like this Mrs. Van Orner has chosen a pretty thankless job."

"Yes, she has. I wonder why she hasn't given it up by now. I don't think I could do it myself."

"I'm glad to hear it."

"Malloy, I know you didn't want me to get involved, but how could I have refused to help that poor girl?"

"You didn't have to get the baby out *yourself*."

"I had to make sure he didn't get sold or shipped out West or something."

"No, you didn't, but that's an argument for another day. Today, I have to figure out what I'm going to tell O'Brien and Mrs. Walker."

"Tell them the truth. I'm not going to betray Mrs. Van Orner."

"Who is this Mrs. Van Orner?"

"Her husband is Gregory Van Orner. I don't know much about them except that they're very wealthy. I could ask my mother—"

"No!" he nearly shouted. "Don't ask your mother anything. I don't need her involved in this, too."

Sarah bit back a smile. Mrs. Decker had occasionally assisted in investigations, but without her husband's knowledge. Obviously, Malloy didn't want to risk him ever finding out.

"Then you'll have to be satisfied with what I know," Sarah said. "She has an office for Rahab's Daughters in the United Charities Building on Twenty-second Street, and she has a group of people who work with her and help her rescue prostitutes."

"Who are these other people?"

"A Mrs. Spratt-Williams, Mr. Porter, Mr. Quimby, and a Miss Yingling, who serves as her secretary. I don't know anything about any of them either, except that they've done this before."

"They've broken into a brothel and kidnapped a prostitute before?" he asked in amazement.

"Yes, but not often. It's dangerous, I'm told."

Malloy didn't appreciate her attempt at humor. "I'm told the same thing. If they don't break into brothels very often, how do they do all this rescuing?"

"They find girls on the street and take them to the house I told you about, where they'll be safe."

Malloy sipped his coffee and considered what she had told him.

"What are you going to do now?" she asked after a moment.

"I'm going to tell O'Brien that Mrs. Van Orner is married to a rich and important man, so we can't touch her either."

"Either?" Sarah echoed. "Who else can't you touch?"

"You."

"Me?"

"Yes, O'Brien wanted me to drag you down to Headquarters to be questioned. I told him who your father is, though, and he changed his mind."

"So he sent you here instead. I'm truly sorry, Malloy."

"Yeah, well, so am I, but there's nothing we can do about it. I'll tell O'Brien what you told me about Mrs. Van Orner and her friends. If O'Brien wants to take on the Van Orner woman and her husband, he's welcome to it."

"I'm not going to tell anyone where that house is," Sarah warned.

"Nobody's going to ask you. I'll tell them you don't know, that you turned the baby over to Mrs. Van Orner and she took it to the mother. If anybody asks you, you should say the same thing."

"Can this Mrs. Walker really take Amy back to her house?"

"If she can find her, she can try." Malloy ran a hand over his face. "Please don't have anything else to do with this, Sarah. People like Mrs. Walker are dangerous, and I can't protect you from her, not when she's got my boss on her payroll."

"I understand." Sarah reached across the table and laid a hand on his arm. "I'm sorry you got involved in all of this."

His gaze met hers and held for a long moment, but before either of them could say anything, the clatter of small, running feet alerted them to the fact that Catherine was about to join them. Sarah withdrew her hand just as Catherine burst into the kitchen.

"Are you still mad?" she asked Malloy.

"No," he said, taking her up into his lap.

She smiled up at him beatifically. "I'm glad."

LATER THAT EVENING, LONG AFTER MALLOY HAD GONE, Sarah and the girls were cleaning up the supper dishes when someone rang her bell. Maeve and Catherine went to answer it while Sarah dried her hands and removed her apron. She was already mentally taking inventory of her medical bag in preparation for going out on a delivery when she heard what sounded like a disturbance in the front room. She was already hurrying out when she heard Maeve say, "You can't come in here!"

When Sarah reached the office, she saw that her visitors had already come in and were facing off with a defiant Maeve and a cowering Catherine, who clung to her skirts and gazed up at them in alarm.

"Mrs. Walker, what are you doing here?" Sarah demanded, quickly stepping between the woman and Maeve. She was only too aware that Jake stood behind the woman, frowning menacingly.

"I came to find Amy, and you're the only one who knows where she is."

"But I *don't* know where she is, and I can't help you, so I must ask you to leave."

The woman jutted her chin out defiantly. "I ain't going anyplace until you hear what I have to tell you."

"Then *we* will leave and go straight to the police," Sarah said, motioning for Maeve and Catherine to move in the direction of the front door, which still stood open.

"The police won't help you none," Mrs. Walker scoffed.

Luckily, Sarah remembered her advantage over Mrs. Walker. "If you think they'll take your side because of the bribes you pay them, let me assure you that my father's influence reaches all the way to the mayor and beyond. Closing down one house of ill repute in the city won't cause much concern to anyone, unless of course you happen to be the owner."

Jake made a threatening noise in his throat and took a step forward, but Mrs. Walker stopped him with an impatient gesture. Then she took a deep breath and lifted a hand to her head, as if she were suffering some sort of distress. "I . . . Mrs. Brandt, I didn't come here to trade threats with you."

"Why did you come, then?"

"To . . . I wanted to talk to you . . . about Amy."

"There's nothing you can tell me about her that I don't already know."

"That isn't true. I think if you know the whole story, you'll change your mind about helping her."

"I doubt that."

Mrs. Walker lifted her chin again. Her eyes were like chips of flint. "Then you shouldn't be afraid to hear me out."

"And if I refuse, will you have your man here force me to listen?" She gave Jake a meaningful glare that he returned with narrowed eyes.

"Jake, go out and wait in the carriage."

"But—"

"Do as I say."

With obvious reluctance, he turned and made his way outside, leaving the front door wide open behind him.

Sarah had no idea what Mrs. Walker intended to say to her, but she knew she didn't want Catherine to hear it. "Maeve, would you take Catherine over to Mrs. Ellsworth's for a little visit?"

"I can't leave you here alone with her!"

"I'll be fine."

"Are you sure?" Maeve asked doubtfully.

Sarah turned to look at them. Catherine's lower lip quivered. In another moment she was going to start crying. Sarah smiled reassuringly. "Wouldn't you like to visit Mrs. Ellsworth? You haven't seen her all day. Just for a few minutes. I'll come and get you when our visitors leave. Go on, now."

Maeve was even more reluctant than Jake had been, but she picked Catherine up and headed for the kitchen. They could go out the back way and Jake wouldn't see them. Sarah was glad she'd thought of that.

Sarah turned back to her visitor expectantly. "What did you want to tell me?"

Mrs. Walker glanced around, apparently noticing her surroundings for the first time. She saw the two easy chairs Sarah had placed by the front window. "Could we sit down? It's been a horrible day."

Sarah didn't want to encourage the woman to stay a moment longer than necessary, but a lifetime of training prevailed. "Of course," she said, glad to hear that she sounded less than gracious, at least.

When they were seated, Mrs. Walker took a moment to study Sarah, as if trying to judge her mood or read her thoughts in some way. Finally, she said, "I know what you think of me, but you're wrong."

"Am I?" Sarah asked. "Are you telling me you don't really own a brothel where you force young women to sell themselves?"

To Sarah's surprise, Mrs. Walker smiled. "You see, that's where you're wrong. I don't force them at all. I don't have to. They come to me of their own free will, begging me to take them in."

"How can you expect me to believe that?" Sarah asked, outraged.

"Because it's true. I have girls knocking on my door every day. Maybe you don't know what it's like to be hungry and desperate, you being from a rich family and all, but there's plenty of girls in the city who do. Poor girls, whose families have thrown them out because they can't afford to feed them anymore. Or girls whose families died or whose husbands deserted them. If they're lucky, they get a job in a factory or they try rolling cigars or making collars in their rooms for some sweatshop, but it ain't long before they figure out they can't afford to eat and keep a roof over their heads both on what they make. Maybe they say no the first time some man offers them a dollar to lift their skirts, but that's more than they make in a week, and when the landlord tells them to pay up or get thrown into the street, that dollar starts to look pretty good."

"I deliver babies all over the city. I know very well how difficult it is for a woman alone to survive," Sarah said.

"Then you shouldn't be surprised that the girls want to work for me instead of being out on the street with no one to protect them, in all weathers where anything can happen to them. I told you before, I take good care of my girls. Nobody beats them or robs them. They eat good and have a clean place to sleep. If I took all the girls who come begging, I'd have a hundred working for me. I have to turn girls away every day."

"Then you shouldn't miss Amy."

Mrs. Walker stiffened. "You don't know anything about her, or you wouldn't say that."

"I know she was desperate to get away from your house."

"She was, but not for the reason you think."

"What other reason did she need?"

"Girls leave my house for lots of reasons. Sometimes they go off with a customer who promised to set them up in style. Sometimes they get lured away to another house. Sometimes I throw them out because they steal from customers or the other girls or me. And sometimes they think they're in love."

"Amy said she hated what you made her do with the customers."

"Of course she did. It's what you wanted to hear, but that's not the reason she wanted to leave."

"What do you think the reason was?"

Mrs. Walker stared at Sarah for a long moment, studying her again. Then she said, "Let me tell you how Amy came to me in the first place. A man brought her."

"What man?"

"A rich man. He'd been keeping her, and he was tired of her. She can be . . . disagreeable when she doesn't get her way."

Sarah had noticed this, but she didn't respond.

"I don't usually do favors for my clients, but this man . . .
I didn't want to refuse him, and he paid me well."

"Did he know she was with child?"

"I don't think she knew herself. If she did, she was stupid
not to tell him, and Amy isn't stupid. Foolish, yes, but not
stupid."

"When did you find out?"

"Not for a long time. She's a plump girl and nobody noticed when she got a little plumper."

"Why didn't she let her protector know about the baby?"

"He didn't want to hear from her, and we don't encourage the girls to write letters. You can understand how much
trouble that might cause. Besides, she was a whore. Why
would he believe the baby was his?"

"How long has she been at your house?"

"Almost six months."

"Then she would have been more than three months gone
when she arrived at your place. The timing should convince
him now."

Mrs. Walker shrugged. "If he wanted to believe it, I
suppose."

"You didn't tell him?"

"Of course not. I make it a habit not to cause problems
for my clients."

"I guess that's why Amy didn't ask you to tell him when
she did realize she was pregnant."

Mrs. Walker sniffed in disgust. "If she'd told me, I
could've taken care of it, but by the time I found out, it was
too late. I had a doctor come see her, but he said she was too
far gone and would probably die if he tried. I should've put
her out then, the ungrateful little bitch, but I let her stay,
out of the goodness of my heart."

"And because some of your customers enjoyed being with a pregnant woman," Sarah guessed.

Mrs. Walker's brown eyes flashed, but she knew how to control her temper. "My girls have to earn their keep. I don't run a charity."

Sarah sighed. "Mrs. Walker, you promised to tell me something to change my mind about helping Amy, but you haven't."

"Yes, I have. I told you she had a baby to a rich man, or at least she's going to try to make him believe that. She's got some romantic notion he's going to take her back or maybe even marry her. I don't know what she's got in her mind, but none of that will happen, I promise you. If she goes to this man with her story, he'll . . . Well, I don't know what he'll do, but it won't be good for Amy, I can tell you that."

Sarah had a difficult time believing Mrs. Walker was so concerned about Amy that she'd come all the way over here to beg for Sarah's help. "I'm guessing he won't be too pleased with you, either, for letting her get out to cause him trouble. In fact, I'm pretty sure that's the real reason you want to get her back, so you can make sure he never finds out."

"If I have reason to be afraid of him, Amy has even more. At least tell me where she is so I can talk to her. She's confused now, but I can set her straight."

"And if you can't, Jake can carry her out bodily."

"The way your people did?" Mrs. Walker countered.

"They weren't my people."

"Then who were they?"

"A group who helps rescue women from the streets. And before you ask, I'll tell you that they've taken Amy to a safe place. I don't know where it is, so I couldn't help you even if I wanted to, and I don't."

"Where did you take the baby? Jake went back to that mission where he'd dropped you off, but they said the baby wasn't there."

"He's with Amy now. I gave him to . . . to the people who helped her."

"Who are these people? How do you know they don't have a brothel of their own? Maybe they rescue whores to take them to their own place!"

"That's ridiculous."

"Not as ridiculous as you might think. A good whore can earn a lot of money."

"The people who rescued Amy are a legitimate charity. It's called Rahab's Daughters."

"Rahab," Mrs. Walker mused. "That's slick. Oh, don't look so surprised. I wasn't born in a whorehouse. I went to Sunday school in my time. Rahab the Harlot. She did all right for herself, if I remember."

"Yes, she did, and Amy will, too, with Mrs. Van Orner's help."

"Whose help?" she asked sharply.

"Mrs. Van Orner. She runs Rahab's Daughters. Maybe you've heard of her."

"No, never," Mrs. Walker said quickly, but Sarah could see she was lying.

She remembered what Amy had said about the girls in the brothel always talking about Mrs. Van Orner. Certainly, Mrs. Walker would have heard of her, too.

Mrs. Walker stood abruptly. "I should be going."

Sarah did want her gone, but something in Mrs. Walker's manner disturbed her. "You'll never find Amy," she tried. "And even if you do, she won't go back."

Mrs. Walker sniffed again. "Fat lot you know about whores, Mrs. Brandt. You should stick to midwiving."

A slender figure suddenly appeared in the front doorway. "What's going on here?" Mrs. Ellsworth demanded, striding determinedly into the room. "Are you all right, Mrs. Brandt?"

"Of course she's all right," Mrs. Walker said haughtily. "Why wouldn't she be?"

Mrs. Ellsworth looked the woman up and down with exaggerated disdain. "Because there's no telling what somebody like you might get up to."

Mrs. Walker flushed crimson, but more from fury than embarrassment, Sarah judged. She lifted her chin and stalked out, taking care to bump into Mrs. Ellsworth, making the older woman gasp with outrage.

"Just who does she think she is?" Mrs. Ellsworth demanded, color blooming in her wrinkled cheeks.

"She thinks she's better than we are," Sarah said. "Where are the girls?"

"I made them stay at my house."

"You should've stayed there yourself."

"I had to make sure you didn't need help. When Maeve told me what was going on . . ." Mrs. Ellsworth shook her head in dismay.

Sarah's first instinct was to remind her neighbor that an elderly woman wouldn't be of much assistance if she really had been in danger, but then she remembered at least one time when Mrs. Ellsworth's assistance had saved her life. "I appreciate your concern, but I wasn't in any danger."

"Is she really a madam?" Mrs. Ellsworth asked, going to close the front door. She stopped when she saw Maeve and

Catherine coming up the front steps. "I told you girls to stay put!"

"We saw the carriage pulling away, so we knew it was all right to come home," Maeve explained. "What did that awful woman say, Mrs. Brandt?"

"Nothing important," Sarah said.

Catherine came running across the room and threw herself into Sarah's arms. Sarah lifted the girl up. "There's nothing to be frightened of, darling."

"Is the mean lady gone?"

"Yes, and she's not coming back."

"I didn't like her."

"I didn't like her either," Maeve said.

"Well, if she comes back here, don't open the door," Mrs. Ellsworth advised.

Catherine didn't allow Sarah out of her sight for the rest of the evening, and she begged Sarah to stay with her until she fell asleep.

When Sarah came back downstairs after putting Catherine to bed, Mrs. Ellsworth was still keeping Maeve company at the kitchen table. Sarah joined them and took this opportunity to tell them about her conversation with Mrs. Walker.

"I can't believe that woman thought you would help her," Mrs. Ellsworth marveled.

"She probably thought she could scare her into it," Maeve said. "She doesn't know you very well, Mrs. Brandt."

"I'm just glad Amy is safe from her now."

"What will happen to her? To Amy, I mean," Maeve asked.

"I don't know. She'll have to find a way to support herself and her baby."

"That won't be easy," Mrs. Ellsworth said. "What kind of a job can a girl like her do? And who will take care of the baby?"

"Mrs. Walker was right about one thing. Amy thinks her baby's father is going to help her."

"How do you know?" Maeve asked in surprise.

"She told me today. She has the idea that once he learns about the baby, he'll want her back or something."

Mrs. Ellsworth shook her head. "He doesn't sound like that kind of man."

"No, he doesn't," Sarah agreed. "But we can't be sure Mrs. Walker was telling us the truth. And maybe Amy knows him better than she does."

"I'd say Mrs. Walker only tells the truth when it suits her," Maeve said. "And it might've suited her this time."

"Yes, it might."

"Are you going to tell Mr. Malloy that she came to see you tonight?" Maeve asked.

"Oh, yes, that's a good idea," Mrs. Ellsworth said. "He'll make sure she never comes back here."

"Unfortunately, I don't think he could." Sarah told them both about her conversation with Frank Malloy earlier in the day.

"You mean the police would actually help her force a girl to go back to her brothel? Against her will?" Mrs. Ellsworth asked.

"So it appears," Sarah said.

"If he was mad before, he'll be even madder when he hears that woman showed up on your doorstep," Maeve pointed out.

"I know, which is why I don't think I'll mention it. I doubt she'll bother us again, at any rate. She knows I can't help her."

"Let's hope," Mrs. Ellsworth said fervently.

"I just wonder if Mrs. Van Orner and her friends will help Amy get in touch with the baby's father," Sarah said.

"If they don't, will you help her?" Maeve asked.

"I think you should take Mr. Malloy's advice and keep out of it altogether," Mrs. Ellsworth said. "You did what she asked you to do and helped her escape from that place. No one can expect anything more."

Sarah wondered if that were true.

T HE NEXT DAY, SARAH WOULD HAVE PAID AMY ANOTHER visit, just to make sure she was doing well, but she was called out on another delivery. When she got back, late the following day, she found a note from Mrs. Van Orner thanking her for her help and telling her Amy was doing fine and Sarah need no longer concern herself. The news made Maeve and Mrs. Ellsworth very happy, and Sarah decided to put the episode out of her mind, as Malloy had begged her to do.

She thought about Amy several times during the next few days, but several more deliveries kept her too busy to do more than that. A week later, she had convinced herself that if Amy had needed her help, they would have sent for her.

She and the girls had just finished cleaning up the supper dishes when someone rang the bell. Maeve and Catherine went to answer it, and Sarah didn't even bother to remind them to check who was there before opening it. All concern that Mrs. Walker would return had evaporated.

Sarah heard the rumble of a familiar voice and quickly removed her apron and smoothed her hair before hurrying out to the front room. Maeve and Catherine were making Frank Malloy feel welcome.

"We have some stew left from supper," Maeve was saying. "We can heat it up for you."

"No, thanks, I can't stay." He looked up at Sarah when she came into the room, but he didn't smile. "I just need to tell Mrs. Brandt something, and then I have to go."

"Girls, would you leave us alone for a minute?" Sarah asked.

Maeve took a reluctant Catherine by the hand and led her back into the kitchen.

"What is it? What's wrong?" Sarah asked, alarm prickling over her.

"It's your friend, the one you did the rescue with."

"Amy? Has something happened to her?"

"Amy? Who's that?"

"She's the girl we took from the brothel. What's happened to her?"

"Nothing that I know of. It's the woman, the one who does the rescues."

"Mrs. Van Orner?" Sarah asked in surprise.

"Yeah, Mrs. Van Orner. She's dead."

6

"DEAD?" SARAH ECHOED INCREDULOUSLY. "ARE YOU sure?"

"As sure as I can be."

"How on earth did it happen?"

"We don't know who did it yet, but it looks like she was murdered."

"Good heavens." Sarah could hardly take it in. "How awful." Then she thought of something else. "Are you investigating?"

"I was put on the case when they figured out this Mrs. Van Orner was the one who kidnapped that whore from Mrs. Walker's place." His expression told her exactly how unhappy that made him. "I think the chief has it in for me now."

"I'm so sorry, but it shouldn't be too difficult to figure out who killed her. I'm sure a woman like Mrs. Van Orner didn't have a lot of enemies."

"No, not a lot," Malloy agreed. "Just every madam in New York City."

"Mrs. Walker, at least," Sarah said, trying to be helpful. "Or that man Jake who works for Mrs. Walker."

"If somebody had cracked her skull, I'd suspect Jake, but it's more likely she was poisoned. Poison is a woman's way of killing someone. Women don't like making a mess."

She didn't miss the sarcasm in his voice, but she ignored it. "Can I help you somehow?"

"No," he said sharply, his dark eyes flashing. "That's why I came to tell you. I want you to stay out of this, Sarah. We're dealing with dangerous people, people who don't think twice about killing the wife of a very powerful man. People like that wouldn't think twice about killing a midwife either."

"Nobody wants to kill me, Malloy," she scoffed.

"I think Mrs. Walker, for one, would be very happy to see you dead. I haven't seen you in more than a week, so by now you could've made a dozen new enemies I don't even know about yet."

"I haven't made any enemies at all, thank you very much. I've been working very hard delivering babies."

"Good, keep doing that, and stay out of the Tenderloin."

Sarah was going to promise to do just that but then she remembered her last encounter with Mrs. Walker. "Oh, no!"

"What?" Malloy asked. He looked like he was bracing himself.

"Mrs. Walker came to see me last week."

"What do you mean, came to see you?"

"She came here to the house, to talk to me."

Malloy muttered something that might've been a curse. "What did she want?"

"She was trying to convince me to tell her where Amy was so she could get her back."

Malloy closed his eyes as if praying for strength and drew a fortifying breath. "And what did you tell her?"

"I told her what you said I should tell her, that I didn't know where they were keeping Amy. But I also mentioned Mrs. Van Orner's name. Oh, my heavens, I betrayed her to that woman! I'm responsible for her death!"

"We don't know who killed Mrs. Van Orner yet. It could have been her maid for all we know."

"I doubt it was her maid. She'd be out of a job if she killed her mistress."

"Which probably explains why more rich women aren't murdered by their maids. I'm serious, Sarah. You weren't responsible and you should forget you ever met any of these people. And if anybody bothers you again, let me know."

"You said she was poisoned. Where did it happen?"

"In her carriage."

"Her carriage? How does someone get poisoned in a carriage?"

"She drank something from a flask she had in her purse while she was going from the house where she keeps the rescued whores to her own house."

This made no sense to Sarah. Why would she be drinking anything at all from a flask? Unless . . .

"Could she have committed suicide?"

"Anything's possible. I'm guessing that would be too easy a solution, though."

"What does her husband say?"

Malloy frowned. "You're much too interested in this. I told you to forget about it, and I mean it. I have to go now."

Sarah should have felt guilty for keeping him from

his very important work, but she just felt frustrated. She wanted to know what had happened to Mrs. Van Orner. She couldn't imagine anyone wanting to kill her, not even the madams of New York City. Mrs. Van Orner had said herself that she rarely had the opportunity to rescue a woman from a brothel. Usually, she rescued the common streetwalkers. The men who pimped for those women would hardly have had an opportunity to poison Mrs. Van Orner.

Malloy was walking toward the door. Sarah followed him.

"The girls will be disappointed. I'll tell them you had to go back to work."

"Thanks. Tell Catherine I'll bring Brian over to see her soon," he said, referring to his son.

"She'll like that."

Malloy settled his hat on his head and opened the door. He stopped, turned back, and for a moment she thought he was going to say something else, probably something about being careful. Then he appeared to think better of it, and he left without another word. Sarah sighed and closed the door behind him. She knew she should forget all about Mrs. Van Orner. She would, too. Just as soon as she'd visited her mother tomorrow to see what she knew from her high society friends.

Malloy sighed as he walked down Sarah's front steps. He hoped he'd impressed her with how dangerous it would be to get involved in this murder. He'd known her long enough to realize that her own natural sense of self-preservation wouldn't be enough to keep her away. He only hoped her concern for Catherine would keep her away.

If only he believed it.

He strode quickly down Bank Street, heading for the Ninth Avenue Elevated Train Station at Little West Twelfth Street. The train whose track ran on pillars two stories above the street would take him quickly uptown to the Van Orner house, where he would try to find out what Mr. Van Orner knew about his wife's murder. And if he even wanted the police to find out anything about his wife's murder. Frank hadn't told Sarah that his only knowledge of the crime came from the report of the beat cop, who had come running when Mrs. Van Orner's driver had opened the carriage door to find her lying in a heap on the floor of her carriage, her body already growing cold. Would Van Orner have even notified the police if he'd found her dead in her bed or slumped over at her dressing table? He would never know.

An hour later, Malloy stood on the front stoop of the Van Orner home. Dusk was falling, and the hour was much too late for callers. A wide-eyed maid took his card and left him waiting in the small, uncomfortable room just off the front entrance hall where they put visitors the maid suspected the family didn't want to see.

After a few minutes, a young woman came into the room. Frank could usually tell from a person's clothing alone what their place in the household was. This woman carried herself like one of the upper classes, back erect, chin up, hazel eyes confident and steady as she took his measure. She held her hands folded primly at her waist. Her clothing betrayed her, however. Her dress fit poorly, obviously a cast-off from someone larger and older, judging from the style, and it was a sickly green that reminded Frank of old moss. She hadn't done anything with her hair either. He thought it might be pretty and shiny if she'd let it down, but she had it pinned up just like his mother wore hers. Frank had the odd feeling she was *trying* to be unattractive. He'd never known a young woman who didn't want to appear at her best at all times.

"Detective Sergeant Malloy?" she asked in a well-modulated voice that made him think of Sarah's mother and her friends. Who could she be?

"That's right. I'd like to speak with Mr. Van Orner about his wife's death."

"Mr. Van Orner is very upset at the moment, as you can imagine. Perhaps I can answer your questions."

"Perhaps you can," Frank said, keeping the sarcasm out of his voice. "Who are you, miss?"

"Oh, I'm sorry. I'm Miss Tamar Yingling. I am . . . I was Mrs. Van Orner's secretary." Her voice caught at just the right moment, and she appeared to be controlling her emotions with difficulty, just the way Mrs. Van Orner's secretary should.

"I'm sorry, Miss Yingling. You must be pretty upset yourself."

"I am, but Mrs. Van Orner didn't approve of unseemly displays of emotion."

Or maybe Miss Yingling didn't really feel like making an unseemly display of emotion. He glanced around the inhospitable room. "Would you like to sit down while you give me the information I need, Miss Yingling?"

"If you think it will take a while, I suppose I'd better." She perched on the edge of one of the two straight-backed chairs that were almost the only furnishings in the room. She sat perfectly erect, the way upper-class women did, with her back not touching the chair.

Frank took the other chair and reached into his coat pocket for the small notebook and pencil he carried to jot down details. "How long have you worked for Mrs. Van Orner?"

"Two years. I admired her very much, and I felt privileged that she chose me to help her with her work."

"What work did you help her with?"

"Her rescue work. Perhaps you don't know. Mrs. Van Orner had dedicated herself to assisting young women in escaping from a life of shame."

"I understand she rescued prostitutes," Frank said.

"Yes," she admitted, obviously offended by his bluntness.

"Was that what she was doing today?"

"No, she . . . she was visiting the house she had purchased to give these unfortunate young women a safe place to live until they can support themselves with honest work."

"Visiting the house or visiting somebody in particular?"

Miss Yingling didn't like his questions. "She was visiting the young women who are living there now, to see how they're adjusting to their new lives."

"Were you with her?"

"I . . . I had gone with her from our office."

"Your office?"

"Yes, her organization, Rahab's Daughters, has an office in the United Charities Building. Her carriage picked us up and took us from there to the house."

"Where is this house?"

"The location of the house is a secret. The young women who live there would be in terrible danger if—"

"Where is the house?" Frank repeated.

"Mrs. Van Orner would never allow me to—"

"Mrs. Van Orner is dead," Frank reminded her. "She died

after leaving that house. If you want me to find out who killed her, I have to talk to the people who saw her there."

"Oh, my, I hadn't thought of that, but Mrs. Van Orner would never—if she were alive, that is—would never allow us to reveal the location, and even if I told you the address, you couldn't enter it anyway."

"Why not?" he asked in surprise.

The color rose in Miss Yingling's pale cheeks, a modest young woman forced to discuss a topic she found embarrassing. "Mr. Malloy, because of the lives the women who live in this house used to lead, Mrs. Van Orner decreed that no male would ever be allowed inside the house. She wished to avoid any hint of impropriety that might affect the ability of these women to return to respectability."

That made sense, Frank supposed. He'd figure out what to do about visiting the house later. "So you were with her today. Can you tell me if she seemed concerned about anything? Had she had an argument with anyone or trouble of any kind?"

"Mrs. Van Orner disapproved of displays of emotion."

"So you said. What does that mean exactly?"

"It means that if Mrs. Van Orner was upset about anything, she would never allow anyone else to suspect."

"But you knew her very well. Maybe you could read her moods when other people couldn't."

Miss Yingling frowned.

"Or maybe you saw or heard someone bothering her."

"Mrs. Van Orner was very concerned about the well-being of a young woman who had recently been rescued. She has a child, you see, and she will have a difficult time of it, I'm afraid."

"Who is this woman?"

"Her name is Amy. I'm not sure what her last name is."

The woman Sarah had helped rescue. "Did this Amy have an argument with Mrs. Van Orner?"

"Not an argument, no. Mrs. Van Orner doesn't engage in emotional displays. This Amy is a difficult case, however. She isn't nearly as grateful as she should be for what Mrs. Van Orner has done for her."

"Do you know why?"

Frank had a feeling she knew perfectly well, but she said, "No, I don't. We've seen this kind of thing before. Women beg us to rescue them, and when they realize how difficult their lives will be, they become angry. They often blame Mrs. Van Orner for their own troubles."

"Is Amy angry at Mrs. Van Orner?"

"Not angry exactly. She refuses to make any plans for her future. She . . . she seems to think the father of her baby is going to take care of her, you see, and that . . . well, that isn't very realistic."

"Does she know who the father is?"

Miss Yingling hesitated a moment, long enough to let Frank know with a glance how inappropriate it was to ask a respectable young woman such a question. Then she said, "She claims to, but considering how she made her living . . ." She shrugged eloquently.

Frank figured if a prostitute claimed he'd fathered her baby, he'd be more than a little skeptical. Any man would. "Did Mrs. Van Orner try to make her see reason?"

"She had a private conversation with Amy today. I have no idea what happened, but afterwards, Amy was very angry and Mrs. Van Orner was very quiet."

"Then what happened?"

"Mrs. Van Orner asked to speak with Mrs. Spratt-Williams, and the two of them went into Mrs. Van Orner's office—the room she keeps as an office at the rescue house, not her office at the United Charities Building."

"Who is this Mrs. Spratt-Williams?"

"She is one of the ladies who helps Mrs. Van Orner in her work. We have several ladies and gentlemen who support us."

"Did she help rescue Amy?"

"I believe she did."

"What did she and Mrs. Van Orner talk about?"

"You'll have to ask Mrs. Spratt-Williams about that, I'm afraid. Mrs. Van Orner didn't confide in me."

"What did Mrs. Van Orner do after she met with Mrs. Spratt-Williams?"

"She spoke briefly with Lisa and—"

"Who's Lisa?"

"Lisa Biafore. She's the . . . I suppose you could call her the house mother at the rescue house. She manages the place and looks after the women who live there."

"Did they have an argument?"

"Not an argument, but Lisa was upset. She doesn't like Amy. Amy is . . . demanding."

"Was this Lisa complaining?"

"I suppose you could call it that, although Mrs. Van Orner is . . . *was* very impatient with complainers. If you saw a problem, she expected you to take action to help resolve it."

"Was she impatient with this Lisa?"

"No, in fact, she was very patient. She told Lisa not to worry, that Amy would be leaving soon."

"Was she going to throw her out?" Frank asked, thinking

this Amy might've had a good reason for doing Mrs. Van Orner in.

"I really don't know. Perhaps the baby's father really was going to help her," she said with a small, unfriendly smile.

"All right," Frank said, making careful note of the order of Mrs. Van Orner's conversations. "What did Mrs. Van Orner do then?"

"I . . . I'm not sure. She may have spoken to someone else, but I didn't see her after she started talking with Lisa. I went back to her office to straighten up some things. I remember being surprised because she'd left without me. I live here, you see, and she always takes me in the carriage with her when she goes home."

This was interesting. "Why do you think she left without you?"

"I have no idea. As I said, I didn't see her leave. I didn't even know she'd gone. I had to make my way home on my own, and by the time I got here . . ." She stopped, her voice breaking delicately, and she lifted her fingers and pressed them to her lips, as if trying to hold back a sob.

"By the time you got here, Mrs. Van Orner was dead," Frank supplied for her. "Who found her?"

"Herman, her driver. He'd stopped the carriage in front of the house, as he always does, and got down to open the door and help her out. He—"

"I'll question him myself," Frank said, not wanting to hear the story secondhand. "Who told you Mrs. Van Orner was dead?"

She hesitated, as if she was trying to remember, but nobody forgot something like that. She was hesitating because she was trying to decide whether to tell him the truth or not. "Mr. Van Orner broke the news to me."

"I'd like to speak to him."

"He can't tell you anything. He hadn't seen Mrs. Van Orner since early morning."

"I still need to talk to him. I need to know what he wants from the police."

"What do you mean?"

"I mean does he want us to find out how his wife died?"

"Of course he does!" she said, genuinely surprised.

"Did he tell you that?"

"No, but . . . I'm sure he does."

"Even if it causes him some embarrassment?"

Her eyes widened as understanding dawned. "Mrs. Van Orner was above reproach. You'll find nothing embarrassing, I assure you."

"She took in prostitutes, Miss Yingling. That alone must've caused him some embarrassment." Frank could only imagine how the man's wealthy friends would have ribbed him about it.

"Does it really matter? Don't the police have to find out what happened to her anyway?"

"No." He let the word hang in the air for a long moment, studying her very real surprise, and then he said, "Men like Mr. Van Orner can tell the police not to investigate and we won't. They can tell us to arrest somebody—anybody—and solve the case. Or they can tell us to find out the truth. We do whatever they want."

"Because they have money," she guessed. He heard the trace of bitterness beneath the words.

Frank saw no reason to reply. He simply waited.

"I'll speak to him," she said at last.

He wondered how much influence Van Orner's wife's secretary would have with him, but she was his only hope at
the moment.

"It may take a while," she added.

"I need to see the driver, Herman. Maybe I could talk to
him while I'm waiting."

"I'll send for him."

"I'd like to see the carriage, too. Could you ask one of the
servants to take me to the stables?"

She rose from her chair. "Wait here," she said, and then
she was gone.

Now he knew her name and her position in the household, but he still didn't know who she really was. He had
the odd feeling that he never would.

A few minutes later, a maid came to fetch him. She took
him to the kitchen and out the back door and across the yard
to the mews. They found Herman in his quarters, a couple
of rooms above the stable. He'd hastily buttoned his livery
jacket before answering the maid's knock, but Frank could
tell he'd been drinking. Even if he hadn't been able to smell
it on him, he could see the red-rimmed eyes. Or maybe he'd
been crying.

The maid made a hasty escape, leaving the two men facing each other in the doorway to his rooms. "What do you
want?" Herman demanded belligerently. He looked to be in
his early twenties, handsome in a rough way.

"Let me in and I'll tell you," Frank said, keeping his voice
mild and reasonable.

"Why should I?"

"So I can be sure you're not the one who killed Mrs. Van
Orner."

The color drained from his flushed face. "I never! You can't say that I did, neither!"

"I can say whatever I want," Frank said quite truthfully, "but I'd like to see the right man punished for killing Mrs. Van Orner. Wouldn't you?"

"Of course!"

"Then stop acting like a fool and let me in."

The boy rubbed the back of his hand across his mouth and stepped aside so Frank could enter. The room was small and sparsely furnished and neat as a pin. He had a stuffed chair that someone had probably thrown out, a table with an oil lamp, some mismatched straight chairs, and a few more odds and ends. Frank pretended not to notice the whiskey bottle and half-empty glass sitting on the table beside the chair.

"What do you want to know?"

"Sit down," Frank said, motioning to the stuffed chair. Frank took one of the straight chairs, turned it around, and straddled it, folding his hands across the top slat.

The boy sat warily.

"I'm Detective Sergeant Frank Malloy, and don't bother trying to lie to me because I've been lied to by men a lot better at it than you, and I'm never fooled."

"I don't have no reason to lie!"

"Good. Now tell me what happened today."

"The whole day?" he asked with a frown.

"Let's start with when you first saw Mrs. Van Orner."

"I saw her right after luncheon. She'd sent word she wanted me to take her out. I took the carriage to the front door and she got in just like she always does."

"Was she alone?"

"No, Miss Yingling was with her."

Something about the way he said Miss Yingling's name told Frank he didn't like her much, but he let it pass for now. "Where did you take them?"

"To Mrs. Van Orner's office at the United Charities Building first. She told me to wait because they'd need me later. They stayed there an hour or so, then they come down, and I took them to that house where they keep the whores. That's what Mrs. Van Orner does, you know. She rescues whores."

Frank nodded, sharing the boy's wonder at such a calling. "Where is this house?"

"Over on . . . I'm not supposed to say," he remembered.

"I'm going to need to go there to question the women who live there."

Herman smiled slightly. "Won't do you no good. They won't let you in. They won't let any men inside. They don't want the neighbors getting the idea it's a whorehouse, don't you know." Plainly, he thought this ridiculous.

"Let me worry about that. Where's the house?"

Herman gave him the address of a neighborhood on the Lower East Side of the city.

"Miss Yingling said Mrs. Van Orner came home without her."

"Yeah, that was funny. They's always together, like two peas in a pod. Miss Yingling, she's always got her nose . . . Well, you know."

Frank did know. "Did Mrs. Van Orner say why she was leaving Miss Yingling behind?"

"No, and I didn't ask. Wasn't my place to look out for Miss Yingling. For all I know, she had some reason to stay behind at the house."

"Did Mrs. Van Orner seem upset when she came out of the house?"

"What do you mean, upset?"

"I mean was she angry or unhappy or—"

"Mrs. Van Orner was a lady," Herman said wisely. "Ladies don't show what they really feel."

"But you've worked for her for a long time, haven't you?"

"Three years now. I drive her someplace almost every day."

"Then you know what she's usually like. Did she seem different?"

Herman considered the question. "I . . . She seemed like she was thinking about something."

"Like she had something on her mind?" Frank suggested.

"Yeah, that's it. Something on her mind."

"Did she seem happy or sad or—"

"I told you, she didn't show how she was feeling, but she wasn't smiling when she told me to take her home. I remember that now. She's always pleasant to the help, real polite and never mean like some I could name. But she didn't smile that time. She just said, 'Take me home, Herman,' real quiet like."

"So you took her home. How long did it take?"

"I don't know. It takes as long as it takes. Some days longer and some shorter. Depends on how crowded the streets are."

"Today, did it take longer or shorter?"

"Maybe a little longer than usual."

"Did you have any idea something was wrong?"

Frank watched the color drain from Herman's young face. "No. She . . . she didn't need to tell me anything because I was just taking her home. I didn't hear nothing from her, but I don't usually."

"What happened when you got home?"

"I stopped the carriage at the front door, just like always. I got down and opened the door and . . ." He stopped. The tears Miss Yingling hadn't shed welled up in Herman's eyes and he struggled to keep his composure.

Frank reached over and snagged the glass of whiskey and put it into the boy's hands. He took a gulp. "Take your time. Tell me what you saw."

He coughed a little after the whiskey and wiped his mouth with the back of his hand again. Then he swallowed the lump in his throat and said, "She was laying on the floor in the carriage. I couldn't see her face at first. I thought maybe she'd fallen and hurt herself. I reached in to help her, but she didn't move when I called her name. I tried to lift her up and . . ." He had to take another sip of the whiskey. "I kind of turned her over and that's when I saw her face. She was white as a ghost and her eyes was open, just staring. She looked kind of surprised, I guess."

"You knew she was dead?"

"Maybe. I don't know. Not at first, I guess. I started yelling for help. I wanted somebody from the house, but that copper come running and got there first. He's always sticking his nose in where it don't belong."

Frank let that pass. "The cop said Mrs. Van Orner had drunk something from a flask in her purse."

Herman stiffened in silent resistance. He wasn't going to reveal any family secrets. "I don't know nothing about Mrs. Van Orner or her purse. All I know is I found her dead. Me and some of the other servants carried her inside and took her to her room, but she was dead all right. Never blinked, not once, and she wasn't breathing. One of the maids started screaming and somebody slapped her."

"Was Mr. Van Orner at home?"

"No, they sent for him."

"What about Miss Yingling?"

"No, she come later."

"What happened to Mrs. Van Orner's purse?"

"I don't know. Somebody picked it up, I guess. I never saw it. It wasn't in the carriage when I put it up. I always check to make sure Mrs. Van Orner didn't leave nothing behind. She appreciates that . . ." His voice died as he realized she couldn't appreciate anything anymore. He took another slug of whiskey, draining the glass.

"Do you like working for the Van Orners?"

Apparently, Herman had never given much thought to such a thing. "I guess so. They treat us fair. Mrs. Van Orner was always polite. I told you that already."

"What about Mr. Van Orner?"

"He's like most rich men. If you do your job and keep your mouth shut, he don't bother you."

"I'd like to see the carriage."

Herman couldn't understand why, but he took Frank down and let him look. Frank saw at once that Herman took even better care of the carriage than he did of his rooms. It gleamed. All the tack was in excellent repair. The animals were well tended. He saw nothing inside the carriage at all that didn't belong there.

Frank thanked the boy and made his way back to the house, rapping on the kitchen door before entering, not waiting for someone to answer it. A stocky woman in a stained apron was busy preparing a meal. She looked up from her work to glare at Frank in disapproval. Her eyes were red from recent weeping. She was sorry to see her mistress dead.

Frank introduced himself. "I'm waiting for Miss Yingling."

"Seems like somebody's always waiting for Miss Yingling," she sniffed.

Another person who didn't like the secretary. They probably resented her superior status in the household when she was really no more than a servant like them. And maybe she lorded it over them, too. That would be natural.

"Miss Yingling was going to ask Mr. Van Orner if he would see me," Frank offered, wanting to see her reaction.

The woman paused in her work and studied Frank a moment, judging his sincerity. "She'd be the one to ask, I reckon," she said carefully.

Now what did that mean? "Miss Yingling seems very efficient."

The cook smiled slyly. "Is that what they call it now?"

Intrigued, Frank opened his mouth to ask another question, but a maid came rushing into the room. "Miss Yingling said I was to take you back to the receiving room to wait." She looked a little desperate. Maybe Miss Yingling didn't want him chatting with the rest of the servants. He took his leave of the cook, determined to find out what else she might know. If he got to see Mr. Van Orner, he'd ask permission to question the rest of the staff.

He tried to chat with the maid, but she kept insisting she didn't know anything and left him to kick his heels in the ugly little room where he'd met with Miss Yingling earlier.

What, he couldn't help wondering, was taking so long? All she had to do was ask him a simple question.

Finally, the door opened, and a lovely young woman stepped in. This, he decided, must be the Van Orners' daughter. She wore an expensive dress in some light purple color with lace trim. It fit her well, showing off a shapely figure. Her dark hair was in a fashionable Gibson girl knot, with occasional loose curls brushing her cheeks and the back of her neck. She held herself erect, her hands clasped demurely at her waist.

"Mr. Van Orner will see you now, Mr. Malloy," she said.

He had to stare at her for another moment before he realized the truth. This vision was Miss Yingling.

7

FRANK RECOVERED QUICKLY AND FOLLOWED MISS YIN-gling upstairs to wherever Mr. Van Orner was waiting for him. As they climbed the stairs, Frank's mind was racing as he tried to make sense of what he knew about Miss Yingling.

While she had worked as Mrs. Van Orner's secretary, she'd tried her best to be unattractive. Or at least she'd made no attempt to make herself attractive. Today, however, with Mrs. Van Orner dead, she had made herself as beautiful as possible before speaking with Mr. Van Orner. Frank could think of several reasons for this, none of which reflected well on Miss Yingling. Or on Mr. Van Orner, for that matter.

They reached a closed door, and Miss Yingling knocked before opening it.

"Mr. Malloy is here to see you," she said, then stepped aside for Frank to enter and closed the door behind her as she left. The spacious room was furnished in the current style, which meant it was stuffed with enormous furniture and cluttered with knickknacks of every description sitting on every flat surface. Dull paintings in heavy frames covered portions of the busy pattern of the wallpaper. A thick and richly patterned carpet stretched across the floor. Heavy velvet drapes shielded the occupants of the room from any hint of sunlight.

Frank needed a moment for his eyes to adjust to the dimness before he found Mr. Van Orner. He sat in a wing chair near the fireplace, a glass in his hand resting on the arm of the chair. A thick-chested man whose good looks had softened with age and whose dark hair was thinning, he wore a silk smoking jacket, and he'd changed his shoes for slippers.

He studied Frank through narrowed eyes and made no move to rise or otherwise acknowledge him. He seemed remarkably relaxed for a man who'd just lost his wife.

Frank introduced himself. "I'm very sorry about your wife."

"Did you know her?" he asked.

"No."

"I thought perhaps . . . because of the charity work she does. Did." He lifted the glass to his lips and took a sip of the amber liquid. "What do you want?" he asked when he'd lowered the glass again.

Frank wasn't sure exactly how to start. He took a stab at it. "The circumstances of your wife's death are . . . unusual."

"I guess they are. Healthy women don't usually drop over dead while riding home in their carriages."

Frank hated asking right out, but Van Orner wasn't giving him any indication of his wishes. "Would you like for me to find out exactly how she died?"

"That's what Tamar said you were going to do."

"Tamar?"

"Miss Yingling," he said impatiently. "She said you thought my wife had been murdered and you were going to find out who did it, so by all means, find out. That's what the police do, isn't it?"

"Yes, it is. Do you mind if I ask you a few questions?"

Irritation flashed in his eyes, but he said, "I don't know anything about my wife's little project, if that's what you want to know."

"I was wondering if you knew if she had any enemies? Anyone who might wish her harm?"

"Vivian? Of course not. She was a saint. Everyone loved her." The words were right, but the tone of them was all wrong. Van Orner sounded almost angry and certainly disgusted.

And obviously, if she'd been murdered, at least one person didn't love her at all.

"Do you know what became of Mrs. Van Orner's purse? The one she had with her when . . . in the carriage?"

"I have no idea. Ask the servants. Ask Tamar. She knows everything that goes on." He looked up at Frank, his eyes suddenly shrewd. "And ask her for your fee. She'll take care of it." He looked away and took another sip of his drink.

Frank felt his face burning. Everyone on the police force accepted "rewards" or even outright bribes. Since no one could live comfortably on the salary the City of New York paid, the arrangement was a necessity. Most people treated the matter in a businesslike way, but Van Orner was purposely making Frank feel cheap, like a tradesman who was demanding more than his product was worth.

"Mr. Van Orner—"

"That's all."

Frank had been dismissed. Having no other choice, he turned and left the room. Miss Yingling was waiting for him in the hallway.

"I told you he'd want you to investigate," she said.

Frank hadn't gotten that impression at all. Van Orner seemed more resigned to the fact than anything. "He said you'd show me Mrs. Van Orner's purse."

"Her purse? Why do you need to see her purse?"

"The report said she had a flask with her, that she carried it in her purse. If she was drinking from it, maybe there was something in it . . ."

"Oh, I see. Mary!" she called. A young maid appeared, breathless, to answer the summons. "Take Mr. Malloy back to the receiving room." She turned back to Frank. "I'll join you there."

A few minutes later, Miss Yingling found him waiting once again in the grim little room. She carried a ladies draw-string purse and a silver flask.

"I think this is what you were looking for."

"Do these belong to Mrs. Van Orner?"

"Yes. She carried the flask in her purse. She . . . Mr. Malloy, I hope we can count on your discretion. I wouldn't want Mrs. Van Orner's memory to be tarnished by idle gossip."

Frank was starting to see the problem. "I'm not interested in gossip, Miss Yingling." He held out his hand for the flask. With apparent reluctance, she gave it to him. "Why did she carry this?"

"Mrs. Van Orner hated displays of emotion."

"So you've said."

"She . . . she found that when she was upset, a few sips of . . ."

Frank had unscrewed the top of the flask and sniffed. "Whew! What is that stuff?"

"A liqueur."

"I know it's liquor. What kind is it?"

"I told you, it's a *liqueur*. A special kind of drink. It's served after dinner, I believe. It's very sweet and mint flavored, so . . ." She gestured vaguely.

"So it goes down easier than whiskey," he guessed. "And she drank it whenever she needed to calm down?"

"She found it calming, yes," Miss Yingling admitted with apparent reluctance. "No one knew, of course. She was very careful to never let anyone see her."

"And today she had that argument with this Amy woman at the rescue house, so she probably felt the need for something calming." He shook the flask. Only a tiny amount of liquid remained in the bottom. "I don't suppose it spilled in the carriage."

"I wasn't here when Mrs. Van Orner got home. I can ask Herman, but . . . Well, it wouldn't have been unusual for her to empty an entire flask at one time."

This was all beginning to make sense now. Herman must have known about Mrs. Van Orner's tippling. That was why he claimed no knowledge of the flask when Frank asked him about it. "Will he tell you the truth?"

"Of course he will. But I can't see that it matters. Drinking from her flask wouldn't have harmed her. She did it all the time."

"Maybe she got a bad batch or something. Can you show me where she kept her supply?"

"Of course not. She kept it in her bedroom."

Frank had searched a lot of ladies' bedrooms, but he figured he wasn't going to get to search this one. "Can you bring me the bottles that are left? Especially any that are open?"

Miss Yingling stepped into the hall and gave the maid some instructions. When she returned, Frank was trying to think of anything else he might need before he left the house. He knew his chances of getting back in were very small. "Can you think of anybody in the house who might wish Mrs. Van Orner harm?"

"Which house?"

Frank remembered the rescue house where she'd been just before she died. "Either one."

Miss Yingling pressed her lips together and lowered her gaze, just the way any well-bred young lady would if she was asked to blacken the character of another person. "I really hate to gossip."

"If somebody killed your mistress, you want them to be punished, don't you?"

She looked up, startled at his bluntness. "Well, of course!"

"Then tell me what you know. Is there anybody in this house who might've wanted Mrs. Van Orner dead?"

She flinched but she said, "I don't believe so. Mrs. Van Orner always treated her staff kindly."

"What about her family?"

"Mrs. Van Orner has no living family."

"Not even any children?"

"She was never able to have children."

"What about her husband?"

Miss Yingling took offense at that. "Mr. Van Orner was devoted to her."

Frank hadn't gotten that impression at all, but Van Orner

wasn't likely to give Frank permission to investigate if he'd killed his wife himself. "All right, what about the rescue house? Anybody there have it in for her?"

"Everyone there admired Mrs. Van Orner. The work she did—"

"Not everybody admired her," he reminded her.

Plainly, she really didn't like speaking ill of other people. "I guess you mean this Amy person, the one who met with Mrs. Van Orner today."

"You said you didn't know what they talked about, but you must have some idea."

After a brief internal struggle, Miss Yingling decided to help him. "I told you, Amy refuses to do anything to help herself. She's convinced the father of her baby is going to help her. She even named her baby after the man. She named him Gregory."

Frank needed a minute to remember. "That's Mr. Van Orner's name. Did she claim he was the baby's father?"

"Not exactly. She hasn't named the father, at least not right out, but I don't know what she might have said to Mrs. Van Orner today. If Amy had made such a claim, Mrs. Van Orner would certainly have been upset. Oh!" she exclaimed suddenly. "I just realized, that might explain why she left without me today. She wouldn't have wanted anyone to see how upset she was."

"And she would've needed a nip or two from her flask."

A knock distracted them. Miss Yingling opened the door to the maid, who carried in a small wooden crate and set it down on one of the chairs. Miss Yingling dismissed her.

Frank lifted the lid of the crate to find half-a-dozen decoratively shaped, emerald green bottles packed carefully in straw. They might have held fancy perfume, but when Frank picked one up to examine the label, he saw they were, as Miss Yingling had said, some kind of liqueur called crème de menthe. Five of them were still sealed, but the sixth was more than half empty.

"I'll need to take these with me to have them tested."

"Do you think . . . Could there be something in it that killed her?"

"Only if somebody put it in there."

"Oh!" She lifted her fingers to her lips again.

"Is it all right if I take them? And the flask, too?"

"Of course," Miss Yingling said, taking a step back, as if afraid of contamination. "I'm sure no one else will be interested in them now."

Frank slipped the flask into his pocket and picked up the crate. "Thank you for your help, Miss Yingling."

"I almost forgot, Mr. Van Orner told me to take care of your fee."

Frank tried not to let his annoyance show. "We can talk about that later."

She let the maid show him out.

SARAH HAD INTENDED TO VISIT HER MOTHER THE NEXT day, to find out what she knew about the Van Orners, but her mother arrived on her doorstep that morning, before Sarah had even finished her breakfast. She'd brought a bakery box of petit fours, which were just the right size for a doll tea party. Mrs. Decker had helped Catherine eat them as they sat around the small table and drank water from the tiny china cups Mrs. Decker had brought on one of her many previous visits.

When the petit fours were gone and Catherine had tired

of the tea party and moved off to play with something else, Mrs. Decker came back downstairs to drink coffee with her daughter. After some polite inquiries after her father's health and her mother's activities, Sarah finally asked the question she'd been longing to ask.

"Do you know Vivian Van Orner?"

"Gregory Van Orner's wife? Of course I do. Why?"

"She died yesterday."

"Good heavens! I hadn't heard a thing about it."

"It happened late yesterday afternoon. I don't suppose they've had much time to tell people."

"What happened to her?"

"They aren't sure yet. She was alone in her carriage, and when they got to her house, the driver opened the door to let her out and she was dead."

"She was so young." Mrs. Decker shook her head in dismay. She was still an attractive woman, although her blond hair was threaded with silver, and fine lines had begun to form around her eyes. "Oh, dear!"

"What?" Sarah asked.

"Was she murdered? Oh, my, of course she was. That's why you're interested in her."

Sarah had to admit it was a logical conclusion, considering how many murders she'd helped Frank Malloy investigate. "I told you, they aren't sure yet."

"But if you're involved . . . You *are* involved, aren't you?"

"Not exactly."

"Mr. Malloy told her she better not be either," Maeve offered as she came into the kitchen. She'd brought the dirty plates and cups from upstairs to be washed.

Mrs. Decker's face lit with interest when she looked at Sarah again. "You must tell me everything."

"It started when Mrs. Brandt delivered a baby in a brothel," Maeve said, carefully setting the fragile dishes down in the sink.

Mrs. Decker pretended to be scandalized. "A brothel! Sarah, how could you!"

Sarah glared at Maeve, who ignored her and started to tell Mrs. Decker the story, forcing Sarah to interrupt and tell her own version. After a few confusing minutes, Mrs. Decker had a condensed version of everything that had happened.

"How did she die?" Mrs. Decker asked when they were finished.

"Mr. Malloy thinks she was poisoned," Maeve said. At some point during the narrative, she had taken a seat at the kitchen table with them.

"That's what Malloy suspects," Sarah corrected her. "She could have died of natural causes for all we know."

"Did you know her, Mrs. Decker?"

"Not well, but all of the old Knickerbocker families know each other," she said, referring to the original Dutch families who had settled the city of New York. "I knew Gregory's mother very well, but she died last year, and I didn't know Vivian's family at all. In fact, I didn't meet her until she married Gregory."

"Did you know about her charity work?" Sarah asked.

"Oh, yes. I'm afraid not many people admired her for it either."

"I'm sure her husband's friends teased her about it," Sarah said.

"Yes, but the women were worse. Women can be very . . . judgmental about others of their sex who have fallen. They didn't believe women like that really wanted to be rescued, you see."

"They should have seen the girl whose baby I delivered. She was desperate to get out of there."

"I'm sure she was. What a horrible life that must be." Mrs. Decker shuddered.

"Mrs. Van Orner did have some friends who helped her. Two gentlemen named Porter and Quimby and a Mrs. Spratt-Williams."

"I never heard of them, but I'm not surprised she found helpers. All the causes with offices in the United Charities Building have dedicated followers. They're extremely organized, too, I understand."

"Organized?" Sarah asked.

"They have to be, so people don't take advantage of them."

"How would people take advantage of them?" Maeve asked.

"By getting help from one charity until it was worn out and then moving on to a new one. Too much charity encourages sloth. People must learn to make their own way in the world."

"Mother! Do you really believe people are poor because they're lazy?"

Her mother looked at her with a puzzled frown. "What other explanation could there be? If they'd just get jobs, they wouldn't be poor."

"Oh, Mother, most poor people in the city do have jobs, but they don't earn enough to support a family, not even when everyone in the family works. In the tenements, little children roll cigars and make paper flowers and do all kinds of piecework for the sweatshops, working twelve hours a day, because everyone has to contribute to supporting the family."

"That's outrageous!"

"Yes, it is, but it's true. The poor in New York are the least lazy people on earth!"

"I had no idea . . . Or I suppose I should say, I never really thought about it."

"Very few rich people do," Sarah said.

Mrs. Decker sat back in her chair, considering what her daughter had just told her. "I suppose you're going to say the women who work in brothels aren't really depraved creatures who have chosen their lot in life either."

"Actually, they often do choose that life, but not because they're depraved."

"Why then?"

"Because they're starving."

"Starving? But what about their families?"

"Most of them don't have families or their families can't afford to keep them."

"But I know hundreds of young women work in those sewing factories. Surely a woman can earn an honest living if she wants to."

"The girls who work in those factories don't earn enough to keep a roof over their heads. They live with their families, and they're working to contribute to their support. They could never afford even a room in a boardinghouse on what they earn, though. If a girl is alone in the world, she has a very hard life."

"That's horrible," Mrs. Decker said, obviously moved, "but still, to sell yourself . . . Oh, I'm sorry. I shouldn't have said that in front of Maeve."

The girl had been very quiet during Sarah's explanations, sitting with her hands folded and staring at the table. She looked up now. "Don't worry about me. Lots of the girls at the Mission had been whores. I was lucky I had my grandfather to look after me, and when he died, I found the Mission. Otherwise . . ."

"Oh, Maeve!" Mrs. Decker laid her hand over Maeve's where they were folded on the table. Maeve looked up in surprise, and Mrs. Decker smiled warmly. "We're very glad you came to us."

"I . . . I'm very glad, too."

"I thank God every day that we have her," Sarah said, "but Maeve is only one of thousands of girls in the city. The woman who runs the house where I delivered the baby claims that dozens of them come knocking on her door every week, begging her to let them work for her."

"I had no idea." Mrs. Decker shook her head again. "I was unkind to Vivian. Not to her face, but I laughed at her behind her back. We all did. We made ugly jokes about her dedication to eliminating all the prostitutes in New York. They said her husband . . ." She glanced at Maeve and bit her lip, obviously loath to say whatever she'd been going to say in front of the girl.

"Maeve," Sarah began, but the girl was already rising from her chair.

"I'll go check on Catherine," she said. "I enjoyed the little cakes, Mrs. Decker. Thank you for bringing them."

"My pleasure, my dear."

They waited until Maeve was truly gone before continuing the conversation.

"What about her husband?" Sarah asked, afraid she already knew the answer.

"I don't know for sure, of course, but the gossip . . . there's always been gossip about him, about how he preferred the company of ladies of the evening."

"If we can judge by the number of brothels in the city, many men do."

"It was an ugly thing to talk about, and I'm ashamed now."

Sarah considered what her mother had told her. "I didn't tell you everything that happened after Amy was rescued. I didn't tell you what Amy named her baby."

"Is this something I would be happier not knowing?"

"She didn't name him Felix," Sarah said wryly. Felix was, of course, her father's name.

"Let me guess. She did name him Gregory."

"And she told Mrs. Van Orner she was naming him after his father."

Mrs. Decker sighed. "How cruel of her. But the girl was a prostitute. How could she possibly know who the father was?"

"According to Mrs. Walker, the woman who ran the house where she worked, Amy had been a rich man's mistress. He'd brought her to Mrs. Walker when he got tired of her. Mrs. Walker said Amy must have already been pregnant when she arrived there."

Mrs. Decker stared at Sarah for a long moment.

"What is it?" Sarah asked finally.

"Sounds like this Amy person had a very good reason for wanting Vivian Van Orner dead."

MRS. DECKER HAD TO LEAVE TO HAVE LUNCH WITH SOME friends. Sarah and the girls were preparing their own meal when the front bell rang. Sarah went to answer it, with Catherine at her heels, eager to see who their visitor might be. Thinking it was probably someone summoning her to a birth, Sarah felt a stab of pleasure to see Frank Malloy standing on her doorstep.

"Malloy," she said in greeting, unable to stop the smile that formed on her lips.

Catherine gave a squeal of joy and threw herself into his arms. He picked her up and returned her hug, but when he looked back at Sarah, he wasn't smiling.

"Catherine, will you go ask Maeve to set an extra place at the table for Mr. Malloy?"

Malloy set the child on her feet, and she scampered off back to the kitchen.

"I haven't done a single thing about Mrs. Van Orner's death except gossip with my mother," she assured him.

"I know," he said grimly.

"Then why do you look the way you always look when you're going to yell at me for doing something you didn't want me to do?"

"I never yell at you," he protested.

She crossed her arms. "All right, if you aren't here to yell at me, then why are you here?"

His expression was pained, as if he'd had a hard time at the dentist's office, and the words sounded as if they were being pulled from him like a bad tooth. "I came because I need your help investigating Mrs. Van Orner's murder."

Sarah couldn't believe what she was hearing, but she knew better than to tease him about it. He wouldn't be here if he weren't desperate. "You know I'd be happy to help in any way I can. Do you have time for some lunch first? We were just going to eat."

"I'd be honored," he said with just the slightest trace of irony.

The girls were both thrilled to have him, and Catherine

told him all about the tiny cakes Mrs. Decker had brought for her tea party—she called them "patty fours"—and Malloy pretended to be mightily impressed. Sarah didn't want to talk about the murder in front of the child, so she waited until they'd eaten and she'd changed her clothes and allowed Malloy to escort her from the house.

This was going to be a very interesting afternoon.

MALLOY COULDN'T BELIEVE HE WAS DOING THIS. How many times had he sworn he'd never let Sarah Brandt get involved in another murder investigation, and here he was, asking for her help.

"Where are we going?" she asked as they made their way down Bank Street. He always forgot how good hearing her voice made him feel, even when she was saying something that completely infuriated him.

"To the rescue house."

"Do you know where it is?" she asked in surprise.

"I was there this morning." He had to swallow down his frustration. "They wouldn't let me in."

Sarah started coughing, and he knew it was to keep from laughing out loud. "I see," she finally managed.

"I'm sure you do. I believe you were the first person who warned me about that."

"But not the last?"

"No, Miss Yingling did, too. She did give me the address, though."

"I suppose you thought the power of your office would overcome their objections." She was smirking.

"Don't you dare laugh at me," he warned her, only half joking. "I've had a pretty bad morning."

"I wouldn't dream of it. Tell me all about it."

Frank sighed. "Well, I guess it started last night, when I went over to the Van Orner house."

"I'm sure they were happy to see you."

"Oh, yes. Van Orner was drinking himself into a stupor, but he gave me permission to investigate his wife's death. He even offered me a *fee*."

"Oh, dear." She knew how sensitive he was on that subject. "But at least he wants it solved. That probably means he didn't do it."

"Probably. And I found out Mrs. Van Orner's dirty little secret."

"Dirty?" Sarah asked uneasily.

He wondered what she was imagining. "She drank."

"She *what*?"

"She drank. Miss Yingling—that's her secretary—"

"I know Miss Yingling."

"Miss Yingling explained how Mrs. Van Orner didn't like to let other people see her when she's mad or upset, so she carried a flask around with her. When she started feeling out of sorts, she'd take a little swig or two to make herself calm again."

He waited, but she didn't say anything. "You don't seem real surprised. Did you know she was a drinker?"

"No, I didn't even suspect, but I'm afraid it's far too common among women who have too much time and too much money to spend."

"How can you have too much time?"

"When you have days and days to fill and nothing meaningful to do except visit with other women just like you who also don't have anything meaningful to do except gossip about the women they know who aren't with them at the moment."

"I always thought it would be fun to be rich."

"Maybe it is for men. They can get into politics or business or whatever interests them. Women have to sit at home and plan parties and knit socks for the poor. I might've taken up drinking myself if I hadn't managed to escape."

"So that's why Mrs. Van Orner started rescuing whores."

He'd expected to get a rise out of her with that, but she just looked unhappy.

"What is it now?" he asked.

"Mrs. Van Orner may have had another reason for her charity work."

Frank remembered she said she'd been gossiping with Mrs. Decker. "What did your mother tell you?"

"She didn't know Mrs. Van Orner drank, but she did say that their friends always claimed Mrs. Van Orner tried to rescue prostitutes because her husband was so fond of them."

Frank overcame the strong urge to swear.

"I suppose this means you're sure Mrs. Van Orner was murdered," she said after a moment.

"Yes. The medical examiner said she was poisoned, and they found laudanum in her flask."

"Laudanum? Oh, dear."

"What is it?"

"It's probably nothing, but when Amy arrived at the rescue house, she was nearly hysterical, and Mrs. Van Orner suggested giving her laudanum to calm her down, so they must keep some on hand."

"That's pretty common." Almost every home in New York would have a bottle of laudanum handy to treat everything from headaches to tuberculosis.

"Laudanum is awfully bitter," she said suddenly. "Why didn't Mrs. Van Orner notice the taste?"

"Probably because it was mixed in with her favorite drink, crème de menthe. It's a liqueur," he added when she gave him a puzzled look.

"I know what it is. It just seems like an odd choice for secret drinking."

"According to the medical examiner, it's popular with ladies because it tastes so good, unlike whiskey and its near relatives."

"I just remembered, she always carried peppermints with her. That would account for the minty smell of it on her breath, too."

"And the strong flavor would've covered up the bitterness of the laudanum. Doc Haynes said it only takes two or three spoonfuls of the stuff to kill you."

"It's very dangerous. Suicides often use it because it's cheap and easy to find and works so quickly and painlessly. Could Mrs. Van Orner have committed suicide?"

"I guess it's possible," Frank said, "but I don't have any reason to think so yet. I have to find out what happened at the rescue house that day."

"Which is why you need me to go with you." He could tell she was trying not to gloat, but he guessed she couldn't help it.

Frank swallowed down his frustration again. "Tell me what you know about the women in this house."

"I don't know much. I told you about Amy. She's the girl whose baby I delivered. An Italian girl named Lisa manages the place. I didn't meet anyone else who lives there."

"What about a Mrs. Spratt-Williams?"

"She's one of Mrs. Van Orner's followers, I guess you could say. She helps with the rescues. Was she at the house yesterday?"

"Yes, and according to Miss Yingling, she met with Mrs. Van Orner right before she left."

"She's a friend of hers, I believe. My mother didn't know her, but she's a respectable matron, just like Mrs. Van Orner."

"Whose husband also likes prostitutes?" Frank guessed.

"You'll have to ask *her* about that," Sarah replied with a knowing smile.

"What do you know about Miss Yingling?"

"Nothing except that she was Mrs. Van Orner's secretary. She worked in her offices at the United Charities Building."

"And she lives with the Van Orners."

"She does? How odd."

"I thought so, too, but I wasn't sure how close rich women like to keep their secretaries."

"They don't usually have secretaries, so I can't really say."

They interrupted their conversation to cross a particularly busy street, an act that required complete concentration to keep from being crushed to death by a horse or wagon. When they had arrived safely on the other side, Frank asked, "I guess this girl Amy was pretty grateful to Mrs. Van Orner for getting her out of Mrs. Walker's house."

"Yes," she agreed with an odd tone in her voice. "I thought so, too, until she named her baby after Mrs. Van Orner's husband."

8

Frank whistled. "I don't suppose she was just showing her respect for Mrs. Van Orner."

"Not that I noticed. In fact, I got the feeling she knew exactly how much she was hurting Mrs. Van Orner when she announced it."

"Could Van Orner really be the baby's father?"

"Only two people know that for sure, and I doubt Mr. Van Orner will be very happy to discuss the matter with us."

"I think you're probably right. If he is the father, though, then this Amy had a good reason to want Mrs. Van Orner dead."

"That's what my mother said, too, but Amy would be foolish to do something so dangerous. She was a prostitute. She surely can't expect Mr. Van Orner to marry her, even if the baby *is* his."

"She's young, isn't she? Young women get foolish ideas."

"I suppose they do. Is that what you want me to find out?"

"I want you to find out who spent time with Mrs. Van Orner yesterday, what they talked about, and what her state of mind was. I also want you to find out where her purse with the flask in it was while she was meeting with these people."

"To find out if someone could have put the laudanum into it while she was busy doing something else."

"Yes, but don't ask anybody if they did it."

The look she gave him would've curdled milk. "I'm not an idiot."

"I know you're not, but one of those women is a murderer, and I don't want you to be next."

"Don't worry. I don't even like crème de menthe."

"They could put it in anything," he said, exasperated.

"I won't eat or drink anything in that house. Will that make you happy?"

"I wouldn't say *happy*, but it's a start."

"Is there anything else you want me to find out?"

"If you think I should talk to any of them myself, see if you can get them to come out and meet with me."

"I doubt any of them will be particularly interested in meeting with a police detective."

"Then lie to them."

She pursed her lips to hold back a smile, an expression he knew well. "Where will you be?"

"A coffee shop on the next block. We'll pass by it on our way, so you'll know where it is. I'll wait for you there."

"I just happened to think, I doubt Mrs. Spratt-Williams will be at the house today. Maybe you can see her at her own house."

If this Spratt-Williams woman was as rich as Van Orner, he doubted she'd be particularly happy to see him. "Maybe."

They crossed another busy street, and Frank went over some of the questions he wanted her to ask of the women in the house. Then he showed her the coffee shop where he'd be waiting, and accompanied her to her destination, standing out on the sidewalk to make sure they let her in. Then he walked back to the coffee shop, prepared for a long, boring afternoon.

LISA BIAFORE ANSWERED SARAH'S KNOCK. THE POOR girl looked frazzled, her dark hair straggling down out of its bun, her eyes red-rimmed and sad. "Oh, Mrs. Brandt, isn't it? I almost didn't recognize you. Have you heard about poor Mrs. Van Orner . . ." Her voice broke, and she pressed a hand to her lips to hold back a sob.

"Yes, I did," Sarah said, taking this opportunity to step inside. "I'm so sorry. I came to see if there was anything I could do to help."

"I don't know of anything," Lisa said, using the tail of her apron to wipe her eyes. "Unless you can tell us what's going to happen to Mrs. Van Orner's work now that she's gone."

"What do you mean?"

"This house and all of us. Will they shut it down? Where will we go? Nobody's told us anything, and there's not enough money here to keep us for more than a week. After that . . ."

Her concerns were legitimate, and Sarah couldn't imagine Mr. Van Orner continuing to finance a houseful of former prostitutes. "Have you seen Mrs. Spratt-Williams?"

"No, not yet. Just Miss Yingling. She came by late last

night to tell us about Mrs. Van Orner. She looked so different, I hardly recognized her. Acted different, too, like butter wouldn't melt in her mouth. She didn't seem sad at all about poor Mrs. Van Orner either."

"I'm sure she was just trying to put on a brave front," Sarah said. "Mrs. Van Orner wouldn't have approved of any displays of grief."

"You're right about that, Mrs. Brandt. I never saw her even look angry until yesterday and then just for a minute, before she caught herself."

"When was that?" Sarah asked, trying not to sound too interested.

"After she had a talk with that Amy. What a piece of work she is. I don't know why Mrs. Van Orner didn't throw her out into the street."

"I can see this has been very hard on you, Lisa. Can I make you some tea?"

"Oh, Mrs. Brandt, I couldn't let you do that!"

"Of course you could. That's what friends are for. Come along and let me take care of you."

The girl allowed Sarah to escort her back to the kitchen, but she insisted on helping prepare the tea things, since Sarah didn't know where anything was. After a few minutes, they were seated at the kitchen table, waiting for the tea to steep.

"Can you tell me what happened here yesterday?"

"You mean about the fight Amy had with Mrs. Van Orner?"

"I mean everything, from the time Mrs. Van Orner arrived until she left."

"I suppose," the girl said doubtfully.

"I'll help you remember," Sarah said. "What was the first thing Mrs. Van Orner did when she arrived?"

Lisa screwed up her face with the effort of remembering. "What she always did. She went into her office with Miss Yingling, and they looked over the accounts."

"She kept track of how much you spent here?"

"Oh, yes. Her husband didn't give her any money for this house, you see. He didn't like her doing this sort of work at all."

"How did she pay for it then?"

"She had some money of her own, I think, and her friends helped. But we had to be very careful. Sometimes she had to bring us food from her own house so we'd have enough."

"So she and Miss Yingling were in her office together. Was anyone with them?"

"They called me in and asked me some questions about some things I'd bought, but just for a minute. Then I told her Amy wanted to see her."

"Why did Amy want to see her?"

"I don't know, probably to complain. That's all she ever did. She didn't like the food, she didn't like her room, she didn't like the clothes we got for her. Nothing was ever good enough for her. You'd think she'd forgot she'd been a whore when she came here with nothing but the clothes on her back."

"How is her baby doing?" Sarah had to ask.

"Oh, he's doing fine. Fat little thing, cute as a button. Not that she cares. She complains about having to feed him, too. If it was up to her, he'd never have a clean diaper either. The other girls and me, we look after him."

"That's very nice of you."

"It's only natural, ain't it? To want to take care of a baby, even if it's not yours?"

"Yes, it is, or at least it should be."

Sarah checked the tea and judged it to be ready. She poured each of them a cup, remembering too late her promise to Malloy not to eat or drink anything. Of course, she'd prepared this with her own hands, so she thought it was pretty safe. "Where are the rest of the girls?"

"There's only two here now, and they're in their rooms. I think they're scared of what's going to happen to them. We've all been real quiet today."

"So Amy and Mrs. Van Orner had a talk. Was Miss Yingling with them?"

"Oh, no. Mrs. Van Orner sent her out. Amy wouldn't have nothing to do with Miss Yingling, and Miss Yingling didn't have much use for Amy neither."

"Did you happen to overhear anything?"

"Do you mean were they shouting? Oh, no, Mrs. Van Orner was too well bred to shout. Not like my family was. They'd scream about every little thing. I had a hard time of it when I first come here. Mrs. Van Orner always says a lady doesn't raise her voice. Took a long time for me to learn that."

"I still have a difficult time with it," Sarah confided. "So you didn't hear anything they said. How did Amy act when she came out?"

"You mean was she mad or something?"

"Yes, that's what I mean."

"She wasn't mad, that's for sure."

"Happy?"

"No, not that. I never seen Amy happy. Seems like nothing pleases her."

"Sad? Disappointed?"

"Oh, no, just the opposite. She . . . she looked like the cat who swallowed the canary."

"Satisfied?"

"That's it. Satisfied, like she got her way about something."

"Did she say anything about it?"

"Her? Not likely. She kept to herself. Never wanted nobody to know her business. Of course, we all figured she didn't have any business. She liked to pretend she had secrets, but nobody ever coaxed her to tell them."

"What do you think her secrets were about?"

"I don't know. She called her baby Gregory. That's Mr. Van Orner's name, and she knowed it, too. That's why she did it, I'm sure. She was mean that way."

"Maybe she named her baby after Mrs. Van Orner's husband out of gratitude for what Mrs. Van Orner had done for her."

Lisa snorted rudely. "Not likely. If she was grateful, she never let on. No, I think she did it to be mean. It hurt Mrs. Van Orner, too. You could tell, even though she never said a thing. She never had children of her own, you know."

"No, I didn't know that."

"She never talked about it to me, of course, but Miss Yingling told me never to mention it to her. Said it was one of the biggest disappointments of her life."

"I was here the day Amy named her baby," Sarah reminded her. "She said she was naming him after his father."

"Oh, law, did she? That little witch! I don't suppose she's ever set eyes on Mr. Van Orner neither. I'm glad she's gone."

"You're glad Mrs. Van Orner's gone?" Sarah asked in surprise.

"Oh, no, I'm glad Amy's gone, and good riddance to her, too."

"She's *gone*? What happened to her?" If Mrs. Van Orner had thrown her out . . .

"She packed up and left this morning right after breakfast. Never said nothing to nobody."

"Did she take the baby?"

"Oh, yes. She wouldn't part with him. She said he was her future, whatever that meant. I just wonder who's gonna change his diapers now. Not her, I'm sure."

"Where would she have gone?"

"Lord knows, maybe back to that house where she worked before. Girls always think they'll take them back, but they never do. They can't trust them no more. I don't see why it matters, since they never trusted them to start with, but that's how it is. She'll be on the street, I suppose."

Sarah thought of the poor, innocent baby, and her heart ached. They were getting off the subject, though. Malloy would never let that happen. "So you thought Amy looked satisfied after her meeting with Mrs. Van Orner. How did Mrs. Van Orner look?"

"That's when I told you she looked mad. Not like a normal person would, mind you, but mad for her. She had her mouth all pinched together and her eyes was all bright, like she had a fire inside of her. Then she saw me looking at her, and she quick went back in her office and shut the door."

Sarah remembered the way Mrs. Van Orner usually calmed herself down. "Did she have her purse in the office with her?"

"Her purse?"

"Yes, her purse. I know it doesn't sound important, but it is."

Lisa looked confused but she gave the question some thought. "I don't know for sure. I wasn't looking for it."

"Where did she usually put it when she was here?"

"Oh, I know. She usually put it on the table in the hall.

I remember because the first time I saw her do it, I said she should keep it with her, considering the type of women who live in this house, and she said to me—I'll never forget—she said, 'Miss Biafore, we must treat these women the same way we would treat them if they was respectable if we ever hope they will become respectable.'"

"So she usually left her purse out where anyone could have found it?"

"Yes, and as far as I know, nobody ever bothered it."

Sarah didn't mention that someone had undoubtedly bothered it yesterday. "So what else did Mrs. Van Orner do after she met with Amy?"

"She was only in the office alone for a few minutes before Mrs. Spratt-Williams went in to see her."

"Had Mrs. Spratt-Williams just arrived?"

"Oh, no, she was here for a while. She'd brought over some things for the baby and some clothes she'd collected at her church. For the women. They never have decent clothes when they come here."

"Do you know what she talked with Mrs. Van Orner about?"

Lisa stiffened slightly. "No. They don't tell me their business."

"But you have an idea."

"How could I have an idea? They don't tell me nothing."

"Miss Yingling said you were the last one to speak with Mrs. Van Orner before she left the house yesterday."

"I guess I was," she said unhappily.

"Did she seem angry or upset about anything?"

Lisa shook her head. "She was always kind to me. I told her Amy was causing all kinds of trouble, and she said I shouldn't worry about it. She said Amy would be gone soon."

"And that's all?"

"Yes, she seemed like she was in a hurry, and she left right after that. Miss Yingling came asking after her a few minutes later and was real surprised that she'd left without her. I was, too."

"So she must have had something on her mind that distracted her. Can you think of what it might have been?"

Lisa stared at Sarah for a long moment, as if trying to judge her intent, and then she shook her head.

Sarah knew she was lying. She reached over and laid her hand on Lisa's arm. "You've been in charge of this place for a long time. I'm sure you know everything that goes on here. You're not being disloyal to talk about it now, and you might help us find out who killed Mrs. Van Orner."

Lisa's dark eyes widened. "*Killed?* You don't mean she was *murdered*!"

Sarah wanted to bite her tongue. "Well, they don't know for sure," she hedged quickly.

"Miss Yingling never said nothing about murder. She said Mrs. Van Orner died real sudden, that's all."

"That's all she knew then. As I said, we aren't really sure yet."

"What do they think killed her then?"

"She may have eaten something that . . ." Sarah gestured vaguely.

Lisa's eyes widened with horror. "She was *poisoned*?"

"It's possible."

"Not from something she ate here. She never ate nothing here. She and Miss Yingling, they was always real careful not to use up our supplies. She'd hardly drink a cup of coffee here."

"Did she drink any yesterday?"

"Not that I know of. She was pretty busy. No, if somebody poisoned her, it was probably somebody at her own house."

"Why do you say that?"

"Because that's where she ate her food, isn't it? She didn't get no poison here."

"Do you keep anything here that could be poisonous?"

"You mean like rat poison?"

"Yes, or . . ." Sarah pretended to think. "Or medicines. Some medicines can be dangerous if you use too much."

"We keep Lydia Pinkham's Vegetable Compound, of course. When you've got a houseful of females, you need to be prepared for female complaints. We've got Dr. Morse's Indian Root Pills, I think, and I know we've got some Pine Toothache drops. I used them myself last month."

"Mrs. Van Orner mentioned laudanum to me when Amy first came here. I remember because I told her I didn't like to use it because it passes through the milk and makes the baby sleep too much."

"Oh, yes, I think we do have some."

"Could you check and see?"

Lisa frowned. "I told you already, it don't matter. Mrs. Van Orner never got poisoned here."

"I know, but could you check anyway? Just to be sure? We don't want anyone here to be falsely accused of anything."

This was something Lisa could understand. "I never thought of that! I'll check right away." She jumped up and went to the pantry. Reaching up to the top shelf, she pulled down a small wooden box that contained an assortment of patent medicine bottles and started sorting through it. "Here it is." She pulled out a small brown bottle and held it up. Then she shook it and looked at it more closely. "That's funny."

Sarah felt the hairs on her arms prickling. "What?"

"It's empty."

FRANK HAD READ THREE NEWSPAPERS AND FELT NO BETter informed than he had been before. He looked up automatically when the coffee shop door opened and was surprised to see Sarah. For a minute, he thought she might have brought someone for him to question, but she was alone. He rose from his chair and pulled out another at his table for her. "That didn't take long."

"There was a bottle of laudanum at the house, but it's empty. Miss Biafore is certain it was nearly full the last time she noticed it. She would have bought more if she knew someone had used the last of it."

"So that could be what killed her. Did you find out where her purse was?"

"Not for certain, but Miss Biafore said she usually just laid it on the table in the hallway. She wanted the women who lived there to think she trusted them."

"But you don't know for sure?"

"No. I'll have to ask Miss Yingling and Mrs. Spratt-Williams if they remember."

"Either of them could be the killer, you know."

She raised her eyebrows. "Miss Yingling is the one who convinced Mr. Van Orner to let you investigate, and I can't think of any possible reason why Mrs. Spratt-Williams would want to kill her friend."

"Just because you can't think of it doesn't mean it isn't there. What did that girl Amy have to say for herself?"

"I didn't see her. She's gone."

"What do you mean, she's gone?"

"I mean she packed up herself and her baby and left this morning."

"Where did she go?"

"They don't know. She didn't even tell anyone she was leaving. Lisa—Miss Biafore—thinks she may have gone back to Mrs. Walker's house."

"Why would she go there? Mrs. Walker was going to give her baby away."

"I didn't say she did. I said that's all Lisa could think of. I don't think Amy had any money of her own, and if she had family, why didn't she go there before? Nothing else makes sense."

"What about the other women in the house?"

"I talked to both of them, but they're too frightened to be much help. They don't remember anything that happened yesterday or even who was in the house. They never noticed Mrs. Van Orner's purse or who she talked to. I can't imagine either of them would want to kill her. Without her, they don't have any hope at all."

"You're probably right, and Amy running away doesn't look good for her," Frank said.

"But we still don't know any reason why she'd want Mrs. Van Orner dead, and if she did have one, wouldn't she stay around to benefit from it?"

"Maybe she's afraid of getting caught."

"When Miss Yingling came over last night to tell them the news, she didn't say Mrs. Van Orner was murdered, only that she'd died suddenly. It's possible nobody would have ever figured out she was poisoned. Why run away until there was real danger?"

"I don't know, and I don't think we'll figure out the answer until we find Amy."

"And if she killed Mrs. Van Orner, we may never find her." Sarah sighed. "What should we do next?"

Frank flinched inwardly at the "we," but he had to admit he still needed her help. "Would Mrs. Spratt-Williams see you?"

"I'm sure she would. She may not even know Mrs. Van Orner is dead yet. I think a condolence call would be in order in any case. I can even express concern about the future of Rahab's Daughters. The women at the rescue house are terrified they'll be turned out."

"They probably will be unless this Mrs. Spratt-Williams is willing to keep it going."

"Even if she's willing, she may not be able. According to Miss Biafore, Mrs. Van Orner supported it with money of her own, not what she got from her husband, and also some she got from friends. Even still, they were often short of funds."

"So that'll give you a reason to call on Mrs. Spratt-Williams. Miss Yingling gave me her address."

"What will you do?"

"I'll call on those two fellows who helped with the rescues."

"Potter and what was the other man's name?"

"Quimby."

Sarah frowned. "Neither of them were with her at all yesterday. What could they possibly tell you?"

"I won't know that until I talk to them."

"Where shall we plan to meet later?"

"I'll come by your house tomorrow."

Sarah took her leave, so she'd arrive at Mrs. Spratt-Williams's house in time to make a socially acceptable afternoon visit. Frank watched her go with a sick feeling in his stomach. How the hell did she always mange to get mixed up in his cases?

Mrs. Spratt-Williams lived in a town house a few blocks from Sarah's parents' home on the Upper West Side. It was furnished modestly but in good taste. Mrs. Spratt-Williams received Sarah in the family parlor. She wasn't dressed for company, and she looked as if she might have been crying.

"What a surprise, Mrs. Brandt. Please excuse my appearance, but I suppose you've heard about poor Vivian."

"Yes, I did. What a shock. I'm so very sorry."

"You can't imagine how distraught I am. I've known Vivian for years and years. She was like a sister to me."

"I'm sure she must have felt the same way. I know she appreciated your help with Rahab's Daughters."

"Oh, yes. I was the first one she came to when she got the idea for it. She said to me, 'Tonya'—she always called me Tonya. My real name is Antonia, but she shortened it to Tonya when we were girls—she said, 'Tonya, we must do something for all these unfortunate women in the city.'"

"It seems a very unusual thing for ladies like you to be concerned with," Sarah observed.

"Vivian was an unusual woman, and . . . well, she had her reasons, I suppose," she added with what might have been a hint of distaste.

Sarah decided not to mention the rumors about Mr. Van Orner, at least not yet. "I understand she supported the work with her own money."

"Yes, she had a small inheritance, from an aunt, I think.

She used the income from that and some of her allowance, I'm sure."

"And her friends helped, too, I suppose."

"Those of us who were involved, of course. I gave her what I could. I'm a widow, you see, and I have limited resources. I believe the gentlemen were more generous."

Sarah knew what it cost to run a house like this, and she suspected Mrs. Spratt-Williams's resources were limited only by her own choices. "I was just at the rescue house to see if there was anything I could do to help. Miss Biafore is quite concerned about what will become of Rahab's Daughters now."

"Oh, dear, I'm sure no one has given that a moment's thought. I know I just heard about Mrs. Van Orner this morning."

"How did you hear?"

"Miss Yingling sent me a note. I assume she notified the others as well. Isn't that how you heard?"

Sarah chose to ignore the question. "I believe you were with Mrs. Van Orner just before she died."

"Was I? I had no idea. I didn't know when it happened. Or even where. Was it at the rescue house?"

"No, shortly after she left, I believe. In her carriage."

"In her carriage? How horrible. But of course, Miss Yingling was with her, so at least she wasn't alone."

"Miss Yingling wasn't with her."

"She wasn't? How strange."

"Why was it strange?"

"I . . ." She had to think about that. "Wasn't Vivian going home? Miss Yingling lives with the Van Orners, so naturally I assumed she was with her. They always leave together."

"Not that day. After she spoke with you, Mrs. Van Orner was upset about something, and she didn't wait for Miss Yingling. Do you have any idea what she was upset about?"

The color rose in Mrs. Spratt-Williams's face. "I hope you aren't accusing any of us of causing her to have apoplexy or something."

"Apoplexy?" Sarah asked in confusion.

"Or heart failure or whatever she died of. I assume from your questions that they believe something that happened that day caused her to die very suddenly. A shock of some kind, perhaps."

"Did she have a shock that day?"

"I'm sure I don't know," she insisted, even though her face was scarlet.

"You were one of the last people to speak with her before she died," Sarah reminded her. "Did she seem to be in shock?"

"I . . . I have no idea. Vivian was . . . She wasn't one to let her emotions show."

"Did she seem out of sorts? Not herself?"

"I don't remember."

Sarah took a chance. "Was she drinking more than usual?"

Mrs. Spratt-Williams's eyes widened and the color drained from her face. "Drinking? What are you talking about?"

"Everyone knows about the flask she carried with her," Sarah lied. "And how she would take a sip or two to calm herself."

"You're mistaken!"

"Drinking alcohol when you've had a shock can sometimes cause a . . . an unfortunate reaction," she tried. "If that's what happened to Mrs. Van Orner, then it's no one's fault, is it?"

There, she'd given Mrs. Spratt-Williams a chance to clear her conscience, if she'd been blaming herself.

"Do you think that's what happened?" she asked, almost hopefully.

"It would make sense."

Mrs. Spratt-Williams closed her eyes and sighed, as if a weight had been lifted from her. "I'm afraid that Vivian and I did have words yesterday. I'll never forgive myself if that caused her death."

"What did you discuss? Maybe it wasn't really that upsetting to her," she added, lest she be thought simply nosy.

"Oh, dear, I don't know if it was or not. With Vivian, it was so hard to tell. She never allowed her true feelings to show. Her mother always taught her it was unladylike."

"I'd be happy to give you my opinion," Sarah said, fighting the urge to shake the story out of her.

"Oh, I don't suppose it could matter now. I was only trying to help, you see. She wanted to put Amy out of the house. She was so unpleasant, and the other girls hated her. She even refused to look after her baby, but . . . Well, Amy has had a difficult time of it. I know because she told me her story. When you know what she's been through, you can understand why she's so angry. I'm afraid I've become quite fond of the girl and her darling little boy."

"Did Mrs. Van Orner argue with you?"

"No, not really. She just . . . She simply refused to discuss it. I tried every argument I could think of, but she wouldn't budge."

"And did you see her with her . . . her flask?"

"No, I didn't. I never saw her actually drink from it, not

once in all the years I've known her. I could smell it on her, though. She used those peppermints, and they fooled most people, I suppose, but not those of us who knew."

"And who else knew?" Because, Sarah realized, only someone who knew about the flask would have thought to poison it.

Mrs. Spratt-Williams stiffened at the question, offended in some way Sarah certainly hadn't intended. "I thought you said everyone knew."

Lying always got her in trouble. "I was guessing. As far as I know, only one other person knew."

"Poor Vivian. She'd be mortified to know people were talking about her this way. What difference could that possibly make now anyway?"

Malloy would be furious, but Sarah knew instinctively that she must tell Mrs. Spratt-Williams the truth if she hoped to get any more useful information out of her. "Because Mrs. Van Orner didn't die of shock or apoplexy or heart failure. She was poisoned."

"Poisoned!" The hand Mrs. Spratt-Williams lifted to her heart trembled. "How on earth could she have been poisoned?"

"Someone put the poison in her flask, and when she got into her carriage, she took a drink from it, as she often did when she was upset. By the time she arrived home, she was dead."

Mrs. Spratt-Williams went white to her lips and her eyes rolled back in her head. Sarah was beside her at once, chaffing her wrists and lightly slapping her cheeks to keep her from losing consciousness.

"Some . . . brandy . . ." the poor woman managed, indicting a sideboard.

Sarah hurried over, found the right bottle, and poured her a medicinal dose. She held the glass to Mrs. Spratt-Williams's lips, and after a few sips and a round of coughing, the woman no longer looked as if she was going to faint.

"I'm very sorry," Sarah said. "I shouldn't have been so blunt, but we need your help if we're going to find out who killed Mrs. Van Orner."

This only distressed her more. "Who is this 'we' you're talking about?"

"The police. They're investigating. I've helped them before, and we thought it would be more acceptable to you to answer questions from me than from them."

"It may be more acceptable, but I can hardly imagine it being any more *shocking*," she said, prompting Sarah to apologize all over again.

"But you can see how important it is to find out who knew about Mrs. Van Orner's flask. Only someone who did could have killed her."

Mrs. Spratt-Williams considered this very carefully, leaning back in her chair and watching Sarah closely as she thought it over. Finally, she said, "It was a well-guarded secret, as you can imagine. Only two others knew of it—her husband and Tamar Yingling."

9

Frank waited a few minutes longer at the coffee shop before heading out to visit the two gentlemen. The police didn't have to worry about formal visiting times, and he thought the closer to dinner he arrived, the more likely he was to find them at home. From Sarah's description, they sounded as if they didn't need to work, but they might have other reasons to be out of the house during the day.

He went to Mr. Quimby's first. He lived in one of those apartment buildings on Marble Row, a section of Fifth Avenue where all the buildings were fronted with marble. The doorman didn't want a policeman to enter the building, so Frank had to threaten to come back with a gang of uniformed cops to search the place. After that, the doorman decided Mr. Quimby would be happy to see Frank.

Mr. Quimby had not been consulted, however, and he was actually somewhat less than happy.

"I can't imagine why the police are involved in this. Does Mr. Van Orner know you're questioning his wife's friends?"

They were sitting in a large room with twelve-foot ceilings. Windows stretched up two walls, giving a magnificent view of the city in all its tawdry beauty. The furnishings were heavy and masculine, mostly leather and brass in shades of brown and gold. Frank determined from this that Quimby was a bachelor. He wondered idly if Quimby had ever used a prostitute. He decided not to ask.

"Mr. Van Orner has asked me to investigate his wife's death," Frank said, surprising Quimby. "He believes foul play might be involved."

"Foul play! Miss Yingling's note gave no indication of any such thing."

"Did you think a perfectly healthy woman just dropped over dead for no reason?" Frank asked curiously.

Quimby found the question offensive. He was the sort of man who was easily offended, dignified and quietly respectable, well-groomed and well-mannered. "Of course not. I assumed she had taken ill or that she'd had some sort of attack."

"She died in her carriage on the way home from the rescue house yesterday."

"Then Miss Yingling will know what happened."

"Why do you say that?"

"Because they were always together. Vivian never went anywhere without that girl. I always said I thought she knew more about Vivian's business than Vivian did."

"Miss Yingling wasn't with her."

"She wasn't? That's odd. Where was Mrs. Van Orner going?"

"Home, I understand."

"Then that doesn't make any sense at all. Miss Yingling lived with the Van Orners. Why wouldn't she have gone home with Vivian?"

"Miss Yingling said Mrs. Van Orner was upset and left without her."

"That's ridiculous."

"That Mrs. Van Orner would leave without her?"

"No, that Mrs. Van Orner would be upset. I've known her for ten years, and I've never seen her anything other than completely calm and in control of her emotions."

"She'd had a conversation with that woman Amy, the one with the baby that you rescued a few weeks ago, and another with Mrs. Spratt-Williams. Can you think of anything she might have talked to them about that would have upset her?"

"Of course not. Well, I can't actually speak for the girl, I'm afraid. I only saw her very briefly the day we rescued her from that house where she worked. I haven't seen her since, although Mrs. Spratt-Williams mentioned the other day when I saw her at church that she wasn't doing very well. Many of them don't, you know."

"No, I don't know," Frank said. "Why is that?"

"I've never understood it myself," he admitted. "You'd think they'd be so glad to be freed from their horrible bondage that they'd be grateful for whatever they received. Not all of them are, though. They don't like wearing cast-off clothes, and they get bored with the simple pleasures of ordinary life. Some of them are addicted to drink or opiates, and they get surly when we don't allow them to indulge anymore. But the worst trouble comes when we tell them they must find a job and learn to support themselves."

"Are they lazy?"

"Oh, no, it's not that. They just can't be satisfied with
the frugal lives they must lead. Jobs for women don't pay
very well, I'm afraid. Most employers assume the girls live
with their families and are just helping out until they find
husbands. As soon as they marry, they have to quit their jobs
and make room for the next batch of girls. No one expects
them to support themselves on what they can earn in a factory, but these girls have to."

"I see. That would be discouraging."

"You have no idea. The work is hard, too, which is another deterrent. After a few months, many of the girls are
back on the street, trying to supplement their meager in-
comes. Word always gets back to their employers, and they
lose the factory job, and then . . . Well, they must go back
to their old lives or starve. I don't know what the answer is."

"Better-paying jobs for women would help," Frank said.

Quimby must not have heard him. "So you see, Vivian
was used to the girls at the house complaining. She wouldn't
have been surprised by that, much less upset by it."

"What about her conversation with Mrs. Spratt-
Williams?"

Quimby made a little grunting sound of disgust. "They
were always squabbling about something, the way women
do."

This piqued Frank's interest. "Anything in particular?"

"Oh, Antonia—that's Mrs. Spratt-Williams—she was always trying to ignore the rules."

"What rules?"

"The rules we abide by as tenants in the United Charities
Building."

"What rules did she ignore?"

"She didn't like reporting the women we helped. They

keep track, you know. All the charities keep a list of the people they help so nobody can get help from more than one charity. Antonia didn't think that was right, but she could never convince Vivian. We had to abide by the rules whether we liked them or not."

So, nothing to inspire a murder there. Frank moved on. "Did you know this girl Amy claimed that a man named Gregory had fathered her baby?"

From the look on his face, he hadn't. "Good God! Did Vivian know that?"

"I believe this Amy made a point of telling her. She named the baby after him."

Quimby sucked in his breath with a hiss.

"Do you think it's possible Mr. Van Orner really was the baby's father?" Frank asked.

The color rose in Quimby's plain face. "Why would you ask that?"

"Because rumor has it that Mrs. Van Orner started her rescue house because her husband liked to visit prostitutes."

"I don't know anything about that. Vivian knew my interests lay in helping the less fortunate citizens of our fair city, and she asked me to help her. She said God had laid it on her heart to help these fallen sisters, and I didn't question her further about her motivation."

"But you knew about Mr. Van Orner."

He pressed his lips together until they were white. "I have heard rumors," he finally admitted.

"So you think it's possible Van Orner fathered Amy's baby?"

"The girl worked in a brothel. How could she possibly know?"

"I have no idea, but she might've made that claim to Mrs.

Van Orner. Do you think that would have upset her enough to make her leave without Miss Yingling?"

"I'm sure it could have, although as I said, it's difficult for me to imagine Vivian getting upset over anything."

"What about something Mrs. Spratt-Williams might've said?"

"Good heavens, no. They were the closest of friends."

"You just said they argued all the time."

"I believe I said they squabbled. They weren't fishwives. They didn't argue. They simply disagreed on that one issue. I hardly see what any of this has to do with Vivian's death. You haven't even said what kind of foul play was involved."

"We think she was poisoned."

"Poisoned! Are you insane? Who would have poisoned her?"

"That's what I'm trying to find out."

He considered this for a moment. "Well, I can assure you it wasn't Mrs. Spratt-Williams."

"How can you be so sure?"

"Because ladies might disagree, but they never argue and they never, ever poison each other."

Sarah looked at Mrs. Spratt-Williams. "Are you sure no one knew about Mrs. Van Orner's flask except Miss Yingling, her husband, and you?"

Suddenly, she wasn't sure at all. "Of course, I can't speak for her servants. Servants know so much more than we ever tell them, don't they? I suppose they can't help overhearing and seeing things, no matter how careful we try to be."

"You're absolutely right," Sarah said, hoping to encourage her. "Some of her servants may have known."

"Her maid would have, I'm sure. We can't hide anything from our maids."

"No, we can't," Sarah agreed, remembering the days so long ago when she'd had a maid.

"Servants can take offense, too," Mrs. Spratt-Williams confided. "I've seen it happen. They can be spiteful and vengeful over the slightest little things."

"Was Mrs. Van Orner harsh with her servants?"

"Oh, no, not at all. But if one of them took a notion . . . Well, I'm sure she never did anything intentionally, but you know how they are."

Sarah tried to imagine a maid, having been chastened for not dusting thoroughly enough, pouring a bottle of laudanum into her mistress's liquor bottle. She decided not to tell Mrs. Sprat-Williams how ridiculous that would be. "Could anyone else at the rescue house have known about Mrs. Van Orner's little vice?"

Mrs. Spratt-Williams thought this over carefully. Sarah tried to figure out why she needed to do this. Was she trying to fairly judge who might have discovered Mrs. Van Orner's secret? Did she know someone had and was she trying to decide whether to betray that person? Or was she thinking about something else entirely? "As I said, Vivian never let anyone see her drinking from her flask, but she was always leaving her purse lying about. Someone might have opened it, looking for money or what have you, and found the flask. Even a simpleton could figure out what it was for."

"Did she leave her purse lying about yesterday?"

Mrs. Spratt-Williams opened her mouth to reply and caught herself. "I was going to say yes, because that's what she usually did, but I didn't really notice," she said after a moment. "I'm sure Miss Biafore would know."

"Do you know where she usually left her purse?"

"In the hall, on the table. Anyone could have found it there."

She was right, of course. "Do you remember seeing her purse when you met with Mrs. Van Orner in her office?"

"No, I don't. It must have been out in the hall, as usual."

"So you asked her not to turn Amy out of the house and then you left? Is that correct?"

"Yes, it is. I had an engagement that evening, and I needed to get home."

"Do you think your suggestion made Mrs. Van Orner angry?"

She had to think this over, too. "I wouldn't say angry. Vivian was impatient with me. Yes, that's it. She didn't want to discuss Amy. I can't say I blame her, but really, I was only trying to help."

"Did Mrs. Van Orner speak with anyone else after you left her?"

"I have no idea. I already told you, I went home. This is all so distressing. Poor Vivian. I don't know what we'll do without her."

"I hope you'll decide soon. The women living at the rescue house are very worried."

"I'm sure they are, especially poor Amy. Of course she may not be as concerned now that Vivian is dead."

"She isn't concerned at all. She packed up this morning and left."

MR. QUIMBY HADN'T BEEN MUCH HELP, SO FRANK wasn't expecting Mr. Porter to be either. He was surprised to find him living in a ramshackle house south of Washington Square, in a once fashionable neighborhood that was slowly changing over into rooming houses. A harried maid answered the door, and she didn't seem at all disturbed to find a police detective asking for her master.

As he waited in the front hall for the girl to announce him, he could hear childish screams and lots of thumping coming from upstairs. After a few moments, a man with thinning hair and a thickening waist came hurrying down the hall from a rear parlor, pulling his suit coat over an unbuttoned vest.

"Mary said you're with the police," he said in alarm when he reached Frank. "Has something happened?"

"I'm sorry to tell you that Mrs. Vivan Van Orner died under suspicious circumstances yesterday," Frank said.

Porter blinked several times, trying to make sense of Frank's statement. "I knew she died, but nobody said it was suspicious. Miss Yingling should have warned us!"

"She didn't know," Frank said.

A loud crash from upstairs made both men jump.

"The children are getting ready for bed," Porter explained. "Let's go into the parlor."

This was the formal parlor, reserved for guests and kept in pristine condition, even though the furnishings were starting to show their age. No fire had been laid, and a distinct chill hung in the air. Porter offered Frank a chair by the cold fireplace and took one opposite.

"What's this about Mrs. Van Orner now?" he asked, leaning forward. "There must be some mistake."

"No mistake, I'm afraid. Mrs. Van Orner died in her carriage yesterday afternoon as she was traveling from the rescue house to her home."

Porter shook his head, his expression inexpressibly sad.

"Miss Yingling just told us she died. I couldn't imagine why. I still can't believe it. She was never sick a day in her life."

"Have you known her all her life?"

"Oh, yes. Our families were great friends. We saw each other in church and at parties, everywhere really." He shook his head, lost in memories.

Frank couldn't help comparing the Van Orner home to this one and wondering why, if their families had been so close, Porter's position in life was now so much less prosperous than the Van Orners'. "Did you ever court Mrs. Van Orner?" he asked, probing to see if he could find some romantic rivalry that might have soured through the years.

He looked up in surprise. "Heavens, no! We were children together. Nothing kills romance quicker than remembering how somebody looked in short pants. Besides, Vivian had higher aspirations. Once Van Orner noticed her, no one else had a chance."

"How did you get involved in her charity work?"

"She asked me to help her several years ago. She needed some men to go with her into a bad part of town. I told her I wouldn't be much help if she was set upon by ruffians, but she wasn't concerned about that. As it turned out, she needed a man to knock on the door of a brothel and pretend to be a customer. She thought I would be perfect for that, and as it turned out, she was right. I've been helping her ever since." He seemed very pleased with himself.

"I understand Mrs. Van Orner used her own money to support the rescue house."

"Yes, she had an inheritance from some relative, I think. She used that for it. Van Orner wouldn't give her a penny to help harlots. Those were his own words. I've heard him say them myself. So she used her own money and asked her rich friends to help her, too."

"Did you help her?"

He shook his head sadly. "I've got six children, Mr. . . . I'm sorry, I've forgotten your name."

"Malloy."

"Mr. Malloy, I've got six children. I inherited my father's business, but I haven't been as successful as he was at it. We manage, but . . . To tell you the truth, one reason I agreed to help Vivian was because I thought it might do me some good with Gregory's friends—that's her husband."

"Did it?"

"Oh, no, not at all. Gregory's embarrassed by her little hobby, as he calls it, and he doesn't have any use for me or the rest of Vivian's helpers."

"But you still kept helping her."

"Yes. As I said, we're old friends." Another crash made them both jump, even though this one was a bit muffled. "And it gives me an excuse to be out of the house," he added.

Frank could readily understand why.

"Can you think of anyone who might want to harm Mrs. Van Orner?"

"Oh, dear, I almost forgot why you're here. I keep forgetting Vivian's dead. She's the last person in the world you'd expect to die. She had so much still to do, you know. And now you tell me someone . . . *Are* you telling me someone killed her?"

"It appears that she was poisoned."

"Good God, you don't say! I can hardly credit it. Why would someone want to do a thing like that?"

"I was hoping you'd tell me."

He gave the matter some thought. "Some of the madams were quite angry with her, as you can imagine."

Frank didn't have to imagine. He'd seen Mrs. Walker in person. "I don't think any of them would have had access to her, though."

"You said she was poisoned. How did it happen?"

"Someone put laudanum in . . . in her drink."

Mr. Porter stared at him, dumbfounded for a moment, and then his eyes grew wide. "In her flask, you mean? Oh, dear heaven, of course that's what you mean."

"You knew about her flask?"

"Oh, yes, we all did. All of us who worked with her, that is. We pretended we didn't, or at least we never said anything to her about it. Who am I to judge, after all? Any woman who had to live with Gregory Van Orner could be excused for just about anything that helped her through the day."

Frank's brief encounter with Van Orner confirmed that opinion. "I know Mrs. Van Orner had made a lot of enemies in the city, but none of them would have had access to her flask yesterday."

"Oh, my, you're absolutely right. But that means some-one who . . . Are you saying someone in the rescue house poisoned her?"

"Someone who had access to her flask at some time yes-terday," Frank corrected him.

Porter nodded. "I see. So it might have been someone at her home, too."

"I have to consider all the possibilities. Her husband asked me to investigate, though."

"He did? I wonder why."

"Maybe he wants the guilty person punished."

"So I guess that means he's not the guilty person. More's the pity, although I don't suppose you'd arrest a man like Gregory Van Orner no matter what he did, would you?"

They both knew the answer to that question, so Frank saw no reason to respond. "Do you have any idea who might want to harm Mrs. Van Orner—either in her home or the rescue house?"

"Besides Gregory, I don't know—not that he really cared enough to murder her, of course, but I'm sure he's not particularly grieved at her death either. Maybe one of the women we'd rescued. Sometimes they get very angry. Vivian did what she could for them, but she couldn't keep them forever. They have to learn to make their way in the world."

"Do you know of one in particular who was unhappy?"

"Not really. I don't even know who's living at the rescue house now. I haven't seen Vivian in over a week, at least."

"Was that unusual?"

"Oh, no. I'm very busy with my business and my family responsibilities. She only called on me when she had a rescue at a brothel, and that rarely happened, I'm afraid. It's very dangerous, you see."

Frank took a chance. "What do you know about Miss Yingling?"

"Miss Yingling? Why do you ask?"

"I just thought it was strange that she lived with the Van Orners."

Mr. Porter smiled slightly. "I thought it was strange, too, considering the rumors about Gregory."

"What rumors?"

Porter leaned forward and lowered his voice conspiratorially. "That he enjoyed the company of harlots."

"What does that have to do with Miss Yingling?"

"Oh, didn't you know? Tamar Yingling was the first whore Vivian ever rescued."

SARAH ARRIVED HOME TO FIND MRS. ELLSWORTH HELPing the girls with supper. They were full of questions about her day spent helping Mr. Malloy, but she couldn't answer them fully until they'd tucked Catherine into bed for the night.

Sarah took the opportunity to read Catherine a bedtime story. When she came back downstairs, Mrs. Ellsworth and Maeve were sitting around the kitchen table, chatting while they awaited her return.

"I already told Mrs. Ellsworth all about how Mr. Malloy came to get you this afternoon," Maeve said as Sarah took a seat at the table with them.

"He must have been desperate indeed," Mrs. Ellsworth said. "I know how much he hates having you involved in his cases."

"He wasn't happy about it this time either, but he needed to question the women who live in the rescue house, and they don't allow men inside."

"Is that the place where they take the fallen women after they've gotten them out of the brothel?" Mrs. Ellsworth asked.

"Yes, they let the women stay there for a period of time. I'm not sure how long, but until they can find a job, I suppose."

"That must be difficult. I mean, if they could find honest work, they wouldn't have had to sell themselves in the first place."

"If only everyone understood that," Sarah said, feeling

grateful that she had a friend who was as open-minded as Mrs. Ellsworth. "So many people think these women are immoral or wicked when they're really just desperate."

"So did you get in to interview the women?" Maeve asked.

"Yes, but I don't think I was much help. I did speak with Miss Biafore, the young woman who manages the house, and two of the rescued girls, but the one I really wanted to speak with was Amy, and she's gone."

"Gone! Where did she go?" Maeve asked.

"Nobody knows. She just packed up her baby and left."

"Is this the girl whose baby you delivered?" Mrs. Ellsworth asked.

"Yes, and I'm very worried about her. I don't know how she can take care of herself and a child, too."

"Do you think she's the one who poisoned Mrs. Van Orner?" Maeve asked. "That would explain why she ran away."

Sarah had been struggling with the same question all afternoon. "We don't have any reason to think she did, at least not yet. We do know she and Mrs. Van Orner had some sort of discussion yesterday, and Mrs. Van Orner was upset afterwards, but nobody else knows what they talked about."

"And a few hours later, Mrs. Van Orner was dead, and Amy has disappeared," Mrs. Ellsworth mused.

"Exactly. As Maeve pointed out, it doesn't look good for her."

The front doorbell rang, and Sarah sighed. She should be happy at the prospect of a delivery. She had a family to support, after all. But she was even happier to see Malloy standing on her front stoop.

"I thought you were coming tomorrow," she said as he stepped inside.

"I found out something very interesting, and I thought you should know it right away. Hello, Mrs. Ellsworth. Maeve."

Maeve and her neighbor had come out to see who'd arrived.

Mrs. Ellsworth was equally happy to see Malloy. "It's always nice to see you, Mr. Malloy. Are you hungry? We can heat up something from supper for you."

"No, thanks, I already ate. I could use some coffee, though."

Mrs. Ellsworth insisted on preparing the coffee, and the rest of them sat around the table.

"What did you learn?" Sarah asked as soon as they were settled.

"Before I tell you, did you find out anything interesting from Mrs. Spratt-Williams?"

"Who's that?" Mrs. Ellsworth asked over her shoulder as she put the coffee on to boil.

"She's one of Mrs. Van Orner's helpers. I went to see her this afternoon, too." Sarah turned back to Malloy. "She told me that she and Mrs. Van Orner were talking about Amy just before Mrs. Van Orner left the house. She said she told Mrs. Van Orner she should be more patient with Amy and not put her out just because she was difficult. Mrs. Van Orner refused to discuss it."

"That's all they talked about?"

"That's what she said, but I had a feeling she wasn't being entirely truthful with me. I did ask her who knew about Mrs. Van Orner's drinking habits."

"Oh, my, this is getting very interesting," Mrs. Ellsworth said, taking her seat at the table while she waited for the coffee to boil. "Don't stop to explain, though. Just keep going."

Sarah thought Malloy wanted to roll his eyes, but he just smiled politely and said, "Who did she say knew?"

"Just herself, Mr. Van Orner, and Miss Yingling."

"Who is Miss Yingling?" Mrs. Ellsworth whispered to Maeve.

"Mrs. Van Orner's secretary," Maeve whispered back.

"More people than that knew about her drinking," Malloy said, resolutely ignoring Mrs. Ellsworth.

Sarah managed not to smile. "I know. Even Mrs. Spratt-Williams realized it when I challenged her. She allowed that the Van Orners' servants probably knew, at least her maid."

"Oh, yes, maids know everything," Mrs. Ellsworth agreed.

"Mr. Porter knew, too," Malloy said.

"Who's Mr. Porter?" Mrs. Ellsworth whispered to Maeve again.

"Another one of Mrs. Van Orner's helpers," Malloy answered impatiently, without waiting for Maeve. "He said everybody who worked with her knew about the flask she carried. They never let on, but they all knew."

"So any one of them could have poisoned her," Maeve said.

"No, they had to have an opportunity to put the poison in the flask yesterday, too," Sarah reminded them.

"Why did it have to be yesterday?" Maeve asked.

Everyone looked at her in surprise.

The color bloomed in her fair cheeks at the sudden attention, but she didn't hesitate. "Just because she drank it yesterday doesn't mean the killer put it in yesterday. They could have put it in anytime before that, and she just happened to drink it when she did."

"Maeve is right," Sarah said. "I guess we've been assuming that she drank from the flask every day."

"Do you know how often she did drink from it?" Mrs. Ellsworth asked.

Sarah looked at Malloy, who shrugged. "Miss Yingling said she took a drink when she got upset, to calm her down."

"She smelled of mint the two times I met with her in her office," Sarah remembered. "She carried peppermints, and she offered me one. I think she must have used them to cover the smell of the liquor on her breath."

"It takes more than a peppermint to do that," Maeve said with authority.

No one asked how she knew this.

"The stuff she carried in her flask was a liqueur that smelled like mint," Malloy told her.

"It's called crème de menthe," Sarah added. "It's very sweet."

"I've tasted that. It's delicious," Mrs. Ellsworth said. "I can't imagine gulping it down from a flask, though."

Sarah smiled. "I'm sure you'd get used to it if you drank it all the time."

"So you need to find out if she drank every day," Maeve said. "And who could've put the poison in her flask."

"According to everyone I talked to, anyone at the rescue house could have done it, since she usually left her purse lying on the hallway table. And now," Sarah added with growing dismay, "it looks like anyone at her home could have done it and maybe other people as well. We don't know where she might have been in the days before she died."

"What kind of poison was it?" Mrs. Ellsworth asked.

"Laudanum," Malloy said.

"Oh, my, anyone could have gotten hold of that, too."

"We found an empty bottle of it at the rescue house," Sarah said.

Malloy shook his head. "That doesn't prove anything. Every house in the city probably has a bottle that's at least half-empty."

"Including the Van Orners," Sarah said. "Oh, the coffee's boiling over."

Maeve jumped up before Mrs. Ellsworth could.

"Could her husband have poisoned her?" Mrs. Ellsworth asked as Maeve started to fill the cups the older woman had set out.

"He's the one who told me to find her killer," Malloy said. "I doubt he would've done that if he was the killer."

"Her servants, then?" Mrs. Ellsworth suggested. "Or somebody else who lives at her house?"

"Miss Yingling lives there," Sarah recalled.

"Why would she want to kill Mrs. Van Orner, though? She'd lose her job," Maeve said, setting cups in front of Malloy and Mrs. Ellsworth.

Sarah tried to think of a reason. "Maybe Mrs. Van Orner had learned something bad about her and was going to let her go. Maybe she was even going to make a scandal and ruin her reputation."

"Yes," Mrs. Ellsworth agreed eagerly as Maeve set down cups for Sarah and herself. "Oh, wait, that one was for Mrs.—" She seemed to catch herself and set about vigorously stirring her own coffee.

Maeve gave her an odd look, then sat down and picked up the spoon from her own saucer. "Oh, look," she said in feigned surprise. "I have two spoons. Doesn't that mean I'm going to get married soon, Mrs. Ellsworth?"

Mrs. Ellsworth also feigned surprise, but since she'd set out the cups and spoons, nobody imagined for a moment that she was. She'd obviously meant the two spoons to go to Sarah. This wouldn't be the first time she'd tried to "arrange" a superstition for her. "Well, yes, it *can* mean that. It can also mean you're going to marry twice, so I hope you don't feel you must hurry to find a beau."

Sarah covered her mouth to hide a smile while Malloy looked on, completely bewildered by the exchange. She wasn't about to explain it to him. "So where were we? Oh, yes, we decided that Mrs. Van Orner was going to ruin Miss Yingling and she was desperate to save herself. She was afraid she might end up in a brothel like those other girls, so she had to kill Mrs. Van Orner."

"I see," said Maeve. "And if she killed Mrs. Van Orner before she told anyone about Miss Yingling, someone else would give her a job after Mrs. Van Orner died."

Malloy sighed in exasperation. "That's fine except for one thing."

"What's that?" Sarah asked.

"Miss Yingling was a prostitute herself."

"What!" all three women cried in unison.

"Who told you that?" Sarah asked in amazement.

"Mr. Porter. She was the first prostitute Mrs. Van Orner rescued. That's what I came here to tell you."

10

Sarah shook her head, trying to understand. "Did the other people at Rahab's Daughters know Miss Yingling had been a prostitute? Oh, wait, of course they did. Now it all makes sense."

"What makes sense?" Malloy asked.

"The way they treated her, that day we had the meeting in Mrs. Van Orner's office to plan how we were going to rescue Amy from the brothel. Mrs. Spratt-Williams and the two gentlemen, they acted like she wasn't even there. I don't think they even looked at her unless they had to. I thought they were just too proud to speak to a lowly secretary, but that wasn't it at all."

"How did Mrs. Van Orner treat her?" Maeve asked.

Sarah tried to recall. "She treated her like she was a servant, but that didn't seem strange, because in a sense, she was."

"Except she lived in the Van Orners' house," Malloy reminded her.

"So do their other servants," Sarah said. "What I can't understand is why Mr. Van Orner allowed it."

"You're forgetting the rumors about Mr. Van Orner," Malloy said. "They say he likes prostitutes."

"But would he like one living under his own roof?" Mrs. Ellsworth scoffed. "He'd be a laughingstock."

Malloy refused to give in. "Maybe *his* friends didn't know. Maybe *he* didn't even know. I can't imagine his wife telling him."

Sarah shook her head. "And I can't believe Miss Yingling was a prostitute. She's one of the most prim and proper young women I've ever met."

"That's what she'd want Mrs. Van Orner and everybody else to think," Malloy argued back. "You didn't see her last night, though."

"What do you mean?"

Mrs. Ellsworth and Maeve leaned forward eagerly.

"I mean when I asked if Mr. Van Orner would let me investigate his wife's murder, she said she would ask him, but it would take a long time. I didn't know what she meant at first. I thought she needed time to convince him, but when she came back an hour later, I realized that she needed the time to get herself fixed up. I didn't even recognize her. She'd changed completely."

"Changed how?" Maeve asked.

"She was beautiful, with her hair all curled and a nice dress on, one that showed off her figure instead of hanging on her. I don't know what she said to convince Van Orner, but she made sure she looked pretty to do it."

"Oh, my," Mrs. Ellsworth said. "That gives her a good reason to kill Mrs. Van Orner."

Sarah frowned, not following at all. "What does?"

"Why, she must be in love with Mr. Van Orner and wanted to get his wife out of the way so he could have him for herself."

Sarah frowned. "Mrs. Van Orner had saved her and given her a job and kept her in her own house. She had a lot of reasons to be grateful to Mrs. Van Orner. She also couldn't possibly think Mr. Van Orner would ever want to marry her, no matter how much he might like prostitutes."

"And we're forgetting all about Amy," Maeve said.

"What about her?" Mrs. Ellsworth asked.

"You're right, Maeve. Amy wasn't grateful to Mrs. Van Orner at all, and she'd been hinting for weeks that Mr. Van Orner was the father of her baby," Sarah said. "We might be sure Mr. Van Orner wouldn't believe her and that he would certainly never marry her even if he did, but she might not have known any of that. As you said, Malloy, young girls get silly ideas."

"She was at the rescue house yesterday, and she had the opportunity to put the poison in Mrs. Van Orner's flask, too," Maeve reminded them.

"Except for one thing," Mrs. Ellsworth said. "How could she know about Mrs. Van Orner's drinking problem in the first place?"

MALLOY DIDN'T LIKE HER PLAN, BUT SARAH THOUGHT IT was brilliant. She didn't even need to convince her mother, who was only too happy to assist. Mrs. Decker agreed instantly when Sarah showed up at her house the next morning to ask her.

"A condolence visit to Gregory Van Orner," she repeated when Sarah suggested it. "I'm ashamed I hadn't thought of it myself."

Sarah filled her in on everything she knew while her mother got herself properly dressed for a visit.

"I'm not complaining, mind you," her mother said while her maid pinned up her hair, "but why didn't Mr. Malloy just go to the house himself?" They were in Mrs. Decker's lavishly furnished bedroom.

"Because they might just refuse to see him, and even if they did let him in, Mr. Van Orner and Miss Yingling might get angry and refuse to answer his questions. I could go alone, but Mr. Van Orner doesn't know me, and Miss Yingling doesn't have any reason to confide in me, but you . . ." Sarah smiled sweetly at her mother's reflection in the dressing table mirror.

"Gregory wouldn't dare refuse to see me, and this Miss Yingling might be awed enough by my name to speak with you, too."

"Mother, you amaze me."

"Perhaps I should speak to Theodore about giving me a job on the police force . . . Oh, dear, I keep forgetting he's not there anymore. He's joined the Navy or something," Mrs. Decker said, referring to their old family friend, Theodore Roosevelt, who had once been the police commissioner.

"He's the Assistant Secretary of the Navy in Washington, D.C., now," Sarah reminded her. "I'm sure if you want to work for the police, Mr. Malloy can tell you who to speak with, though," she added with a grin.

"I'm sure he could. Perhaps we should see how this trip goes before I make any plans," Mrs. Decker said, making her maid sigh in dismay.

Even though the Van Orners lived only a few blocks away from Mrs. Decker, they took the carriage. Mrs. Decker wanted to make an impression.

The maid who answered the door escorted Sarah and her mother straight upstairs to the front parlor, where they had to wait awhile for Mr. Van Orner. The maid brought tea and cake to occupy them. At last, Mr. Van Orner came in, looking a bit harried and still smoothing the lapels of his black mourning suit.

"Elizabeth, how good of you to come," he said, going straight for Mrs. Decker and taking the hand she offered him. He had once been a handsome man who was now going soft in his middle years. His features seemed slightly blurred with the puffiness that comes from too much drink.

"I'm so sorry to hear about poor Vivian. I came at once to see if there's anything I can do to help."

"We're all still in shock, I'm afraid. I've been trying to decide on funeral arrangements, but it's so difficult. I don't have any idea what she would have wanted." He noticed Sarah. "Is this your daughter?"

"Yes, Mrs. Brandt. She helped Vivian in her work at Rahab's Daughters."

Sarah saw the emotion flicker across Mr. Van Orner's face. She thought it was distaste, but he recovered quickly. "I'm sure Vivian appreciated your help very much."

"I was grateful for the opportunity. She'll be greatly missed."

"Yes, well, I see the servants have brought you some refreshment. Can I refill your cups?" He took a seat on a chair opposite the sofa where they sat and proceeded to pour, fill-ing a cup for himself in the process.

"Vivian's death was so sudden," Mrs. Decker said. "Had she been ill?"

"No, not that anyone knew. She . . . Well, I suppose you'll hear sooner or later. The police believe she was helped along."

"Helped along?" Mrs. Decker said with creditable inno-cence.

"You know, murdered."

"Good heavens! Who would do such a thing?"

Van Orner glanced at Sarah. "Vivian had made a lot of enemies with her little hobby, people who wouldn't think twice about murder."

"How was she murdered?" Mrs. Decker asked, still look-ing suitably shocked.

"They believe she was poisoned somehow. At least that's what Miss Yingling tells me. Miss Yingling was Vivian's secretary."

"How on earth could someone have poisoned her?"

"I have no idea. I've left everything up to the police."

Sarah could see they'd get nothing from Mr. Van Orner. "I would like to express my condolences to Miss Yingling, if I may. I met her while I was working with Mrs. Van Orner, and I know she must be devastated."

Mr. Van Orner seemed a bit surprised, but he shrugged. "I'm sure that would be fine." He rang for the maid and sent her to fetch Miss Yingling.

Mrs. Decker made polite conversation with their host while they waited for Miss Yingling. When the door opened, Sarah managed not to gasp at the transformation in the young woman. After what Malloy had told her, she'd been prepared for a change, but the difference was still shocking.

Malloy hadn't done justice to her when describing the change, but Sarah could see every detail. The drab, ill-fitting suit was gone. In its place she wore a fashionable flowered gown that fit snugly enough to accentuate all of her womanly curves, curves Sarah hadn't even suspected she possessed. Her hair had been restyled into the modern, more flattering Gibson girl knot on the top of her head. Soft curls adorned her forehead and trailed down her cheeks and the back of her neck. The faintest touches of rouge brought out the color in her lips and cheeks. She was, Sarah acknowledged, a lovely young woman. Sarah had to consciously close her gaping mouth.

Miss Yingling seemed equally surprised. "Mrs. Brandt," she said. "I didn't know you were here."

"I heard the news about Mrs. Van Orner. I'm so very sorry."

Miss Yingling just stood there.

Conscious of the uncomfortable silence, Mr. Van Orner said, "Mrs. Brandt said she knew you, Tamar." He seemed unsure if he'd made a mistake by summoning Miss Yingling.

"Yes, of course she does," Miss Yingling quickly confirmed. "Mrs. Brandt helped us with our last rescue."

"The one with—"

"The one I told you about," she said sharply, cutting him off. The glance she gave him could only be described as a warning.

Sarah had never seen a servant give such a look to her master, but Mr. Van Orner didn't seem outraged or even surprised. He just nodded once and fell silent.

Miss Yingling turned her attention back to Sarah, suddenly and belatedly gracious. "Thank you for coming, Mrs. Brandt. How did you hear about Mrs. Van Orner's death?"

"From the police," Sarah said.

"The *police*? Why were you talking with the police?"

"They wanted to know what I knew about Mrs. Van Orner's activities." That much was true, at least.

Miss Yingling frowned. "I wonder how they got your name."

"I understand they're questioning all the people who helped Mrs. Van Orner at Rahab's Daughters."

"That's not necessary, I'm sure," Van Orner said, finally finding a reason for outrage.

"They're trying to find out who might have wished Mrs. Van Orner harm," Sarah said. "Her friends would know the people she had offended."

"That seems reasonable," Miss Yingling said to Van Orner.

He seemed to accept her judgment.

Sarah soldiered on, wondering how to get some information out of one of them. Maybe if she could get Miss Yingling alone . . . "I stopped by the rescue house yesterday, as soon as I heard, to see if I could be of any assistance. I was particularly worried about Amy . . ." Miss Yingling stiffened slightly. Sarah pretended not to notice. "But she wasn't there. It seems she'd packed up and left the house that morning."

Miss Yingling didn't seem surprised. She glanced at Mr. Van Orner before replying. "Did she? I wonder where she went."

"No one seemed to know. She didn't even tell anyone she was leaving."

"That's a shame, but some of the women simply refuse to

be helped. We can't make them change, as much as we may want to."

Somewhere, a door slammed, not a sound one expected to hear in a home where the occupants were in mourning. A servant would probably find herself turned out of the house for the lapse.

"Miss Yingling, I know it's not my place to say anything, but Miss Biafore is very concerned about what's going to happen to the rescue house now that . . . Well, with Mrs. Van Orner gone . . ."

Miss Yingling glanced at Mr. Van Orner again, and this time he looked away, clearly not pleased by the subject.

"I'm afraid we haven't really had time to give the matter any thought," Miss Yingling said.

Sarah wanted to press the issue, but before she could say anything, they heard a disturbance out in the hall and then the parlor door burst open. Sarah could hardly believe her eyes.

Amy strode into the room, her cheeks red with fury, but she stopped dead at the sight of Sarah and Mrs. Decker. She wore a muslin housedress that barely contained her full breasts, and her golden hair was loose around her shoulders. "I . . . I thought . . ." she stammered in mortification.

"I'm sure no one cares what you thought," Miss Yingling said, obviously furious and also embarrassed at being proved a liar. "Mr. Van Orner has visitors. You have no business here."

Sarah jumped to her feet. "Amy, I'm so glad to see you. How is the baby?"

Amy looked around wildly, searching for some clue as to how she should react. Mr. Van Orner and Miss Yingling simply glared at her, but Mrs. Decker apparently sensed an opportunity to be of service to her daughter.

"Is this the young lady whose baby you delivered at the——" She caught herself and covered her near-disastrous error with a charming smile. "Mrs. Brandt has been very worried about you."

"Yes, I have," Sarah said. "I would love to see the baby. May I?"

Amy was still looking somewhat desperate and finding no friendly face except Sarah's. "If you'd like, I . . . Of course you can see him." She whirled around and made her escape. Sarah had to hurry to catch up with her.

As she followed Amy up the stairs, she saw the girl was barefoot. She was making herself quite at home here. Amy didn't look back until they'd reached the top of the stairs and gone down the hallway to one of the doors. Amy pushed it open and entered, leaving Sarah to follow.

Sarah saw at once it was a bedroom, furnished in the impersonal style used for occasional guests. A large market basket sat at the foot of the unmade bed. Sarah recognized it as the one she'd carried the baby in from the Mission the day they'd rescued Amy. Amy stopped beside it, turning back to Sarah.

"Here he is."

Sarah closed the bedroom door behind her. She didn't want anyone to hear the questions she needed to ask Amy. She went over to the basket and looked down. The tiny boy was sleeping peacefully, snuggled into his makeshift bed. "He looks well."

"He's fine. Did you think I wasn't taking care of him?" She was still angry and taking it out on Sarah.

"I knew you'd take good care of him, but babies can get sick for no reason at all, and he's been through a lot in his young life. When I heard you'd left the rescue house,

I couldn't imagine where you'd gone. I was very worried about you."

She stuck out her lower lip like a spoiled child. "I couldn't tell them I was coming here, could I?"

"I suppose not. Did Miss Yingling invite you here?" she tried.

"Miss Yingling!" she scoffed, amused by the thought. "Not likely."

"But you did know Mrs. Van Orner was dead."

"Sure. Miss Yingling was kind enough to send us a note, so we'd know the old witch was gone."

Sarah managed not to wince. "It must've been a shock."

"We were all surprised, if that's what you mean. That Lisa, she bawled like she'd lost her own mother. You never saw such carrying on. The other girls, too, but I don't think it was for the witch. They were just worried about who was going to feed them now."

"And you decided Mr. Van Orner was going to feed you," Sarah guessed.

Amy smiled the sly little grin Sarah was coming to know. "I told you little Gregory's father was going to take care of us."

Sarah glanced down at the child in the basket, her heart aching for the innocent babe who hadn't asked for any of this.

"Oh, that's just temporary," Amy said, apparently thinking Sarah was judging her success by the quality of the baby's sleeping arrangements. "He's going to get a cradle and a nurse and everything brand-new."

"That's very nice."

"I'm going to get everything brand-new, too, now that she's gone."

How very convenient for Amy. "Do you know what happened to Mrs. Van Orner?"

"She died. That's all I need to know."

"Miss Yingling said you had a conversation with her right before she left the rescue house the other day."

"So what if I did?"

"I was just wondering what you talked about. Miss Biafore said Mrs. Van Orner was upset afterwards."

"Upset? Is that what she claims? I don't know how she could tell. The witch never let on that she was feeling anything at all. I never even saw her smile. She was a cold fish. I know everything about her. Gregory told me."

Sarah's stomach twisted at the thought of a man discussing his wife's shortcomings with his mistress, but she managed not to betray her true feelings. "What did you and Mrs. Van Orner talk about that day?"

Amy smiled, apparently enjoying the memory. "She told me I was going to have to leave the rescue house. She said the other girls were complaining about me, but I knew the real reason. She couldn't stand looking at me and my baby. She hated me because I had his baby and she never could."

That conversation may have upset Amy, too. She wouldn't have liked being threatened. "You must have been frightened at the thought of leaving the rescue house and having no place to go."

"She couldn't scare me. I told her she wouldn't dare put me out because I'd tell Gregory what she'd done. I was going to tell him anyway—about the baby, I mean—the first chance I got. I knew he'd take care of me, too. He used to take good care of me, and I knew he would again, because of the baby. He always wanted a son, and now he has one."

This certainly explained what Lisa Biafore had observed. Mrs. Van Orner would have been furious to hear her husband's mistress challenge her. "Were you trying to hurt her?"

The question surprised her. "I just wanted her to know she couldn't treat me like she treated all the other whores."

"Do you know how she died?" Sarah asked again.

"I already told you . . . Wait, are you saying that's why she died? Because I got her so mad? Did she have apoplexy or something?" The thought seemed to please her.

"No," Sarah said, feeling sick. "She didn't have apoplexy."

Amy's eyes lit up. "Oh, I know, she got drunk and fell down! Gregory told me how she drank all the time. She drank something funny, something with mint in the name. He told me but I can't remember. And then she ate peppermints so people wouldn't know. He told me all about it, and when I smelled the peppermint on her, I knew it was all true. We used to lay in bed and laugh about how she carried a silver flask in her purse and took a nip whenever things didn't go her way. That's what happened, wasn't it? After I told her what for, she took too many nips and fell down and broke her neck."

"No, that's not what happened."

Someone tapped on the door, and it opened before anyone could respond. Miss Yingling stood in the doorway. "Mrs. Brandt, I'll show you out."

Sarah thought she should probably stay and question Amy further, but she wasn't sure she wanted to hear any more of her answers. Grateful to Miss Yingling for the rescue, she bade Amy good-bye. "You can send for me if you need anything," she added as she stepped out into the hallway.

Amy smiled. "I won't need anything."

Miss Yingling closed the door behind them with more force than was necessary. "I'm sorry."

"There's no need to be," Sarah said. "I really am glad to know she and the baby are safe. I was picturing her carrying him around the streets and begging for food."

"Amy isn't very bright, but she knows how to take care of herself."

Sarah decided not to comment. "Do you think there's any chance that Rahab's Daughters will continue its work?"

Miss Yingling raised her eyebrows, surprised at the question. "That's up to Mrs. Spratt-Williams and the others, and they aren't likely to consult me when they make their decision."

"I don't suppose Mr. Van Orner would help in any way."

Miss Yingling came as close to laughing as Sarah had ever seen. "No, and I believe I can be certain about that."

They'd reached the stairs, and Sarah stopped, forcing Miss Yingling to stop as well. She gave Sarah a questioning look.

"I've been thinking about Mrs. Van Orner's death," Sarah began, feeling her way carefully. "I got the idea that the police believe someone at the rescue house put the poison in her flask the day she died, but that's not the only possibility."

Miss Yingling held herself very still. "What other possibility is there?"

"Someone in this house might have done it. They could have even done it the day before, maybe *days* before, and Mrs. Van Orner just happened to drink from the flask that day."

"Why are you telling me this?"

"Because you would know if that's possible. Could she have been carrying the poisoned flask around for days?"

Miss Yingling considered the question carefully. "No."

"You seem very sure."

"She filled her flask every morning. You can ask her maid, if you like. She filled it every morning because it was empty from the day before. She filled it that morning as well."

"You saw her?"

"No, of course not, but I know her habits. Mrs. Brandt, someone at the rescue house put the laudanum in her flask. That's the only place it could have happened."

"But who would have wanted her dead?"

Miss Yingling slowly turned her head until she was looking at the closed door to Amy's bedroom. Then she slowly turned back to Sarah. "Someone who had something to gain by her death."

Unfortunately, Sarah was starting to believe that, too.

"GOOD HEAVENS," MRS. DECKER EXCLAIMED WHEN they were safely ensconced in the Decker carriage again. "I've never seen a prostitute before in my entire life and today I saw two."

"And what do you know now that you didn't know before?"

"That they look exactly like everyone else."

Sarah couldn't help smiling. "What were you expecting?"

"I don't know. I suppose I thought they'd look . . . depraved or something. That girl Amy did look like a trollop, the way she was dressed, or rather, *not* dressed, but I gather she'd been resting or something."

"I'm sure she was. According to the other women at the rescue house, that's one thing she's good at."

Mrs. Decker leaned closer to Sarah, even though they were completely safe from eavesdroppers. "Did you get the impression when she burst in that she thought Van Orner and Miss Yingling were having a tête-à-tête?"

"I did. I'm sure that's why she was so angry. She was quite shocked to see us sitting there with them."

"I can't imagine what Gregory plans to do with those two women now."

Sarah rolled her eyes. "I think you could if you gave it a moment's thought."

"Oh, Sarah, I don't mean that. I mean how does a gentleman explain the presence of two young women in his home with no wife to serve as a chaperone?"

"Hundreds of gentlemen live with unchaperoned young women in their homes. They're called maids."

"Those women aren't maids."

"No, they aren't, Mother, but he could pretend they're some sort of servants."

"His dead wife's secretary and a woman who used to be his mistress and now has a child named after him?"

"I'll admit, that is a bit difficult to explain."

"And whatever her past, I'm sure Miss Yingling would like the world to believe her to be a respectable young woman now. Will she jeopardize that to remain in Gregory's home?"

"I have no idea," Sarah said with a weary sigh. "I don't understand any of these people."

"Did you learn anything at all while you were upstairs?"

Sarah mentally reviewed her conversations with Amy and Miss Yingling. "I learned that Amy did know about Mrs. Van Orner's drinking. It seems Mr. Van Orner told her all about it, for her amusement."

"That cad!" Mrs. Decker exclaimed.

"I suppose if you're unfaithful to your wife in one way, it's not a very big step to be unfaithful in all ways."

"I believe I could forgive your father for seeking the delights of another woman's bed, if he were truly repentant, but I would never forgive him for speaking about me to a trollop!"

"I know. That's a completely different kind of betrayal. Amy said they'd lie in bed and laugh about her drinking."

Mrs. Decker gasped in outrage.

"But all of that aside," Sarah continued, "the fact is that Amy did know about Mrs. Van Orner's flask."

"Did you find out if someone could have put the poison in the flask the day before?"

"Miss Yingling said Mrs. Van Orner emptied her flask daily, so it seems likely someone put the laudanum in it the same day she died."

"Someone at her house still could have put it in before she left home that morning."

"Yes, but who?"

"Miss Yingling, for one. I don't like her at all. She's a bit of a . . . a *prig*, although it sounds odd to say such a thing about a woman with her past."

"I know what you mean, though. I think she's just trying very hard to be what she thinks a respectable woman should be."

"Do you think she imagines Gregory is interested in her?"

Sarah considered this. "I have no idea, of course, but it's interesting that while Mrs. Van Orner was alive, she took great pains to make herself plain and unattractive, but as soon as Mrs. Van Orner died, she changed her clothes and her hair and every part of her appearance to make herself as beautiful as possible."

"A woman only does that when she wants a man to notice her," Mrs. Decker said.

"Or when she wants to influence him," Sarah said. "According to Malloy, she first made the change when she went to speak with Van Orner about allowing the police to investigate the murder."

Mrs. Decker considered this. "Gregory could easily have forbidden the police from getting involved. He could have just claimed Vivian died of some mysterious ailment and let her be buried quietly. Even if he suspected she'd been murdered, no one wants their family secrets dragged through the newspapers, and they certainly don't want to be involved with the police . . . No offense to Mr. Malloy, but you know very well—"

"Yes, I know very well what people in your social set think of the police, and you're right, no one with the means to prevent it would allow them to be involved in their lives."

"So Vivian's death could have passed with little notice from any but her closest friends, and yet Gregory chose to let Mr. Malloy investigate."

Sarah was beginning to see the point her mother was trying to make. "Yes, why would he do such a thing? If he was devoted to his wife, he might want justice, but . . ."

"Believe me, he was not devoted to Vivian."

"Then it doesn't make any sense."

"Just as important, why did Miss Yingling work so hard to convince him to accept Mr. Malloy's assistance?"

"And she did work hard. She changed her entire appearance, becoming a woman he couldn't fail to find appealing before making her case to him."

"Even more amazing, she succeeded," Mrs. Decker said. "She must have some influence over him, more than his wife's secretary should have, at any rate."

"Miss Yingling thinks Amy poisoned Mrs. Van Orner."

Mrs. Decker looked at Sarah in amazement. "Does she? How do you know?"

"She made it very clear to me that she believes Amy is the only one with something to gain from Mrs. Van Orner's death."

"I don't know if she's the only one, but she certainly did stand to gain. She'd get nothing but crumbs as long as Vivian was alive. Gregory might have taken her as his mistress again, but he'd never acknowledge the child openly. Vivian would have made sure of it. She'd never allow him to humiliate her like that."

"How could she have stopped him?"

"She would make sure he understood that she would win the support of the wives of all his friends. He'd be socially ostracized. Even though his friends might not care what he had done, their wives would make certain he was never invited anywhere. The threat of such a fate would be enough to ensure his discretion."

"Now he doesn't have to worry about that," Sarah mused.

"No, he doesn't, but I still don't understand why he's letting the police investigate the murder."

"I got the feeling the whole thing was Miss Yingling's idea. She dressed up and went to see him, sort of like in the Bible, the way Queen Esther dressed up to go see the king to plead for the safety of her people."

"It's a trick as old as time."

"And she convinced him to do it."

"Yes, she did," Mrs. Decker said with a frown. "But why? Why would she care so much?"

"Maybe we misjudged her. She had good reason to be grateful to Mrs. Van Orner, who'd rescued her from the depths of degradation and given her a place in her own household and a respectable way to earn her living. I can't even imagine how grateful I'd be to someone who had done that for me."

"You're right. I hadn't thought of it that way before. She hasn't shown it, but she must be devastated that Vivian is dead."

"And if Vivian was murdered, Miss Yingling would surely want to find out who did it and see them punished."

"That would be perfectly natural, and the only way to find the killer is to involve the police."

Sarah nodded. "So that explains why she went to so much trouble to make sure Mrs. Van Orner's death was investigated."

"And if they find out Amy is the killer, she'll be rid of an annoying problem into the bargain."

"Yes, everything would work out very neatly for Miss Yingling . . . but only if Amy is the killer."

II

"Mother, could you have your driver drop me off someplace?" Sarah asked, even though they were almost back to the Decker home.

"Of course, dear. Where would you like to go?"

"I need to see Mrs. Spratt-Williams. She was very concerned when I told her Amy had left the rescue house, and I'd like to let her know she and the baby aren't in any danger."

"I'm sure she'll be surprised to learn she landed at the Van Orner house."

"Maybe not. Amy certainly gave plenty of hints that she was involved with Mr. Van Orner."

"Still, hinting and moving in with the man are two very different things."

"Would you like to go in with me?"

"Yes, but I don't know Mrs. Spratt-Williams and I have a feeling I don't want to. She'll surely be looking for patronesses to replace Vivian. Your father would never permit me to support such a cause, and I'd rather not have to refuse her."

"Since when do you worry about what Father approves and doesn't approve?"

Mrs. Decker shook her head in mock dismay. "Sarah, I was trying to be discreet. When I don't want to do something, I always blame your father. How unkind of you to make me admit it."

"I'm so sorry," Sarah said with a grin. "Then I won't force you into an acquaintance with Mrs. Spratt-Williams. Do you know anything about her? She said she's a widow."

"Hmmm, I seem to remember some scandal about her husband. He's been dead a number of years, though, and there have been so many scandals in the meantime that they've started running together in my memory. I could be completely mistaken, too. I do know she doesn't go out in society. She's probably one of those widows who devote themselves to good works."

That seemed to describe Mrs. Spratt-Williams perfectly.

Mrs. Decker gave her driver the address, and they chatted about Catherine for the rest of the drive. Mrs. Decker had taken a healthy interest in the child who would likely be the closest thing to a grandchild she would ever have. Mrs. Decker instructed the driver to wait until Sarah had been admitted into Mrs. Spratt-Williams's house, and Sarah waved good-bye before stepping through the front door.

Mrs. Spratt-Williams looked much better today than she had yesterday. She was dressed and groomed, and her color was good and her eyes clear.

"Mrs. Brandt, what a delightful surprise. Please come in and sit down. I'll order some tea."

"Oh, don't go to any trouble for me. I can only stay a few minutes. I just thought you'd want to hear some good news for a change."

Mrs. Spratt-Williams looked oddly wary. "Good news?"

"Yes, we've found Amy."

"Amy?"

"Yes, and her baby. They're both safe and sound."

"Oh, my, that is good news," she said, although she didn't seem as relieved as Sarah had expected. "Where has she gone?"

"I'm afraid this may be a bit shocking to you, but she's staying at the Van Orner home."

She did find this shocking. "At Vivian's house?"

"Yes, she . . . Mr. Van Orner has taken her in."

The older woman's expression hardened. "The scoundrel!"

Sarah decided to withhold comment. "I knew you were worried about Amy and the baby, so I wanted you to know they weren't out on the streets."

"I almost wish they were. Oh, dear, I suppose this means Amy's claims were true, that Gregory is the father of the child . . . Or at least that he was involved with her and has reason to believe he could be."

"I learned long ago not to make assumptions," Sarah said.

"Vivian knew he had a mistress, but so many men do, you know. They get tired of us when we aren't young and pretty anymore, and to tell the truth, most women are relieved when their husbands turn their attentions elsewhere, if you know what I mean."

Sarah knew exactly what she meant. "So she didn't mind?"

"She never said. Vivian kept the secrets of her heart very closely, but I don't think she was jealous, not of Gregory, at any rate. She was desperately jealous of the child, though."

"Amy's child?"

"Yes, she wasn't able to have any of her own, you see. She suffered several miscarriages, and then her physician told her she shouldn't even try anymore. Her life could be in danger if she lost another one."

"So seeing Amy's baby and knowing it might be her husband's child . . ." Sarah gestured vaguely, encouraging her to go on.

"I'm sure that's why she was so determined to turn the poor girl and her baby out. She never would have been that heartless with anyone else."

"Do you think Amy was frightened?"

Mrs. Spratt-Williams looked at Sarah in surprise. "Frightened? I'm sure she was, but Amy wasn't one to simply quake in her boots. She gave as good as she got from Vivian. That's why Vivian hated her so much."

"Did Amy hate her, too?"

Sarah waited while her hostess considered the question. "What are you really asking me, Mrs. Brandt?"

"Someone poisoned Mrs. Van Orner. Do you think Amy would do something like that?"

Plainly, Mrs. Spratt-Williams wasn't used to answering such frank questions. "I can't say for certain, of course. I didn't see her do anything, and she hasn't confessed to me, but as I told you before, Amy has had a difficult life. She came from a respectable family, but her father was involved in some unsuccessful business dealings and lost all their money. He couldn't stand the disgrace, so he killed himself, leaving Amy and her mother destitute. They struggled for a time, but when Amy started blossoming into a lovely young woman, her mother arranged for her to be taken in by a protector, a man who had been a friend of Amy's father, I believe."

"Mr. Van Orner?"

"No, Gregory got her later. Her first protector passed her along to him. I've heard that's fairly common."

"And when he tired of her, he gave her to Mrs. Walker," Sarah said, telling the part of the story she knew.

"Such a sad story, but all too common, I'm afraid. We try to help these girls, but by the time they come to us, they're often so hardened by life that they've lost their feminine natures."

"So you're saying that Amy might have poisoned Mrs. Van Orner."

"I have no idea, but I would like to see her for myself. Perhaps we can decide then."

MRS. SPRATT-WILLIAMS EXPLAINED THAT SHE NO LONGer kept a carriage, so they walked out to Fifth Avenue and found a hansom cab to take them back to the Van Orner house. Sarah would have walked all the way, and they would have gotten there much sooner if they had, given the state of the New York City traffic at midday on a Saturday, but Sarah deferred to her companion. While the weekday traffic was impatient and urgent, the weekend traffic seemed more relaxed and somehow happier, if no less congested as city residents did their shopping and errands in preparation for the Sabbath and another week.

The Van Orners' maid recognized both of them, but she frowned in confusion when Mrs. Spratt-Williams asked to speak to Miss Cunningham.

"Oh, you mean Amy," the maid said after a moment. "I don't know if she's receiving. We're in mourning, you see."

No one could have missed the gigantic black wreath on the front door or the maid's black armband.

"Just tell her I'd like to see how she is," Mrs. Spratt-Williams said.

A few minutes later, the maid returned to escort them upstairs to the front parlor, where they found Amy ready to receive them as if she were the lady of the house. Only her gown gave her away. She still wore the shabby castoff she'd received at the rescue house.

"Mrs. Spratt-Williams and Mrs. Brandt, how kind of you to come," she simpered, offering each of them her hand in welcome.

No sooner had they returned her greeting than Miss Yingling hurried into the room, catching herself in the doorway and slowing to a sedate pace as she entered, although her cheeks were flaming with indignation. Except for her expression, she looked the picture of demure womanhood in a gown that surely must have once belonged to Vivian Van Orner. "Amy, you should have told me we have visitors."

Amy ignored the rebuke in her tone. "They asked to see *me*."

Miss Yingling looked at the two guests, obviously not sure she was telling the truth.

"Mrs. Brandt was kind enough to tell me Amy was here," Mrs. Spratt-Williams said. "I wanted to hurry right over and make sure she was all right. I've been very worried since Mrs. Brandt told me yesterday that Amy had disappeared from the rescue house."

"As you can see, she's perfectly fine," Miss Yingling said, although her expression said she wouldn't have been disappointed had things been otherwise.

"I can speak for myself," Amy said crossly. "Won't you sit down. I've ordered some tea to be brought up."

This made Miss Yingling even angrier, as Sarah felt sure Amy had intended for it to. Amy was assuming all sorts of authority.

"How is the baby doing?" Sarah asked when they were all seated.

"I told you, he's fine," Amy said. "We're getting a nurse for him. She'll be here the day after tomorrow. Then I won't have to think about him at all."

"Not that you do now," Miss Yingling muttered.

"Is she a wet nurse?" Sarah asked.

"Oh, no, they couldn't get one so quickly. She's going to give him a bottle, though, so I don't have to feed him anymore."

"It's so much better for the baby if you nurse him," Sarah said, thinking it would be better in so many ways. If nothing else, his mother would be forced to acknowledge him several times a day at least.

"Oh, they have these scientific formulas now that they give the babies. They're even better than mother's milk. Besides," she added when Sarah would have protested, "Gregory doesn't want me tied down."

"The baby doesn't want you tied down?" Mrs. Spratt-Williams asked in confusion.

"Mr. Van Orner doesn't," Miss Yingling said through stiff lips. The emotion burning in her eyes was so clear, Sarah would not have been surprised had she sprang up from her seat and strangled Amy with her bare hands.

"That's what I said. Gregory." Amy smiled sweetly. "Things have changed a lot in a few days, haven't they, Mrs. Brandt? Mrs. Van Orner was so mean to me, and now I never have to worry about her again."

Sarah couldn't manage a reply.

Mrs. Spratt-Williams exchanged a quick glance with Sarah, then turned back to Amy. "Mrs. Van Orner was a wonderful and generous woman. Many people will miss her very much."

"I don't suppose you'll be one of them." Amy's eyes shone with merriment . . . or deviltry. Sarah wasn't sure which.

"Me? Of course I will!"

"But now you don't have to worry about her telling on you."

Mrs. Spratt-Williams's face flooded with color. "I don't know what you mean!"

"Yes, you do. I heard you arguing with Mrs. Van Orner that day she died, but now she can't cause trouble for anybody ever again."

Mrs. Spratt-Williams gave Sarah a desperate glance that told her she had no idea what Amy was talking about.

Apparently oblivious to her guests' distress, Amy chatted on. "Mrs. Brandt, what should I do to stop my milk? I'll be so glad to not be leaking all over myself anymore."

Sarah hated giving these instructions to a perfectly healthy woman with a perfectly healthy baby, especially when she knew the baby wouldn't do nearly as well on the bottle, but she very quickly gave Amy the instructions.

When she was finished, Amy turned to Miss Yingling. "I hope you were paying attention, Tamar. I'll never remember all that."

Sarah knew a moment of pity for Tamar Yingling. If Gregory Van Orner really did intend to keep this girl as his mistress under his own roof, her position here would be impossible, even if Van Orner would agree to let his dead wife's secretary remain.

"Tamar is taking me shopping on Monday, after the nurse gets here," Amy said. "Gregory wants me to have some new clothes. He said he's tired of looking at this old rag." She giggled.

"We're going to Macy's Department Store," Miss Yingling said, in case they were imagining she would take a harlot to a dressmaker.

"I'm sure you'll find some very nice things there," Sarah said.

"Just to tide me over," Amy clarified. "I'm sure Gregory wants me to have the very best. That's what he always used to say." She turned to Miss Yingling. "Don't let me forget I'll need a black dress for the funeral, too."

The three other women stared at her for a long moment in mute horror, and then someone tapped on the door.

The maid stuck her head in. "I'm sorry, Miss Yingling, but the baby's crying something awful."

"Why are you telling Miss Yingling?" Amy demanded, jumping to her feet. "He's *my* baby!"

The maid looked stricken. "Yes, miss."

"Thank you, Mary," Miss Yingling said with a long-suffering sigh.

"I'm sorry I must leave my guests, but duty calls," Amy said. "Thank you so much for your visit. Please, come back to see me anytime."

When she was gone, Miss Yingling sighed again. "I'm so sorry."

"There's no need to apologize," Sarah said. "She's young and . . ."

"And silly," Mrs. Spratt-Williams supplied. "No one takes her seriously."

"I can't believe she's behaving like this. I assure you, no

one has given her any reason to think she's the mistress of this house."

"Of course not," Sarah said, but she wondered if that might happen. Was Mr. Van Orner as desperate for a child as his wife had been? Would he accept Amy to claim her boy somehow? And had Amy gotten rid of Mrs. Van Orner to make all of this possible?

"Mrs. Spratt-Williams, I'm so sorry for what Amy said to you about arguing with Mrs. Van Orner. I'm sure she was making it all up, all that about overhearing secrets. She's always looking for ways to make other people feel bad."

"Don't think anything of it. The only secret I have is my age, and I assure you, Amy doesn't know it."

The three women smiled, although Miss Yingling's was strained.

Mrs. Spratt-Williams asked about the funeral arrangements, and Miss Yingling told them the service had been delayed because the coroner still had Mrs. Van Orner's body. They had scheduled it for Tuesday.

After they'd run out of things to talk about, Sarah and Mrs. Spratt-Williams took their leave.

Out on the street, Sarah and her companion strolled back toward Fifth Avenue, where they could find a cab. Sarah would be heading the opposite direction this time, anxious to get home to her family and some normalcy.

"Thank you for coming with me, Mrs. Brandt."

"I'm glad you suggested it. What an unusual situation."

"Exactly what I was thinking."

"What do you suppose Mr. Van Orner is going to do?"

"I have no idea, but he can't imagine he can marry that creature, even if he thinks the child is his. He'd be shunned by everyone he knows."

"I doubt his friends would look too kindly on his keeping a mistress in the home he'd shared with his wife either," Sarah said.

"I'm sure someone will talk sense to him once people begin to realize the situation. He may just be in shock right now, after all that's happened."

Sarah doubted this, but she wasn't going to argue the point. "I hate to ask this, but have you given any more thought to Rahab's Daughters?"

"I have indeed. We can't allow Vivian's work to die with her. She would have hated that. I will be honored to step into her place as leader of the organization. I intend to approach everyone who has been involved with the charity and ask them to continue their support. We'll need funds, first of all. Vivian provided the majority of that, so the need will be much greater than before. I should also go see Miss Biafore and assure her they will not be forgotten."

"I know she would appreciate that. She was very worried when I saw her."

"I'll go right after church tomorrow. Mrs. Brandt, I hope you will continue your association with Rahab's Daughters."

"I have limited resources, I'm afraid, but I'll be glad to contribute my widow's mite."

"And can we count on you to help us with rescues in the future?"

"I'm afraid the nature of my work makes me unreliable, but anytime I'm able to help, I certainly will."

"You're very kind." Mrs. Spratt-Williams looked oddly relieved, as if a burden had been lifted since they'd left her house earlier today. They'd reached Fifth Avenue. She hailed a cab rumbling by and took her leave. Sarah wished her well.

* * *

Sarah lay awake part of Saturday night, going over what she knew about Amy Cunningham. She needed to share this new information with Malloy as soon as possible. She was sure he would chasten her for choosing someone as the killer simply because she didn't like her. In the past, she'd also been guilty of refusing to see the evidence against a killer whom she did like. He would probably tell her that's why they didn't allow women to be detectives. Still, the evidence against Amy was compelling, and Malloy would need to know it.

Sarah, Maeve, and Catherine enjoyed the rare opportunity to attend church together, then came home to the meal Maeve prepared. Sarah was trying to think of something they could do together that afternoon when the front doorbell rang.

Maeve and Catherine moaned, thinking it was a client summoning Sarah to a delivery, but they were all delighted to discover Frank Malloy and his son, Brian, on their doorstep. At four years of age, Brian was a little younger than Catherine, although no one was exactly sure how old Catherine was. Brian was a handsome lad with red hair and bright blue eyes. He had been born deaf, and was attending a special school, where he was learning to speak by making signs with his hands.

At the sight of the girls, Brian's hands started flying.

"What's he saying?" Sarah asked.

Malloy chuckled. "I have no idea."

"Aren't you learning the signs, too?"

"I know a few, but he's going way too fast for me." Malloy tapped Brian on the shoulder to get his attention, then made a few slow, simple signs to him. "I told him to go play," he said to Maeve.

Catherine clapped her hands in delight and started up the stairs at a run. Brian didn't hesitate an instant, following at her heels. Maeve followed more sedately, as befitted her position as an adult.

"I'm so glad you came," Sarah said when they were alone in the entrance hall. She couldn't help smiling. She was simply too happy to see him. "Catherine's been asking me when she'd see Brian again."

"My mother needed a day of rest. She's not getting any younger, and I know it's hard for her taking Brian back and forth from school every day."

"Did she know where you were taking him?"

"No." He returned her smile. Mrs. Malloy didn't approve of his friendship with Mrs. Brandt.

"Come and have some coffee. There's some cake for later, too."

"Mrs. Ellsworth?" Sarah's neighbor often brought them desserts.

"Oh, no, Maeve and Catherine made this one themselves. They're getting very good. I have some news for you, too, about Vivian Van Orner's murder."

"What?"

"It'll keep for a few more minutes," she teased.

Malloy followed her into the kitchen and took a seat at the freshly scrubbed table while Sarah made the coffee and set it on the stove to boil. Then she sat down opposite him at the table. How often had they sat just like this, talking about such important things? It felt entirely too natural.

"I found Amy," she said.

"You did? Where is she?"

"At Van Orner's house."

His surprise was almost funny. "Van Orner? How many women does he have there now?"

"Not counting his maids? Just the two, Tamar Yingling and Amy Cunningham. That's her last name."

"Just *two*? Good God! Not many women would say *just two* when they're talking about whores. Are you saying this Amy packed herself and her baby up and sashayed straight over to Van Orner's house as soon as she heard his wife was dead?"

"Something like that, although I'm not positive she actually sashayed."

Malloy didn't smile. He was still too stunned. "I suppose you discovered this when you and your mother went to visit Van Orner."

"Yes, against your advice, I might add. Look at what we would have missed if we'd listened to you." Malloy just glared. She ignored him. "I don't think Van Orner intended for us to know Amy was there. I asked to see Miss Yingling, and he sent for her. Amy must have thought she and Van Orner were meeting alone or something. She came barging into the front parlor barefooted in her dressing gown."

"Your mother must have loved that," he said with a grin, imagining the scene.

"Oh, she did. I managed to get Amy alone for a few minutes. I asked to see the baby, and she took me upstairs. She told me Van Orner is going to hire a nurse for him and in general gave me the impression she's there to stay."

Malloy gave a low whistle.

"She's not very sorry Vivian Van Orner is dead. And poor Miss Yingling is mortified that we discovered Amy is living there. She also hinted—very strongly—that she thinks Amy is the one who poisoned Mrs. Van Orner."

"I thought her running away made her look guilty, but running to Van Orner might even be worse."

"I thought the same thing. After Mother and I left, I realized I needed to tell Mrs. Spratt-Williams that I'd found Amy. She's been very worried about her."

"She's the only one."

"Yes, she is. Everyone else wishes Amy would disappear. Amy made a friend in Mrs. Spratt-Williams, though. She told the woman her sad tale, how her father killed himself after financial ruin and her mother sold her to a family friend to become his mistress when she was still a young girl."

"That is sad, but lots of girls have it much worse," he reminded her.

"I know, I know. I'm not trying to win your sympathy. I'm just telling you how Amy won Mrs. Spratt-Williams over. I have to say, though, that after Mrs. Spratt-Williams and I talked about it, she also decided Amy was probably the one who killed Mrs. Van Orner."

"Amy is winning the vote," he observed.

Sarah folded her hands on the table. "I keep thinking there must be someone else who had a reason that we don't know about to want Mrs. Van Orner dead."

"That's always possible. But if they killed to keep it secret, we aren't likely to find it out now."

The coffee started to boil, and Sarah got up to take it off the stove and pour them each a cup. When they were settled at the table again, Malloy carefully examined his spoon.

"What are you doing?"

"Making sure I only have one."

Sarah gave a yelp of laughter before she could stop herself.

"What are you going to do now?" she asked when she had composed herself. "About Mrs. Van Orner, I mean."

"I have to go see Mr. Van Orner and tell him what I know. He might want to get rid of Amy by charging her with his wife's murder, but he might not. If he doesn't, there's no point in arresting her because he'll just bail her out and the whole thing will get pigeonholed."

"It will get what?"

"Pigeonholed. Don't you know how the courts work?"

"Apparently not."

"When somebody gets arrested, the judge can set bail. If the arrested person gets bailed out and money is paid to the right people, their case papers get stuck into one of the slots in this big wooden case where they're supposed to be stored—they call them pigeonholes—except nobody ever takes them out again."

"You mean the case is forgotten?"

"Completely forgotten. Lots of murderers are walking around free because their case was pigeonholed."

Sarah hadn't thought she could be shocked any more by the level of corruption in the city. "That's horrible!"

"That's the way it is. So I've got to find out what Mr. Van Orner's pleasure is in this matter, and I have a feeling the pleasure he gets from Miss Amy is going to win out over justice for his wife's murder."

"It does seem likely." Sarah sighed. "But if you're going to see Mr. Van Orner, you should wait until midmorning tomorrow. Miss Yingling is taking Amy out shopping, and I'm sure you don't want her around when you're talking to Van Orner."

"Thanks, I'll do that."

"Well," Sarah said, brightening, "let's try to forget all this ugliness for the rest of the day and enjoy ourselves."

"That's a great idea."

The children had a wonderful time, and everyone decided the cake was delicious. Mrs. Ellsworth stopped by to say hello and bring some cookies she had just baked. No one wanted Malloy and Brian to leave, but when the time came, they all gathered in the front hallway to say good-bye.

They were laughing at something Catherine had said when the front doorbell rang.

"Ah, a baby being born, I'll wager," Mrs. Ellsworth said as Maeve opened the door.

The young woman on the doorstep seemed taken aback to find so many people staring out at her, but she said, "Mrs. Brandt?"

"I'm Mrs. Brandt," Sarah said, stepping forward. She realized the girl looked familiar.

"I have a message for you, from Mrs. Spratt-Williams." Of course, she was Mrs. Spratt-Williams's maid. She handed Sarah an envelope. "I'm to wait for your answer," she added.

Sarah opened the envelope and found a note card inside. Written in an elegant hand was an invitation for Sarah to join Mrs. Spratt-Williams for tea the next afternoon to discuss the future of Rahab's Daughters.

"Tell her I'll be happy to accept her invitation," Sarah said. She wasn't sure how much assistance she could offer, but she was flattered to be asked. If she was summoned to a birth, she'd have to send her regrets, but she'd worry about that if it happened.

TAKING SARAH'S ADVICE, FRANK WAITED UNTIL THE MIDdle of the morning to call on Gregory Van Orner. The man seemed annoyed at being bothered, and Frank thought he might have been drinking already today.

"I thought Tamar was taking care of all of this," he muttered, grudgingly offering Frank a seat.

"I thought you'd want to be kept informed of what I've found out so far."

"I suppose," Mr. Van Orner said, leaning back in his chair as if challenging Frank to make this visit worth his time.

"Your wife died from an overdose of laudanum that someone put into the flask she carried in her purse."

Van Orner shifted uneasily in his chair. "Flask? What are you talking about?"

This was going to be more difficult than Frank had expected. Van Orner was going to pretend he didn't know about his wife's drinking. "According to Miss Yingling and some of your wife's friends, Mrs. Van Orner carried a silver flask in her purse which contained crème de menthe."

"What on earth for?"

"To drink," Malloy said, hoping Van Orner wouldn't decide to throw him out for speaking ill of his poor, dead wife. "According to Miss Yingling, Mrs. Van Orner would use it to . . . to calm herself when she became upset about something."

"Good God, no wonder . . . You know, she always smelled of mint. I thought it was those dammed peppermints she was always popping in her mouth." At least he wasn't going to tell Frank he was a liar.

"A fatal dose of laudanum is only two or three spoonfuls, and the strong taste of the crème de menthe would have covered the bitterness of the laudanum, according to the medical examiner."

"So that's what killed her. I'd been wondering."

"She might have been saved, but because she was alone in the carriage, and nobody knew she'd taken laudanum—she didn't even know herself—she died within an hour."

This still wasn't making sense to Van Orner. "But who could've done it?"

"Someone who had access to her purse and the flask."

"Her maid," Van Orner offered. "She has access to everything Vivian owns."

"Did her maid have any reason to want her dead?"

Van Orner frowned. "Oh, I see. No, probably not. She was devoted to Vivian, too. She's been hysterical ever since she got the news. Had to call in the doctor to give her something. Laudanum, probably," he added with a trace of irony.

"Would anyone else in your house . . . who lived in your house *then*," Frank amended, "have any reason to harm your wife?"

"Not that I can think of. She was never . . . She was always too easy with the servants. I told her a hundred times they took advantage of her."

"So no one here had a grudge against her?"

"No, no one. But who else could it have been?"

"She was at her office that day, but nobody else was there except Miss Yingling. Then they went to the rescue house."

Van Orner curled his lip in distaste. "Are you saying that's where it happened?"

"Anyone at that house could have had access to her purse," Frank said, choosing not to answer the question. "From what I've been told, she always left it on a table in the hallway."

"And did they all know about the flask?"

"I've been told they did."

"Who was there?"

"Miss Yingling, of course. Mrs. Spratt-Williams—"

"You can count her out. They've been lifelong friends."

Frank had already eliminated her. "Miss Biafore."

"Who's that?"

"She manages the rescue house."

"Vivian gave that responsibility to an Italian woman? What was she thinking? Those people will steal you blind!"

Knowing better than to respond to that, Frank said, "And three women whom Mrs. Van Orner and her friends had rescued."

"It had to be one of them, then. Everyone knows a whore would kill her own mother for fifty cents."

"One of the rescued women was Amy Cunningham."

12

Sarah and Maeve got up early on Monday morning to do the wash. The day was raw but fair, and they had everything on the line well before noon. They were sitting in the kitchen, warming themselves with hot tea, when Mrs. Ellsworth came to the back door with an offering of a freshly baked cake.

"Ever since Nelson insisted we start taking our clothes to the Chinese laundry, I never know what to do with myself on Monday mornings," Mrs. Ellsworth said, referring to her son.

"Baking a cake was a good idea," Maeve said, admiring the finished product.

"We still have half of the cake Maeve and Catherine made on Saturday," Sarah reminded them.

Mrs. Ellsworth accepted the cup of tea Sarah had poured for her. "I'm sure you'll find a good use for it, Mrs. Brandt.

It's good luck to give someone a cake. Has Mr. Malloy found the murderer yet?"

"He thinks he knows who it is, but he had to go meet with Mr. Van Orner first."

"You didn't tell me he knows who the killer is," Maeve complained. "Who is it?"

"I said he *thinks* he knows."

"Why does he need to talk to Mr. Van Orner?" Mrs. Ellsworth asked.

"Because Mr. Van Orner might not want the killer arrested."

"Good heavens, why not?"

"It's that girl, isn't it?" Maeve asked eagerly. "The one who had the baby."

"As I said, he's not sure."

Maeve wasn't fooled. "But if it is her, Mr. Van Orner might not want her punished. He might be in love with her, and she's the mother of his baby into the bargain."

"How can he be sure it's his baby?" Mrs. Ellsworth asked.

"I don't know," Sarah said. "Maybe he *can* be sure or maybe he doesn't care. At any rate, Mr. Malloy doesn't want to arrest her unless Mr. Van Orner wants her punished." She explained the practice of pigeonholing cases.

Mrs. Ellsworth was outraged. "You mean they just let murders go free?"

"Murderers and thieves and anybody else who has the money," Maeve said, not at all surprised to hear about the practice. "My grandfather always used to say it was *better* not to get caught, but if you did, it's *best* to have your bail money socked away."

"Do you think this Amy is the killer?" Mrs. Ellsworth asked.

"I'm not sure what I think. She may have thought she had a reason for wanting Mrs. Van Orner dead. She knew Mrs. Van Orner drank and carried a flask with her. She had the opportunity to put the laudanum in her flask."

"Other people knew about the flask and the drinking," Maeve said.

"Yes, but who had a reason for killing her? Not Mrs. Spratt-Williams, who was her oldest friend. Not Miss Yingling, who owed her everything."

"Sometimes gratitude is a good reason to kill someone," Mrs. Ellsworth observed.

Sarah looked at her in surprise. "What do you mean?"

"I've seen it happen where a person starts to resent the one who's helped them the most. Sometimes people don't want to remember how much help they needed or how little they deserved it."

Maeve nodded enthusiastically. "The person who helped is always a reminder of how low you were, too. Nobody likes to remember that."

"Especially if how low you were was working as a prostitute," Mrs. Ellsworth added.

"So you think Miss Yingling might have wanted Mrs. Van Orner dead?" Sarah asked them both.

"I can't judge, not knowing her myself," Mrs. Ellsworth replied. "But I wouldn't rule her out just because Mrs. Van Orner has raised her up."

"I see what you mean. Do you have an argument for why Mrs. Spratt-Williams might have killed her?"

"Old friends know our secrets," Mrs. Ellsworth said.

"And we know theirs," Maeve added.

Sarah considered this. "My mother said she thought she remembered some old scandal involving Mrs. Spratt-

Williams's late husband, but if she knew about it, so would everyone else. No secrets there."

"Maybe she has another secret," Maeve said. "Maybe she was stealing money from the rescue house."

"She was *giving* money to the rescue house. Besides, I don't think she would have had an opportunity. She only helped with the rescues." Sarah suddenly remembered Amy's accusations. "When I was at the Van Orner house on Saturday with Mrs. Spratt-Williams, Amy was hinting that she knew a secret about Mrs. Spratt-Williams, but I don't think the poor woman even knew what she was talking about."

"Maybe Mrs. Spratt-Williams was jealous of Mrs. Van Orner," Maeve offered.

Sarah was happy to consider this possibility. "Why?"

Maeve thought for a moment. "Mrs. Van Orner had a rich husband, and she doesn't."

"Does she have a husband at all?" Mrs. Ellsworth asked.

"She's a widow, and there's my mother's memory of a scandal, but we don't know that for certain. On the other hand, Mrs. Van Orner's rich husband had a mistress half his age who gave birth to a child when Mrs. Van Orner couldn't. Does that make you jealous of her?"

Maeve and Mrs. Ellsworth had to agree that it didn't.

"Mrs. Van Orner must've had lots of enemies," Maeve decided after a few minutes of thought. "What about all the madams she rescued prostitutes from?"

"None of those people were at the rescue house the day she died. They don't even know where it is."

"Could one of them have allowed one of their girls to be rescued so that person would have the opportunity to take revenge on Mrs. Van Orner?" Mrs. Ellsworth asked.

"Oh, Mrs. Ellsworth, that's a wonderful plan!" Maeve exclaimed. "There were other rescued women in the house, weren't there?"

"Yes, but both of them were scared witless. Neither of them would have the courage to poison someone like Mrs. Van Orner. The only rescued woman who would is—"

"Amy," Maeve supplied.

"So we're back to her." Mrs. Ellsworth sighed.

"ARE YOU TRYING TO TELL ME YOU THINK AMY POISONED my wife?" Van Orner asked, none too pleased by the thought.

"The person who poisoned your wife was in the same house with her sometime shortly before she died. You don't think it was any of your servants, and neither do I. We know who was at the rescue house. You've already told me Miss Yingling and Mrs. Spratt-Williams wouldn't have done it. Only one person in that house really had anything to gain from your wife's death."

"Amy had nothing to gain!"

"Mr. Van Orner, I know Amy is living here with you now. I know she was your mistress before she went to Mrs. Walker's brothel. She has said she knew about Mrs. Van Orner's flask because you told her about it, and I know she named her baby boy after you."

Color flooded Van Orner's face. "That doesn't mean she killed Vivian."

"I know it doesn't, but it doesn't look good for her either. What I need to know from you, Mr. Van Orner, is what you want me to do if she did kill Mrs. Van Orner."

Van Orner's breath caught in his throat, and he let it out

in a long sigh. "You have to understand about Amy. She's had a difficult time of it."

Frank made no comment. He just waited.

"Her father was in business, but he'd invested his savings in a project that went bankrupt, and he blew his brains out because he couldn't face the shame of it. Her mother tried renting rooms in their house, but then she got consumption. She was going to die and leave Amy alone and penniless, so when one of her husband's friends offered to take the girl as his mistress, what could she say?"

Frank could think of a number of things, but he just shrugged, not wanting to interrupt the flow of the story.

"He paid Mrs. Cunningham's medical bills and buried her when she died. Then he set Amy up in her own establishment. She was fourteen."

Frank thought of the girls even younger than that whom he'd seen sleeping in alleys and servicing bums for a few pennies to keep themselves alive. He had only limited sympathy for Amy.

"She blossomed into a lovely young woman, and when I saw her one evening at the theater . . . Let's just say her protector was more anxious for my goodwill than he was for Amy's company. He was handsomely compensated, and I got Amy."

"How did she end up at Mrs. Walker's?"

Van Orner didn't even flinch. "Amy was amusing at first. I enjoyed satisfying her whims, but *she* was never satisfied. Her parents had spoiled her, you see, and her first protector had done nothing to remedy that. By the time she came to me, she had learned that whining and pouting would get her what she wanted. After a while, I found it more annoying than otherwise."

"She named her baby after you."

Van Orner shifted uneasily in his chair. "I didn't know about the child. She claims she didn't either. I tend to believe her, because if she'd told me, I would never have taken her to Mrs. Walker."

"You believe it's yours, then?"

"Six months ago, she was still under my protection. I have every reason to believe the child is mine. My wife was barren, Mr. Malloy. Even if I were to remarry, I have no guarantee I'll ever have another child."

"I wonder why Mrs. Walker didn't let you know about the baby."

"I told her I didn't want to hear anything else about Amy. I assume she took me at my word. She may even have thought I'd sent Amy to her because I didn't want the child."

"Could Amy have thought you'd marry her if your wife was gone?"

"I certainly never said anything to make her believe that, but you know how women are, Mr. Malloy. One never knows what goes on in the female mind."

Frank could attest to that, at least. "You still haven't told me what you want me to do if I find out Amy poisoned your wife."

The sounds of raised voices, women's voices, and running feet distracted them both. Van Orner rose, his face twisted with fury at the disturbance and ready to call out a reprimand when the parlor door flew open and Miss Yingling burst in.

"Greg, they've kidnapped Amy!"

Then she saw Frank, but instead of being chagrined, she appealed to him. "Mr. Malloy, you have to do something. Mrs. Walker has kidnapped Amy!"

* * *

AFTER LUNCH, SARAH TOOK A LONG LOOK AT THE CAKE sitting on her kitchen table and made a decision. "I'm going to take this cake to the women at the rescue house."

"That's a wonderful idea," Maeve said. "Can I go with you?"

"I don't think it's a good idea for you to go there, Maeve."

"Are you afraid I'll be corrupted by the prostitutes?"

"Of course not, but I don't want you to be seen there. Someone might get the wrong idea."

"Aren't you afraid they'll get the wrong idea seeing you there?"

"Not at all. I'm much too old to be a rescued prostitute."

"You're not that old! You're not even thirty!"

"But very few prostitutes live to even be as old as I am."

This was the sad truth, and Maeve did not dispute it. Instead she said with a sly grin, "You could be a madam."

"No one rescues madams," Sarah replied tartly.

They packed up the cake in a market basket, and Sarah set out for the rescue house.

Lisa Biafore was delighted to see her and even more so when she saw what was in the basket. She called down the other two girls who were still living at the house, and they all enjoyed some coffee and cake. After the other girls had gone back to their rooms, Sarah helped Lisa clean up.

"I hate to ask you again," Lisa said as she stacked the dirty plates, "but do you have any idea what's going to become of us?"

"Hasn't Mrs. Spratt-Williams been to see you yet?"

"No, we haven't heard a thing. We only have enough food for a couple more days, and just a few dollars of spending money left."

How odd, Mrs. Spratt-Williams had said she would visit here yesterday. "I'm going to see Mrs. Spratt-Williams this afternoon. I spoke with her the other day, and she assured me she would be taking Mrs. Van Orner's place and making sure things continued on just as they have been."

"Oh, dear," Lisa said, then looked away.

"What's wrong?"

"Nothing," Lisa said, hurrying to take the dishes into the kitchen.

Sarah followed. "Lisa, if something is wrong, please tell me. Maybe I can help."

Lisa looked stricken. "You won't tell anyone you heard this from me, will you?"

"Absolutely not."

"I shouldn't say anything, I know, but . . . Poor Mrs. Van Orner, she worked so hard to help the women here, and she got very little reward. She deserves better than this."

Sarah was confused. "Better than being murdered?"

"Oh, yes, surely that, but I didn't mean the way she died. I meant Mrs. Spratt-Williams."

"What about her?"

Lisa set the dishes in the sink, took a deep breath, and turned back to Sarah. "I don't think Mrs. Van Orner would want Mrs. Spratt-Williams taking her place."

"Why not? I thought they were friends."

"Oh, they were. Mrs. Spratt-Williams told me time and time again how they'd known each other as girls, but friends don't always see eye to eye, if you know what I mean."

"What didn't they see eye to eye on?"

"You promise you won't tell anyone I told you?"

"Of course," Sarah promised.

"I've heard them arguing more than once about how Mrs.

Spratt-Williams changes the reports they give to the Charity Organization Society."

"Changes them how?"

"She changes the names of the women we rescue. She'll change a few letters or something, just to make it different."

"Why would she do that?"

"So if the girls ever needed help again, they can go to one of those other charities. They keep a list, you see, and they're very strict. Once you get help from one of them, you can't ever go back to any of them."

Sarah remembered that Miss Yingling had explained this at her very first visit. She'd thought it horribly unfair then and still did. In fact, she found herself in perfect agreement with Mrs. Spratt-Williams. She was suddenly glad the woman had asked for her help.

"I suppose Mrs. Van Orner believed in following the rules," Sarah guessed.

"Oh, yes. She was a great one for rules. That's why she wouldn't like it if Mrs. Spratt-Williams took her place."

"I'll talk to her about it when I meet with her this afternoon."

"Oh, please don't mention my name!"

"Don't worry. I wouldn't dream of it."

"Mrs. Spratt-Williams is very sensitive. She doesn't like it when people question her. I didn't understand that at first," Lisa confided, "but Mrs. Van Orner explained it to me. Seems like she was very rich once, back when her husband was alive, and people always invited them to parties and such, the way rich people do. Then something happened with her husband. He cheated people in business somehow. I don't understand how he did it, but lots of people lost all their money. I never had any money to lose, but I guess

some people do. There was a big scandal about it, because
he cheated them. One man even shot himself over it. Now
people don't invite her to parties anymore, not even after
her husband died. Mrs. Van Orner was the only real friend
she had left. So be very careful what you say to Mrs. Spratt-
Williams. Do you understand?"

Sarah nodded. She thought she understood a lot more,
too. The story about the man shooting himself sounded all
too familiar.

FRANK HELPED MISS YINGLING TO A CHAIR. "CALM DOWN
and tell me everything that happened."

Miss Yingling sat down and took a deep breath. "I took
Amy shopping. She needed some new clothes, so we were
going to Macy's Department Store. Herman took us in the
carriage and let us out on a corner. We were walking down
the sidewalk toward the entrance to the store when this
woman approached us."

"Was it Mrs. Walker?" Van Orner asked.

"Yes. Amy wasn't afraid of her or anything. In fact, she
seemed almost happy to see her. She said something like,
'Look at me now, Mrs. Walker.' That's how I knew who she
was."

Van Orner had gone to the sideboard, and he brought
back a small glass of something and put it in Miss Yingling's
hand. She took a sip before continuing her story.

"As soon as I saw her, I knew something was wrong.
How would a woman like that dare approach us on a public
street? But before I could think what to do, a man came up
behind us and put his hand over Amy's mouth."

"Did you get a good look at him?"

"I don't know. I might recognize him again, but it happened so quickly. I expected Amy to put up a fight, but she almost seemed to go limp."

"Did you smell anything strange?" Frank asked.

She looked at him in surprise. "Yes, I did."

"Chloroform," Frank said to Van Orner. "What happened next?"

"Mrs. Walker shoved me out of the way and took Amy's arm. The man took her other arm and together they walked her across the sidewalk to a waiting carriage. I tried to go after them, but there were so many people on the sidewalk, and they didn't seem to notice what had happened and they got in my way. They were all so interested in where they were going, and when I started calling for help, they just started walking faster."

"What kind of a world do we live in?" Mr. Van Orner muttered.

"So they put Amy in the carriage?" Malloy asked.

"Yes, the man almost had to pick her up to get her inside, and then the woman got in and he jumped up into the driver's seat and drove away. By the time I found a policeman, they were gone, and he said he couldn't do anything, so I ran all the way home to tell you."

She looked like she had, too. She was still breathless, and her face was flushed and her hat crooked.

"That was the best thing you could've done," Frank assured her. He turned to Van Orner. "Do you want me to get her back?"

Van Orner was furious. "Of course I do. The nerve of that woman, kidnapping someone in broad daylight on a public street. Amy is my property, and she knows it."

Frank wanted to be sure. "What if Amy's the one who . . ."

He saw the light of understanding in Van Orner's eyes. "Yes, I see, but I don't want Mrs. Walker to have her. Bring her back here, and we'll sort it out. It's just too bad Mrs. Walker isn't the one who poisoned my wife. I'd help you arrest her myself."

Miss Yingling gave a small cry, and both men turned to reassure her.

"Don't worry," Van Orner said. "No one blames you for this."

"What did you mean?" she asked.

"About what?"

"About Mrs. Walker being the one to poison Mrs. Van Orner?"

Van Orner's voice was gentle when he spoke to her, making Frank wonder exactly what their relationship was. "Mr. Malloy was just explaining to me who had an opportunity to poison Vivian, and while I'd be happy to find out Mrs. Walker was the guilty party, she couldn't have been."

"Yes, she could," Miss Yingling said.

Van Orner shook his head firmly. "No, she couldn't. She would have had to be near enough to Vivian that day to put the poison in her flask, but—"

"She was!"

Both men stared at her in surprise. Frank found his tongue first. "What are you talking about?"

"She was here. Mrs. Walker came here to the house that morning, the day Mrs. Van Orner died."

"The Devil you say!" Van Orner cried. "The nerve of that woman, coming to my home! Surely, no one let her in, though."

"I don't know exactly what she said, but the maid put her in the receiving room and went looking for Mrs. Van Orner.

We were getting ready to leave for the day. Mrs. Van Orner went down. She wouldn't have her brought up to the parlor, so she went down to the receiving room, and they talked there."

"Did Mrs. Van Orner have her purse with her?"

"I don't know. I don't remember, but she must have because we were just getting our things to go out."

"Would Mrs. Walker have had an opportunity to be alone with Mrs. Van Orner's purse?"

Miss Yingling looked up at him in despair. "I don't know. I just don't know!"

"She must have. That's it," Van Orner said. "The Walker woman was angry at Vivian for breaking into her house and kidnapping Amy, so she poisoned Vivian and now she's taken Amy back."

Frank turned to Miss Yingling. "Why didn't you tell me this before?"

Guilt flushed her cheeks, but she said, "I'd forgotten all about it. I was so upset after Mrs. Van Orner died . . ."

Frank knew she was lying, but he didn't have time to figure out why just now. "Do you want to come with me?" he asked Van Orner.

"No, I'll leave this to you."

Of course he would. He didn't want his name mentioned if there was trouble and the press got hold of it. "Which house on Sisters' Row is it?"

Armed with directions, Frank refused the offer of Van Orner's carriage. He would make better time on foot and the elevated train.

THE TENDERLOIN WAS QUIET AT THIS HOUR ON A MON-day morning. The seven houses of Sisters' Row sat as if sleeping, their shaded windows like shuttered eyes. Frank counted carefully to make sure he was at the right door and then hammered with authority.

After a few minutes, a voice called out, "We're closed!"

"Not to me," Frank called back. "I'm the police."

"We paid our protection. Go away!"

"Open up or I'll get a squad to break down the door!"

Frank could almost feel the frustration of the person on the other side of the door as she turned the locks, ready to give Frank an earful. As soon as the latch released, however, Frank threw his weight against the door, sending the other person staggering backward as it lurched open.

"Mrs. Walker'll have your job!" the woman screamed, her dark face fierce with fury.

"Just tell her Detective Sergeant Frank Malloy is here because Gregory Van Orner sent him."

Her eyes widened with either fear or amazement. He hadn't figured out which before she turned and ran up the stairs. Frank decided he wouldn't find out anything standing where he was, so he followed her at a more sedate pace.

By the time he reached the top of the stairs, Mrs. Walker was hurrying down the hallway to meet him. "Where's Amy?" he demanded.

"Hush," she cried in a hoarse whisper. "You'll wake the other girls."

Frank wasn't particularly concerned about that. "Just tell me where Amy is and I'll take her back to Van Orner and we'll pretend this never happened."

"Are you crazy? Van Orner is the one who ordered me to bring her back here."

Frank needed a minute to absorb this ridiculous statement, and before he could formulate a reply, a male voice called from downstairs.

"Mrs. Walker? Are you there?"

Frank had left the front door standing open and someone had wandered in.

Mrs. Walker made an exasperated sound, pushed past him, and hurried down the stairs. Before he could decide whether to follow her or stay where he was, she was coming up again. A small man with white hair carrying a doctor's black bag was right behind her.

"Do you have any idea what she took?" he was asking her.

"She didn't take anything. She was perfectly fine and then she just fainted and we can't wake her up."

Frank stepped out of the way to let them pass. Mrs. Walker gave him a dirty look. "Don't try to scare me, copper."

Frank had thought for sure that mention of Van Orner would scare *her*, and he was confused and a little alarmed. Why had Mrs. Walker summoned a doctor?

He waited until Mrs. Walker and the doctor disappeared into one of the bedrooms, then he followed. He wasn't exactly sneaking, just not making more noise than was absolutely necessary. He stopped outside the door, which they'd left ajar.

"What did you use on her, Rowena?" the doctor asked.

"Nothing, I told you."

"Don't lie to me. I can smell the chloroform."

"Just a little, to keep her calm while we brought her here. She came around after we got her in the house, and then she started screaming bloody murder like they sometimes do."

"So you gave her some more?"

"I know better than that. I talked to her until she calmed down. She was mad as a scalded cat and then she said she didn't feel right and laid down on the bed. That's when I called you."

"You gave her too much."

"No, I didn't. I know my business, Arthur. I've never lost a girl yet."

"You've lost one now."

"What are you talking about?"

"She's dead."

"She can't be dead!"

Frank stepped into the room. A pretty young woman lay on the bed, her face white, her body still. "Is that Amy Cunningham?"

Mrs. Walker looked up. "Are you still here? I thought I told you to get out."

"Is that Amy?" he asked again.

"What if it is?"

"If it is, then Mr. Van Orner is going to be very upset."

"I don't see why. He wanted rid of her and now he's rid of her."

"If he wanted rid of her, why did he send me to get her back?"

The doctor was putting things back into his medical bag. "Next time, be more careful, Rowena."

"I told you, I was careful!"

"What did she die of?" Frank asked the doctor.

"I'd say too much chloroform."

"It wasn't that!" Mrs. Walker cried. "I told you, she came around after we gave it to her. She was talking sense and running around the house and everything."

"She was, really," the maid offered. She'd been standing

off to the side, wringing her hands. "She was perfectly fine, then something took her real sudden."

"What do you say, Doc?" Frank asked.

"I don't hold with autopsies, but that's the only way to tell for sure."

"Your opinion," Frank prodded.

"If it was chloroform, she wouldn't have woken up. If she woke up, and they didn't give her any more—"

"We didn't!" Mrs. Walker insisted.

"Then it could've been something else, although she's young to up and die for no reason."

"She just had a baby," Mrs. Walker said. "A couple weeks ago or maybe three."

The doctor pursed his lips. "Maybe complications from that. I've seen it happen."

"Or maybe you killed her," Frank said, "the way you killed Mrs. Van Orner."

"What?" Mrs. Walker gaped at him.

"I know you went to see her the morning she died. Somebody put laudanum in the flask she carried, enough to kill her. Maybe that's what she did to Amy, too," he added to the doctor. "Is that why you kidnapped her today? Because she knew you'd killed Mrs. Van Orner? Or maybe you killed Mrs. Van Orner for revenge for stealing Amy out from under your nose and now you've punished Amy for wanting to get away."

Mrs. Walker looked stunned. "I didn't even know Mrs. Van Orner was dead. What happened to her?"

"I think you know exactly what happened to her."

"I don't! And I didn't need revenge for anything! Gregory Van Orner told me where Amy would be today and said he was sick and tired of her and wanted me to take her back."

Frank gave her a pitying look. "How do you intend to prove that?"

"I don't have to prove anything," she snapped.

"You will when I arrest you for kidnapping . . . and murder."

"Murder! That's rich. Wasn't nobody murdered."

"Mrs. Van Orner was, and now here's Amy lying dead in your house. Are we going to find she died of an overdose of laudanum, too?"

"She didn't have a dose of anything, I'm telling you! I wouldn't hurt a hair on her head. She's worth a fortune to me alive. What kind of a fool do you take me for, to put myself out of business by killing my own whores?"

"We'll let a jury decide that."

"What do you mean, a jury? I'm not going to trial for anything."

"Oh, I suppose Mr. Van Orner is going to stand up for you."

Mrs. Walker gave him a look that could've drawn blood. "I'll prove it to you."

She stomped out of the room and down the hall. Frank glanced at the doctor, who had picked up his bag, ready to leave.

"What should I do with her?" the maid asked, nodding to the body on the bed.

"Call an undertaker," the doctor said.

"Don't touch her," Frank said. "I'll get the medical examiner here."

Frank followed Mrs. Walker, catching up with her at the bottom of the stairs. She kept going until she'd reached a room that was apparently her office.

She picked up a piece of paper from her cluttered desk and thrust it at him. "See for yourself."

It was a sheet of expensive stationery. The words had been printed carefully in a steady hand. Just as Mrs. Walker had said, it contained the information on where Amy could be found that morning and the request to fetch her back to Mrs. Walker's house so he would never have to see her again. The signature said, "Gregory Van Orner."

"See, just like I told you. Do you think I'd mess with the likes of the Van Orners all on my own?"

Frank studied the note, trying to make sense of this. "Van Orner didn't send you this note."

She looked down her nose at him. "How would you know?"

"Because I was with him when he got the news about Amy being kidnapped, and he was furious. He sent me here to bring her back and have you charged with kidnapping."

"You're lying! And if you think you're getting anything from me for covering this up, I'm not giving you a cent."

Frank sighed in exasperation. "I'm not lying. Van Orner didn't want Amy kidnapped. As soon as Mrs. Van Orner died, she left the house where Mrs. Van Orner took her for safekeeping and went to live with Van Orner. He wanted me to bring her back there."

The color drained from her face. "It wasn't my fault! I was tricked. You can see that for yourself!"

"And now Amy's dead."

"I didn't have nothing to do with that. It was an accident, I tell you."

Frank's mind was spinning, trying to put all the facts he knew into some sort of order that would make sense. Someone killed Mrs. Van Orner. Someone wanted Amy out of the way and sent this note to make that happen, knowing the kidnapping would make Mrs. Walker look suspicious. And someone had just told Frank about Mrs. Walker's visit to Mrs. Van Orner on the day she died, to make her look even more suspicious. Had that really happened or was it an effort to make someone else look guilty of murder?

Tamar Yingling had known exactly where Amy would be this morning, and Frank hadn't forgotten she'd called Van Orner "Greg" in an unguarded moment. The two of them were closer than he should have been with his wife's secretary. She probably even knew how to sign his name.

"Do you have a telephone?"

"Of course I do!"

"I need to call the medical examiner."

"Why would you do that?" she asked in alarm.

"To prove Amy was poisoned . . ."

"I never poisoned her!"

"I know. She was probably poisoned by the same person who killed Mrs. Van Orner."

Frank waited impatiently for the medical examiner. He wanted to get back to the Van Orner house and talk to Miss Yingling again.

13

Sarah gathered up her things, getting ready to leave the rescue house. Lisa thanked her again for the cake as she handed Sarah the now-empty basket.

"I'll be happy to return the plate to you in a day or two."

"Don't worry about it. I'm sure I'll be back to visit in a few days. I'm going to be helping Mrs. Spratt-Williams, remember."

Lisa frowned. "You won't tell her what I said, will you?"

"Oh, no. I appreciate your honesty, and I wouldn't dream of betraying your trust in me."

"Thank you. And I hope you'll remind Mrs. Spratt-Williams that we're running short of supplies. The girls are getting nervous, and I'm afraid they might be tempted to run away."

"Please assure them that they'll be taken care of."

Lisa sighed. "I will. At least I don't have to worry about keeping Amy happy anymore, now that she's gone."

"Oh, I almost forgot to tell you, I know where Amy went after she left here."

Lisa made a face. "To the Devil, I hope."

Sarah managed not to smile. "She went to Mr. Van Orner's house."

Lisa gasped and covered her mouth with both hands. "You aren't teasing me, are you?"

"No, I'm not. Apparently, she really did name her baby after his father."

Lisa crossed herself. "Poor Mrs. Van Orner. She didn't deserve that, not at all! Do you think she knew?"

"I don't know. I'm sure Amy was trying to make her suspect, but we'll never know if Mrs. Van Orner believed it or not."

"Oh, I hope not. I'd hate for her to have that hurt in her heart when she died, poor lady. And what's going to become of Amy now?"

Sarah had a good idea, but she said, "I don't know."

"Oh, dear, is Miss Yingling still living there, too? They must be like two cats in a sack!"

If they weren't yet, it was only a matter of time, Sarah thought. "Yes, she is."

"Does Mrs. Spratt-Williams know she's there? She'll want to know, I'm sure. Amy was her pet," Lisa added with distaste.

Sarah remembered what Lisa had said earlier, about one of the men Mrs. Spratt-Williams's husband had cheated shooting himself . . . just the way Amy's father had. Could that have been just an unfortunate coincidence? "I did notice that she took a special interest in Amy, but I suppose she did that for all the rescued girls."

"Oh, no, she didn't usually pay much attention to any of the women we rescued after we got them here. She was only interested in the rescues themselves. I think . . ."

"What?"

Lisa obviously didn't like expressing an opinion about someone who might have power over her.

"I won't tell anyone," Sarah promised.

"I think she just liked the excitement of it. She didn't seem to care if the women got jobs or if they found a place to live afterward. She didn't even mind when we found out one of them had gone back to walking the streets. Mrs. Van Orner would be sad, but Mrs. Spratt-Williams wasn't even disappointed. The only thing she cared about was when they were going out again to rescue someone."

Which was, Sarah had to admit, the only thing over which Mrs. Van Orner and her friends had much control. Once the women were here and safe, the rescuers could only offer encouragement. Success or failure would depend on the women themselves.

Still, the unusual interest in Amy was interesting. "Do you suppose Mrs. Spratt-Williams singled Amy out because she had the baby?"

Lisa considered this. "I don't think so. The rest of us fussed over him. He's so cute. But Mrs. Spratt-Williams didn't pay him much mind. She just fussed over Amy. You remember how Amy complained about everything?"

"Oh, yes."

"Well, Mrs. Spratt-Williams, she kept trying to make her happy, finding her extra things to eat and apologizing that the place was so shabby. That's what she called it, *shabby*. Mrs. Brandt, all the other women who come here are grateful for every little thing, but not Amy. And Mrs. Spratt-Williams just made it worse."

"I'm very sorry."

"You don't need to be, and besides, Amy's gone and not likely to be back, considering where she is now."

"What do you think killed her, Doc?" Frank asked the medical examiner when he'd had a chance to look at the body. They were standing over where Amy still lay on the bed while Mrs. Walker glared at them, silently daring them to accuse her of murder.

"Not the chloroform," Doc Haynes said, glancing at Mrs. Walker.

She nodded. "I told that quack it wasn't."

"How can you be sure?" Frank asked.

"Chloroform doesn't work that fast, for one thing. She would've lingered for hours, maybe even a couple of days."

"What else could it be, then?"

"Look at her eyes." He raised one of her eyelids. "See the pupil?"

Frank peered at the filmy orb. "It's really small."

"We call it pinpointing. That's what happens when you take an opiate."

"My girls don't take opium," Mrs. Walker snapped. "I won't allow it in my house."

"Nevertheless, she died from an overdose of some compound of opium."

"Like laudanum?" Frank asked, thinking of Mrs. Van Orner.

"Exactly. Women often use laudanum to commit suicide because it's readily to hand. Could she have killed herself?"

Mrs. Walker snorted. "That one never killed herself, I guarantee you. She thought too much of herself to do something like that."

Frank agreed. "I think she might've been poisoned."

"She wasn't poisoned here," Mrs. Walker said, outraged at the thought. "She never had nothing to eat or drink since she walked in the door. She was too busy yelling and screaming and pitching a fit. Then she said she felt light-headed and sort of fainted. I sent for the doctor, but he said she was already dead when he got here."

"Well, I'll leave it up to you to figure out how it happened," Doc Haynes told Frank. "If I find out anything more when I cut her open, I'll let you know."

Mrs. Walker made a strangled sound. "You're not going to cut her up, are you?"

"I'm going to do an autopsy to find out the cause of death," Doc Haynes explained patiently.

"You already told us the cause of death!"

"I told you my theory. Now I have to prove it." He turned to Frank. "I've got an ambulance on the way."

"Do you need me anymore?" Frank asked.

"No, I can handle it from here."

Frank thanked him and hurried out. The arrival of the medical examiner had roused the other occupants of the house, and they hovered in the hallway in their silk kimonos, their hair tied up in rags, eyes bleary and heavy with sleep as they whispered to each other. None of them spoke to Frank as he passed by. Whores had no love for cops, he knew.

Out in the street, he saw the ambulance pulling up. He

pointed to the correct house before setting off for Van Orner's again.

SARAH HAD A LOT TO THINK ABOUT AS SHE MADE HER
way to Mrs. Spratt-Williams's house. If she was going to
be of any help to the women at the rescue house, she'd have
to convince Mrs. Spratt-Williams to take a more personal
interest in all of them, the way she had in Amy.

Sarah kept thinking about the fact that Amy's father had
shot himself after losing all his savings and one of the men
Mrs. Spratt-Williams's husband had cheated had also shot
himself. If Amy's father was the man Mr. Spratt-Williams
had cheated, his wife's guilt over the damage that tragedy
had done to Amy would certainly explain her special interest in the girl.

The maid remembered Sarah and admitted her at once.
She took her straight to the front parlor, where the tea things
had already been laid.

"Mrs. Brandt, how kind of you to come," Mrs. Spratt-
Williams said, rising to greet her. The room was inviting,
furnished in shades of gold and lit by afternoon sunlight. As
Sarah took a seat on the sofa, she noticed some things she'd
missed on her last visit. While the furniture was of excellent
quality and everything was immaculate, the fabric showed
wear in spots. Sarah couldn't help remembering what Lisa
had said about Amy thinking everything at the rescue house
was "shabby." Mrs. Spratt-Williams's home wasn't shabby
but was certainly showing some wear. Maybe she'd been
honest when she claimed her resources were limited.

The two women exchanged pleasantries for a few minutes.
"Have you heard anything from Amy?" Mrs. Spratt-

Williams asked when they had exhausted the topics of each other's health and the weather.

"No, not a thing, although I think the nurse was supposed to arrive today. She'll be a big help, I'm sure."

"Oh, yes, I remember Amy mentioned that when we visited her on Saturday, didn't she?"

The maid tapped on the door and brought in the teapot. Steam coiled gently from the spout and an exotic aroma filled the room before the maid covered the pot with a padded, brocade tea cozy. No American tea service was complete without the use of this recent British import.

"I hope you don't mind," Mrs. Spratt Williams said. "I thought I'd serve you a special blend of tea I've discovered. It has an unusual flavor that I thought you'd find appealing."

"It smells delicious," Sarah said.

"Are you planning to attend Vivian's funeral tomorrow?" Mrs. Spratt-Williams asked while they were waiting for the tea to steep.

"I hope to, unless I'm called to a delivery."

"Oh, yes, I keep forgetting you're a midwife. That's how you met Amy, isn't it?"

"Yes, it is." Sarah silently debated whether to pursue the subject and decided she had nothing to lose. "I appreciate your telling me about Amy's hardships."

Mrs. Spratt-Williams smiled slightly. "I ordinarily wouldn't have violated a confidence, but I thought if you understood, you might feel kinder toward her."

"I'm glad she chose to confide in you. She'd told me a few things about herself, but nothing to hint she'd had such a difficult time of it. For instance, she just told me her father had left them destitute."

"I suppose his death did have that effect. And of course

she'd be ashamed to admit he'd taken his own life. People often hold the family in contempt after an incident like that, instead of giving them the sympathy they truly deserve."

"Did you happen to know Amy's family?"

As she'd expected, her question startled Mrs. Spratt-Williams. "Whatever do you mean?"

"From what you said just now, I thought perhaps you'd known them. I understand she comes from a respectable family, and I thought your paths might have crossed back before . . . before she fell on hard times."

Red blotches of color had bloomed on Mrs. Spratt-Williams's face. "I'm sure I never knew her family. Respectable or not, they were hardly the type of people I would know."

"And yet, you were so kind to Amy," Sarah continued relentlessly.

"I'm kind to all the women we rescue."

That was, of course, a lie. "I'm sure you are, but with Amy . . . Well, I couldn't help noticing that no one else found it easy to be kind to her."

"She was . . . Oh, perhaps you're right, Mrs. Brandt. Amy was difficult, to be sure, but she isn't like the other women we rescue. She was well bred and used to finer things, and she found life at the rescue house very confining. I suppose I couldn't help thinking that there but for the grace of God go I."

"I know what you mean. We aren't shocked when a woman from a poor family is forced to sell herself to survive, but we never expect a girl from a good family to be reduced to such circumstances."

"Yes, it was . . . tragic." She reached over and lifted the

tea cozy and peeked under the lid of the teapot to check on its strength. Apparently not satisfied yet, she replaced the cozy. "What else did Amy tell you about herself?" she asked, elaborately casual.

"Several things, but I'm not sure how much of it was true."

"Such as?"

Sarah got the feeling Mrs. Spratt-Williams was testing her in some way. If Sarah's suspicions about her husband having been the one who cheated Amy's father were true, perhaps she wondered if Sarah knew the whole story. Mrs. Spratt-Williams had denied a connection, but she must be wondering why Sarah had asked in the first place. "Oh, she told me her baby's father was named Gregory, but you knew that already."

Mrs. Spratt-Williams squeezed her lips together in distaste. "I was hoping Miss Yingling was right, that the baby had been fathered by another man named Gregory."

"I think we all were."

"Yes, well, I suppose we must face the truth now, in light of Amy moving in with Mr. Van Orner."

"Yes, we must."

"What else did Amy tell you about herself?"

Sarah hesitated, carefully sorting out what Amy had actually told her and what she'd learned since. "She told me her lover had taken her to Mrs. Walker for safekeeping until her baby was born," she recalled.

"Did she? How extraordinary."

"I thought so, too. Mrs. Walker doesn't run a refuge, after all."

"Certainly not!"

"She also claimed that she wasn't a prostitute—"

"Oh, yes, I remember that. She said it the first day she was at the rescue house."

"Yet she'd told me before how much she hated what she had to do with the customers at the brothel."

Mrs. Spratt-Williams nodded. "I suppose it would be difficult for a young woman to admit to having been a prostitute. As soon as she got away, she'd want to pretend it had never happened."

"I imagine you're right."

"Did she say anything . . . ?" Her voice trailed off as if she realized she'd already questioned Sarah far more than good manners allowed.

"I visited the rescue house today," Sarah said, hoping a change of topic now might allow her to return to the subject of Mrs. Spratt-Williams's connection with Amy later.

She didn't seem pleased. "Did you?"

"Yes, my neighbor had brought over a cake, and I thought the women there might enjoy it, so I stopped on my way over here today."

Mrs. Spratt-Williams didn't say a word, leaving Sarah to continue on her own.

"Miss Biafore told me she hasn't seen you since Mrs. Van Orner passed away. I thought you said you were going to visit there yesterday."

Plainly, Mrs. Spratt-Williams thought Sarah had overstepped. "I had other obligations yesterday," she informed her coldly.

"Miss Biafore is getting quite worried about what will become of them. She's running out of supplies and—"

"She needn't worry. I'll see they're taken care of."

"I know she would appreciate hearing that from you."

"She will, in due time."

Sarah didn't like her attitude. "I'm sorry if I've offended you, but I thought you'd invited me here today to talk about the rescue house."

"Yes, I did, and I'm glad you mentioned the needs there. I'd hoped you would approach your mother about supporting it," she said. "I didn't expect to be interrogated about my oversight of the house, though."

"I certainly didn't intend to interrogate you. I was just trying to remind you of their needs."

"We all have needs, Mrs. Brandt. Charity can extend only so far."

This was just the opening Sarah had been looking for. "This is true, and I know you've always resisted the restrictions of the Charity Organization Society."

"What?" she asked, the color draining from her face.

Sarah wasn't sure what she'd said to cause her such a shock. "I know you don't agree with their rules about not allowing people to obtain charity from more than one group, and I think you're absolutely right."

"Did Amy tell you that?"

"Tell me what?" Sarah asked, confused.

"What else did she tell you about me?"

Amy hadn't told her any of this, but Sarah wasn't going to betray Lisa Biafore. "I know you changed the names of the women you had helped when you wrote up the reports, so they wouldn't be forbidden from getting help if they needed it again. I think that's . . . commendable." She really did, but Mrs. Spratt-Williams didn't respond. Instead she checked the teapot again.

"Well, it looks as if the tea is finally ready."

* * *

THE MAID AT VAN ORNER'S HOUSE ADMITTED FRANK without a word and took him straight upstairs to where Van Orner and Miss Yingling still waited in the parlor. Miss Yingling was drinking a cup of tea while Van Orner paced. They both froze when he stepped into the room.

Van Orner waited a moment then stepped forward and craned his neck to look past Frank into the hallway. "Where is she?"

"Mr. Van Orner, I'm very sorry to tell you this, but Amy is dead."

Miss Yingling gasped and nearly dropped her teacup, but Van Orner just stared at him stupidly. "What?"

"She's dead, Mr. Van Orner. She was poisoned."

"That . . . that's impossible," he said, his face crinkling in confusion. "She was just here."

"Maybe you should sit down," Frank suggested. "Miss Yingling, can you get him some brandy?"

Miss Yingling set down her cup very carefully and went to the sideboard, where Van Orner had gone earlier to get her a stimulant. She poured a generous amount of whiskey into a lead crystal glass and brought it to where Frank had helped Van Orner sit in one of the wing chairs beside the fireplace. Whiskey wasn't as calming as brandy, but he had to assume Miss Yingling knew Van Orner's tastes.

Van Orner took the glass and drank deeply. When he looked up, he was still confused. "What happened to her?"

Frank glanced at Miss Yingling, but she didn't seem the least bit apprehensive. All her attention was on Van Orner as she stood at his elbow, ready should he need anything. "Like Miss Yingling said, Mrs. Walker was the one who took Amy this morning. The man with her probably put a rag soaked with chloroform over her face. That's why she went limp and didn't resist. She was unconscious until she got to Mrs. Walker's house. When she came to, she was furious."

"Of course she was!" Van Orner said. "Who wouldn't be? Imagine being snatched off the street like a . . . like a bag of laundry." He looked to Miss Yingling for confirmation, and she nodded dutifully.

"Mrs. Walker said she started screaming and carrying on when she saw where she was, just like you'd expect. But then she started feeling faint, and she collapsed."

Frank watched Miss Yingling, but she seemed as mystified by all this as Van Orner.

"She's probably just sleeping, from the chloroform," Van Orner said.

"Mrs. Walker called a doctor, but by the time he got there, Amy was dead."

Van Orner's eyes showed no sign of comprehension. "You say she was poisoned?"

"Yes."

Van Orner glanced at Miss Yingling, who still looked as bewildered as he was, then back at Frank. "It's the Walker woman, then. She did it. She poisoned Amy."

"I don't think she did."

"Are you crazy?" Van Orner snapped. The color rose in his face as fury replace the confusion. "Who else would have killed her? Rowena Walker did it out of revenge because Amy left her, but if she thinks she'll get away with it, she's a bigger fool than I thought!"

· "Mrs. Walker didn't kill her."

"Why did she kidnap her, then?" Van Orner demanded. "She wanted revenge, I tell you. She'd know I'd never stand for her taking Amy. I would've torn her house down brick by brick if I had to! She couldn't hope to keep her, so she must've intended to kill her all along. It's the only explanation."

Frank glanced at Miss Yingling. She still don't look worried. "Mrs. Walker kidnapped Amy because she thought you wanted her to," he said.

Now Van Orner was confused again. "How could she think that?"

Frank reached into his coat pocket, pulled out the note Mrs. Walker had received, and handed it to Van Orner.

"What the hell is this?" he demanded when he'd read it. He seemed completely baffled.

"She thought it was from you, telling her you were tired of Amy and wanted her to take the girl back."

"I can see that! But I didn't write it!"

"I know you didn't. You wouldn't have sent me to get Amy away from her if you did."

Van Orner looked at the note again. "She probably wrote it up herself, to throw you off the scent."

"I thought of that, too, but she wouldn't have known I'd be coming after Amy. And besides, how would she have known exactly where Amy was going to be this morning?" Frank looked at Miss Yingling, and this time she took offense.

"Why do you keep looking at me? I didn't tell her where Amy was going to be!"

"Someone did. Someone who knew. Someone who wanted to get rid of Amy because she was causing too many problems."

"Amy always caused problems," Van Orner said wearily.

"But she'd never caused problems for anyone close to you because she'd always been someplace else. First she was in the house you'd provided for her," he reminded Van Orner.

"Then she was at Mrs. Walker's house. Then she was at the rescue house. But when she showed up on your doorstep with her baby in her arms, suddenly she was causing problems for someone new."

"Who?" Van Orner demanded.

Once again Frank looked at Miss Yingling, and this time she took a step back. "Stop looking at me! I didn't have anything to do with this!"

"Didn't you?" Frank asked gently, the way he did when he wanted to disarm a suspect. "You've been waiting a long time to get Mr. Van Orner all to yourself, haven't you?"

Van Orner had been staring at her, too, and now he jumped to his feet. "Tamar? What's he talking about?"

"I have no idea!" she claimed.

"Mr. Van Orner, did you know that Tamar Yingling was the first prostitute your wife ever rescued?"

Miss Yingling winced, but Van Orner wasn't shocked. "Of course I knew. Vivian brought her here so she could keep her under my nose, a constant reminder."

"A reminder of what?"

"Of my weakness, or what she considered my weakness. She thought it abominable that I enjoy the pleasures of the flesh, Mr. Malloy. She thought having a reformed harlot in our house would torment and shame me."

"And did it?" Frank asked, beginning to feel disgust.

"What do you think, Tamar?" he asked her with a sly grin.

She grinned a little herself. "You didn't seem ashamed, although I think I managed to torment you."

Now Frank really was disgusted. "You betrayed your wife under your own roof with a woman she was trying to save?"

"Yes, and it was quite enjoyable for a while, wasn't it, Tamar?"

Tamar Yingling smiled. "Yes, it was, especially when Vivian would lecture me on how I had to conduct myself properly to avoid any suspicion of immorality. She never suspected a thing."

Frank's mind was racing. "You said it was enjoyable *for a time* . . ."

"Yes, but like everything else in life, it ceased to be a novelty. That's when I met Amy, and I turned my attentions to her, leaving Tamar to become the respectable young woman Vivian believed her to be."

Miss Yingling stared back at Frank serenely, as if she'd felt no pain at being rejected for a younger woman. But if she'd thought to convince him of her innocence, she was wrong.

"You must've despised Mrs. Van Orner," he said to her.

He saw the emotions flicker across her face. "She was always very good to me," she said, belying what Frank saw in her eyes.

"I'm sure she was, but that kind of goodness has a price, doesn't it? You always have to earn it, and you never can be quite worthy enough, can you, no matter how hard you try?"

"What does any of this have to do with Amy's death?" she asked, angry now.

"I'm coming to that, but first we have to think about Mrs. Van Orner's death. She was poisoned, too, remember?"

"What does that have to do with this?" Van Orner asked.

"I don't believe in coincidences, Mr. Van Orner, especially when two women living in the same house turn up dead from drinking the same poison."

"You think Amy's death has something to do with Vivian?"

Frank was starting to wonder how a man so stupid had managed to be successful enough to become rich. But maybe he'd just inherited his money. "I think somebody who wanted you all to herself decided to do away with your wife. That somebody slipped laudanum into your wife's flask at the rescue house."

"Amy!" Van Orner guessed.

"That's what I thought at first. She had the opportunity to poison her and she wanted her dead. And the next day she packs up her baby and marches over here and presents herself to you, and you take her in. That made me think she'd planned it."

"Of course she did!" Miss Yingling cried. "She planned the whole thing. Gregory had told her all about Vivian's work, so she told the midwife her sad story and begged her to contact Vivian to rescue her. She was going to kill Vivian all along!"

"I don't know what she planned to do, but even if she did plan it, somebody else beat her to it."

"How can you know that?" Van Orner asked.

"Because the killer didn't plan on Amy showing up on your doorstep or you taking her in. She intended for Amy to get blamed for the murder, because Amy had the perfect reason for wanting Mrs. Van Orner dead. But when you let Amy move in here, the killer couldn't take the chance that you'd protect her. So Amy had to die, too."

Now Van Orner was looking at Miss Yingling, his eyes filled with horror at what she'd done.

Her eyes widened with terror. "It's not true! I didn't do any of that!"

"Who else had something to gain by killing these two women?" Frank asked.

Miss Yingling looked around wildly, as if hoping to find someone to blame lurking nearby. "Mrs. Walker! She's surely the one who killed Amy. She died in her very house."

"That's what you wanted us to think. That's why you sent Mrs. Walker that note and signed Mr. Van Orner's name. You knew you were taking Amy shopping this morning. You also knew Mrs. Walker would do what Van Orner wanted, because she's afraid of him. In fact, she was too afraid of him to kidnap Amy unless she thought that's just what he wanted."

"She's not afraid of him!" she tried, but they all knew it wasn't true.

"And don't forget, the person who killed Amy also killed Mrs. Van Orner," Frank said.

"Mrs. Walker could've done that!" Miss Yingling cried. "She was here the morning Vivian died, remember."

"But why would she want to kill Mrs. Van Orner?"

"I . . . Because she hated her. Because she'd stolen Amy right out of her house."

"And isn't it funny that you didn't remember Mrs. Walker had visited Mrs. Van Orner until this morning."

"That's not true! I remembered all along."

"Then why didn't you tell me before?" Frank asked.

"Because I wanted you to think Amy killed Vivian!" she cried, then clamped her hand over her mouth in horror over what she'd just admitted. She looked to Van Orner for help, but he was staring at her as if he'd never seen her before.

"What have you done?" he roared.

"Nothing! I didn't do anything, I swear!" She was trembling now, her face white and her lips bloodless. She stared up at Van Orner, her breath coming in shallow gasps. "You've got to believe me!"

Van Orner started toward her. "You lying bitch! After all I've done for you!"

She gave a cry and her knees gave way. Frank caught her before she fell. He lifted her into his arms and carried her to the sofa, where he laid her down.

"I didn't do it, Gregory," she murmured. "You've got to believe me!"

"Get her something to drink," Frank told Van Orner.

Reluctantly, Van Orner went to the sideboard and poured something into a glass and handed it to Frank. Frank pressed it to her lips, and she took a sip or two, then turned her head away. "You might as well give me some laudanum, too," she said bitterly.

"You won't get off so easy," Van Orner said. "I'm going to see you hang!"

She gasped, her eyes wide with horror. Frank decided not to mention that in New York State, murderers died in the electric chair, figuring that wouldn't ease her concerns at all.

She turned to Frank, tears flooding her eyes. "You've got to believe me! Why would I kill anyone?"

"Because you wanted me all to yourself," Van Orner snapped.

"But I didn't! I didn't want him at all!" she told Frank. "I was so glad when he got tired of me, and Vivian was giving me a chance to have a real life! I never would've harmed her."

"Then who did?" Frank asked reasonably, ignoring Van Orner's disgruntled frown.

"I thought it was Amy! Truly, I did. That's why I convinced Gregory to let you investigate. I was sure you'd find out she killed Vivian. If I'd killed her, why would I want you to investigate?"

Frank had to admit that did seem to support her innocence, but he still wasn't convinced. "Maybe you thought you'd set it up well enough that I'd think Amy was the killer, but when she showed up here, you decided not to take a chance and got rid of her yourself."

"That would be stupid! Why would I take a chance like that?"

"Who else would have wanted them both dead then?"

"I don't know!"

"Of course you don't. The person who did this had to hate both Mrs. Van Orner and Amy. She had to be in a place where she could sneak the laudanum to them. She had to know about Mrs. Walker and that she would do what Mr. Van Orner wanted. And she had to know where Amy was going to be this morning so she could set it all up. Who could that be but you?"

Miss Yingling was frantic now. Her eyes darted around as her mind raced in search of some way out.

"It's no use, Tamar," Van Orner said. "You're the only person who—"

"No, wait, someone else knew!"

"Knew what?" Frank asked skeptically.

"About Amy, that I was taking her shopping today. Mrs. Brandt knew!"

"Mrs. Brandt?" Van Orner asked. "You mean Elizabeth Decker's daughter?"

"Yes, the midwife! She was here on . . . on Saturday. Yes, I remember. We were talking about it then. Amy was bragging that she was going to get a nurse for the baby, and she asked Mrs. Brandt about . . . about feeding him, and then she told her that we were going shopping first thing on Monday, as soon as the nurse got here. She knew!"

Frank sighed. "You have to do better than that if you want to convince me you're innocent. I know Mrs. Brandt very well. She's been helping me with this investigation. She wouldn't have killed either woman. She didn't have any reason to."

"It's over, Tamar," Van Orner said. "Mr. Malloy, you can take her now."

"No!" she wailed. "No, there's someone else! I almost forgot—Mrs. Spratt-Williams was there, too, that day. She came with Mrs. Brandt. She was worried about Amy, she said, and she came to make sure she's all right."

"Why would Mrs. Spratt-Williams want to kill Amy?" Van Orner scoffed. "Or Vivian either, for that matter. Vivian was her oldest friend."

But Miss Yingling wasn't listening. Frank knew that expression on her face and what it meant. He'd seen it many times before on many other faces. She was remembering something, something important, and putting it together with everything else and figuring it all out.

She sat up on the sofa, and when she looked at Frank, her eyes were clear. The terror had drained out of her, and she almost smiled when she said, "I know who killed them."

14

Mrs. Spratt-Williams turned in her chair so she could reach the tea tray that had been set out on a table beside her. Three cups were stacked on the tray, along with three saucers, three spoons, and three small plates to hold the little sandwiches and cakes her staff had prepared for them.

She picked up the top cup and set it on a saucer, then took the cup from the bottom of the stack and put it on another saucer.

"I'm not sure you realize the implications of your pledge to support my beliefs that charity to the poor should not be limited, Mrs. Brandt."

"Perhaps not, but I do know how shocked I was to learn the philosophy of the Charity Organization Society."

"Their philosophy, as you put it, is based on Mrs. Lowell's belief that 'Gratuitous charity works evil rather than good.'"

Sarah had heard those words before, the first time she'd visited Mrs. Van Orner's office. "Mrs. Lowell?"

"Mrs. Josephine Shaw Lowell. She founded the COS. She believed that if a widow receives too much assistance to support her children, for example, she might lose her love for them because she was relieved of the anxiety of providing for them."

Sarah blinked in amazement at such reasoning, but Mrs. Spratt-Williams wasn't finished.

"She also believed that while giving a handout to an unemployed man would help him for the moment, it would also teach him the dreadful lesson that it's easy to get a day's living without working for it."

As Sarah absorbed this astonishing bit of news, Mrs. Spratt-Williams carefully lifted the tea cozy off the pot.

"The COS has records on over one-hundred-seventy-thousand individuals and families, and they are quite selective and stringent in qualifying people to receive aid. The records of each applicant are carefully examined to determine if their poverty is the result of their own character flaws. Such people are denied assistance, and consequently, they refuse the majority of requests."

Sarah couldn't even imagine the tragedy this policy would have caused to the thousands in the city who were destitute and had no other hope of assistance.

Mrs. Spratt-Williams poured the tea. "How many lumps do you take, Mrs. Brandt?"

"Two, please."

"I think you'll find that with this particular type of tea, more sugar enhances the flavor. If you'll allow me to judge . . ." She dropped four lumps into each cup.

Sarah accepted the cup her hostess offered. "I can certainly see why you took it upon yourself to circumvent the system by reporting false names for the women that you helped."

"What do you think of the tea?" she asked.

Sarah took a sip. She found it unpleasantly bitter and could understand why extra sugar would be necessary. "It's very unusual," she said tactfully.

"It comes from Madagascar, I believe. It's very rare in this country."

Sarah thought it probably wasn't likely to become popular either.

Her hostess tasted hers. "You'll find the flavor improves as you drink it."

Sarah obediently lifted the cup to her lips again, wishing propriety didn't demand that she politely drink something that tasted so awful.

"I had no other choice but to report false names for the women we rescued. As I'm sure you can imagine, Mrs. Brandt, a woman who has worked as a prostitute would never qualify for charity under the requirements of the COS. They would consider her immorality a character flaw and determine that her own weakness had caused her distress."

Sarah nodded. She could see that clearly.

"Do you need more sugar?" Mrs. Spratt-Williams asked.

"Oh, no, this is fine," Sarah lied and lifted the cup again. "I understand that Mrs. Van Orner didn't approve of you falsifying the names."

Distaste flickered over her face, but she managed a small smile. "Yes, Vivian and I did disagree on this matter."

"That's unfortunate, since you were such good friends."

"We were *old* friends, that's true," she said, making a distinction Sarah didn't quite understand. "I may honestly say that Vivian was my last remaining friend in the world."

"I'm sure that isn't true," Sarah said as common courtesy demanded, although she knew from what she had heard that this was probably true.

"Oh, yes, it is. You see, I experienced a tragedy of my own almost a decade ago that cost me practically everything I held dear."

"I'm sorry to hear it." Sarah put the cup to her lips again.

"The worst part is that I had no hand at all in the evil that happened, yet I alone suffered for it."

Sarah nodded her understanding. "That's often the case, unfortunately. But you seem to have risen above it."

"You're kind to say so, but you know nothing of my life before the tragedy. My husband was a wealthy man as a result of his family's business interests. He lacked his father's talents at making money, however, and after his father's death, his businesses ceased to prosper."

"A very common story."

"I suppose so, but that doesn't make it any easier to bear. My husband longed to improve his fortunes, and he learned of a new business venture out West somewhere. I'm not sure exactly what it was. He never confided the details to me, but he invested in it and persuaded many of our friends to do the same. He wanted them to benefit, too, you see."

Sarah thought perhaps the friends might have seen things differently, but she nodded encouragingly. "Of course he did."

"As I'm sure you've guessed by now, this venture was not successful, and all the money was lost. My husband suffered along with everyone else, but our friends had no sympathy for that. Some had lost far more than they ever should have risked, and they were completely ruined, but that wasn't Harold's fault, was it? They should have known better."

They should have, but no one ever blamed their own poor judgment in a situation like this. "It must have been very difficult for you."

"Oh, it was. Not only did we lose our own money, but our friends deserted us. Our lives became very different, as you can imagine."

Sarah could easily imagine. "Was Amy's father one of the people who lost money in the scheme?" Sarah asked.

Mrs. Spratt-Williams smiled slightly. "You're very perceptive, Mrs. Brandt. I knew you were. That is why I invited you here today. I knew you would discern the connection once you had all the facts."

"I can certainly understand why you took such an interest in helping her."

"I didn't do it out of guilt, you understand. I was in no way responsible for what happened to her, but if I could ease her path in any way, I felt an obligation to try. Your tea will be getting cold."

Sarah raised the cup again. "I'm guessing Mrs. Van Orner felt just the opposite about helping Amy."

"Oh, yes, and Amy had no one to blame for that but herself. If she hadn't made such a point of letting Vivian know she had been Gregory's mistress, she would have fared very well."

"She's faring well now," Sarah reminded her.

"Is she?" Mrs. Spratt-Williams said with an odd smile. "Time will tell."

Sarah supposed she was right. Gregory Van Orner had tired of her once, and he might again.

"I'm glad to find you so perceptive, Mrs. Brandt. I do want you to understand, but perhaps I won't need to explain everything to you. When our friends deserted us and our circumstances were so greatly reduced, I was no longer welcome in homes where I had been received for years. I had little opportunity for society or the company of my social equals. All I had left was the service Vivian offered me as a member of her group at Rahab's Daughters."

"She proved to be a good friend to you."

"In her own way, but she never showed me the same compassion she had for the women we rescued."

Sarah couldn't imagine why Mrs. Spratt-Williams would need compassion. "In what way?"

"As I said, we disagreed about reporting the names of the women we helped to the COS. They would never permit one of their members to violate the rules, and when I begged her to allow Amy to stay at the rescue house, she told me she was going to report me for falsifying records. I would never be able to work with any of the charity organizations again."

Miss Yingling swung her feet down to the floor and gazed up at Frank and Van Orner with the self-confidence Frank had come to expect from her. "I know who killed both of them."

Van Orner glared down at her. "Tamar, you can't expect us to—"

"Wait," Frank said. "I'd like to hear what she has to say."

"I just remembered, Mrs. Brandt wasn't the only one here on Saturday. She'd been here earlier, with her mother, and she came back later with Mrs. Spratt-Williams. Mrs. Spratt-Williams had been worried about Amy and wanted to make sure she was all right."

"That's what I would expect from her," Van Orner said.

"Don't you see? She was there, too, so she also knew I was taking Amy shopping this morning."

"You can't think that Mrs. Spratt-Williams would kill anyone," Van Orner said, angry at her for even thinking such a thing. "And why would she want to kill Vivian, who was her closest friend?"

"Because Vivian was going to destroy her life!"

The two men gaped at her. Frank found his tongue first. "How could she do that?"

"By telling the Charity Organization Society that she'd been sending them fake names."

"Fake names?"

"Yes, we had to report the names of everyone we helped through Rahab's Daughters. They keep very careful records, and none of the other organizations ever give charity to anyone without checking the records first. If they feel someone isn't worthy, then that person gets nothing."

Frank frowned. "Would they think women who'd been prostitutes weren't worthy?"

"Of course! They'd think it showed moral weakness. So when she reported the names, Mrs. Spratt-Williams would change them, so if one of the women asked for help later, using her real name, there wouldn't be a record of her."

Frank considered that a very clever way of bypassing an unfair rule, but Van Orner obviously disagreed. "You mean Tonya lied? I can hardly credit it. But then there was that business with her husband."

"What business?"

"He had some company that was digging for gold . . . or maybe it was silver. I can't remember. He told everyone he was going to make a fortune, and a lot of his friends invested. They lost every penny."

"Even him?" Frank asked.

"I suppose so. I didn't see much of him after that. He wasn't welcome in the clubs anymore. He died shortly afterwards, I think. Bad heart, they said, although most people thought it was the shame. One poor devil he'd cheated had shot himself."

"Mrs. Spratt-Williams wasn't welcome anywhere either," Miss Yingling continued. "Vivian was her only friend, and her charity work was her only activity. Vivian was going to take that away from her and make sure she was never allowed back into the fold."

Plainly, Van Orner wasn't impressed. "Are you trying to tell me she'd kill someone over something so silly?"

"It wasn't silly to Mrs. Spratt-Williams!" she cried, jumping to her feet. "I saw her before she left the rescue house the day Vivian died. She and Vivian had quarreled, and she was devastated. I've never seen her so upset. I went to Vivian, to make sure she was all right, and she was so angry, she was trembling. She said she was going to ruin Mrs. Spratt-Williams's reputation."

Van Orner snorted. "This is ridiculous, Malloy. She's just trying to save herself. Take her away."

Frank didn't think it was all that ridiculous. "Would Mrs. Van Orner really have ruined her friend over changing the names?"

"She didn't approve, but I think she was using that as an excuse. She was really mad because Mrs. Spratt-Williams was defending Amy. She was begging Vivian to let her stay at the rescue house, and that made Vivian furious." She looked at Van Orner. "Because Amy made sure Vivian knew you were the father of her baby."

Van Orner just shook his head. "Even if we could believe that a respectable woman like Tonya would murder her friend over some silly argument, why on earth would she kill Amy?"

"Because Amy knew all about it! She'd eavesdropped on their argument that day at the rescue house, and she let Mrs. Spratt-Williams know she knew all about it when she was visiting here on Saturday."

"Are you saying she killed *two* people to keep this stupid secret?" Van Orner scoffed.

Frank's mind was spinning. "So Amy told Mrs. Spratt-Williams she knew her secret. That might give her a reason to kill Amy, too, but how did she do it? Amy didn't die until two days later."

"I don't know, but she was here again yesterday," Miss Yingling said uncertainly.

"Who?"

"Mrs. Spratt-Williams. She visited Amy."

"What did they talk about?"

"I wasn't with them. Amy saw her alone, but . . . Oh, wait, I know something that . . . Oh, my, I know how she killed her!"

"How?" Frank demanded.

"Gregory had hired a nurse to take care of the baby, and Amy wouldn't have to feed him herself anymore. She'd even asked Mrs. Brandt on Saturday about how to stop her . . . her milk," she said, flushing slightly at the delicate nature of the conversation.

"For God's sake, do we have to hear this?" Van Orner asked.

"Go on," Frank said.

"Mrs. Brandt told her what to do and warned her she'd be very uncomfortable for a few days. Amy never liked to be uncomfortable. This morning, Amy told me that Mrs. Spratt-Williams had brought her a potion to take that would dry up her milk instantly, and she wouldn't have a moment of discomfort."

"What kind of potion?"

"I have no idea, but she was bragging about it to me in the carriage this morning. She said Mrs. Spratt-Williams told her not to take it until the nurse arrived, in case she was delayed or something and Amy had to keep feeding the baby for another day or two. She said it worked very quickly, so Amy had waited until the nurse came this morning." She looked up at Frank, her eyes wide. "She must have taken it just before we left the house."

Frank felt the hair on the back of his neck rising. "Where would she have put the empty bottle?"

"Probably in her room."

"Show me," Frank said.

"This is outrageous," Van Orner protested, but Miss Yingling was already across the room with Frank at her heels.

She led him upstairs and down a hallway to one of the closed doors. She threw it open and stopped, taking stock. The bed was unmade, and Amy's few belongings were strewn around. Some toiletries sat on the dressing table. Miss Yingling went straight to it, looking over the bottles. Frank was right behind her. He saw it first.

"This is it." He picked up the small brown bottle. The cork that had stoppered it lay nearby. It was empty except for a drop or two in the bottom. He sniffed. "Laudanum."

"Dear God. But why kill Amy? She actually seemed partial to her. She'd even tried to convince Vivian not to turn her out of the rescue house."

"She must have been worried that Amy would tell what

she knew about her argument with Mrs. Van Orner. Did Mrs. Spratt-Williams know Mrs. Walker?"

"She'd never met her, but she knew all about her from helping to plan Amy's rescue. I know this sounds like I'm just trying to throw suspicion from myself onto Mrs. Spratt-Williams, and you don't have any reason to believe *me*, but Mrs. Brandt can tell you all this is true. You said she's helping you, so I know you'll believe what she says. She was there when they planned the rescue, and she was here when Amy told Mrs. Spratt-Williams that she knew all about her argument with Vivian. Mrs. Brandt knows everything I just told you except about the potion."

Frank felt the truth like a blow to the stomach. Mrs. Spratt-Williams was the killer, Sarah knew all the damming evidence, and she was having tea with her this afternoon!

Sarah stared at Mrs. Spratt-Williams, who was looking back at her with the oddest expression on her face, almost as if she were expecting something from her. Sarah thought she knew what it was. She'd said she was impressed by Sarah's perception, and now she expected Sarah to understand something. Her mind was racing, trying to figure out what it might be.

Mrs. Spratt-Williams had seemed upset after Vivian Van Orner's death. She'd lost her closest—and only—friend. But Mrs. Van Orner's death meant she need no longer fear exposure and expulsion by the Charity Organization Society. It also meant she could take over Rahab's Daughters herself, giving her a higher position in the charitable community.

Sarah felt almost guilty thinking it, but Mrs. Spratt-Williams had good reason for being glad her friend was dead. Not only would she avoid exposure, but she would also benefit.

Yes, she would actually *benefit* from Mrs. Van Orner's death.

The realization must have shown on her face. Mrs. Spratt-Williams smiled. "You know the truth now, don't you?"

Sarah couldn't believe it. Mrs. Spratt-Williams was so much like her mother and all the other women she'd known growing up as the daughter of one of the oldest families in the city. How could a woman like that become a killer? "I'm afraid you've given me the impression that you had something to do with Mrs. Van Orner's death," she said carefully, trying not to show her growing alarm.

"I knew you would figure it out eventually. I just wanted to make sure I was with you when you did."

None of this was making any sense. "Why did you want me to figure it out at all?"

"I didn't, of course, but after what Amy said the other day, I knew it was just a matter of time until you did. I knew Amy wouldn't actually betray me. She was going to blackmail me instead. But you were a different matter. I couldn't have overcome your sense of duty."

"My duty to do what?"

"To report me to the COS."

"But I don't think what you did was wrong," Sarah said. "I have no intention of reporting you to anyone."

She sighed. "I wish I could believe that, but we'll never know now, will we?"

"What do you mean?"

"I mean you're going to die, just as Vivian did."

For some reason, Malloy's warning flashed through her mind. He'd told her not to eat or drink anything at the rescue house, for fear she might be poisoned. She looked down at the cup she held in horror.

"Don't worry, it will be painless," Mrs. Spratt-Williams said. "I'm afraid I'll have to keep you here for an hour or so, just to make sure it's too late for you to get help."

She rose from her seat and started toward Sarah, but Sarah held out the cup for her to see.

"I didn't drink it."

"What?" she asked stupidly, looking down at the nearly full cup.

"I didn't drink it. I only pretended, because it tasted so bad. I'm not going to die."

She blinked, momentarily at a loss. "But you *have* to drink it," she said. She snatched the cup from the saucer and thrust it at Sarah's mouth.

Instinctively, Sarah threw up her arm and sent the cup flying, the deadly liquid spilling out in an arc and falling harmlessly to the floor. The cup bounced silently onto the carpet.

Mrs. Spratt-Williams gave a strangled cry and lunged for Sarah. Sarah jumped to her feet and caught the older woman by the shoulders, shoving her away.

"What are you doing?" Sarah cried into the woman's angry face. She peered into her eyes, and that's when she realized that Mrs. Spratt-Williams was no longer in her right mind.

Her eyes blazed with an unnatural fury as she cast about for a weapon. She grabbed the teapot by the handle and flung it. Tea streamed from the spout, falling to the carpet with a dull thudding sound, but the pot flew harmlessly past as Sarah dodged. It smashed to the floor, at last making the kind of noise that would cause the servants to come running.

"Stop it!" Sarah screamed, but Mrs. Spratt-Williams was beyond reason.

Her wild eyes saw the fireplace tools, and she raced toward them with Sarah at her heels. She yanked the brass poker out of the stand, toppling it with a violent crash, and spun around to face her adversary. She raised the poker over her head, but Sarah rushed in and grabbed her hands where they clutched the handle.

Locked together, face to face, she could feel the other woman's hot breath on her face and see the madness shining in her eyes. Mrs. Spratt-Williams clenched her teeth in the silent, desperate standoff as each woman strained against the strength of the other. Some part of Sarah's mind registered pounding and raised voices, but she couldn't wait for help. She gathered her strength, and with a roar, she threw her weight against her adversary, sending them both crashing to the floor.

The poker went flying, and Mrs. Spratt-Williams cried out—in pain or anguish, Sarah could only guess. Tangled in the weight of her skirts, Sarah kicked her feet in a frantic effort to free them while Mrs. Spratt-Williams thrashed and bucked beneath her.

"Stop it!" Sarah cried again, but her adversary was past reason.

Sarah's hat had slid down, almost covering her eyes, and Mrs. Spratt-Williams grabbed for it, finding the hatpin and jerking it free before Sarah could guess her intent. Sarah caught her wrist as she thrust with it, stopping her just before the lethal tip plunged into her eye.

With a roar of fury, Sarah pulled her knees under her and slammed Mrs. Spratt-Williams's hand into the floor. In a frantic flurry, she captured her other wrist and held it down, pulling herself up so she was straddling her adversary, with both of her hands pinned to the floor. At that moment, the parlor door burst open, and Frank Malloy shouted her name.

Sarah looked over her shoulder, glaring at him under the cockeyed brim of her hat. "It's about time you got here."

"What in God's name is going on?" he thundered, scrambling over to where she was perched on top of Mrs. Spratt-Williams.

"She was trying to kill me."

Malloy glared down at the woman and all the fight drained out of her. Sarah felt her go limp except for her heaving chest as she struggled for air.

The maid had followed Malloy into the room, and now she was weeping hysterically at the sight of her mistress being manhandled.

"Help Mrs. Brandt up," he told her sharply, startling her into action.

She took Sarah's arm and helped her up. Sarah managed to catch her hat before it fell completely off. Malloy reached down and hauled Mrs. Spratt-Williams unceremoniously to her feet, holding on to her arm in case she tried to flee.

"Killing Mrs. Brandt won't help you," he nearly shouted, speaking right into her face as Sarah had seen him do to intimidate people. "I know everything you did and why, and so does Van Orner and Miss Yingling."

She cringed, wrapping her arms around herself as if for protection.

Malloy looked at Sarah. "Are you all right? Did you eat or drink anything?"

"No. I think she poisoned the tea, but I didn't drink it."

Mrs. Spratt-Williams straightened abruptly, lifting her

chin in a pathetic effort at outrage. "That's preposterous! How dare you accuse me of something like that!"

"Amy's dead," Malloy said.

Sarah gasped. "How on earth . . . ?"

"Mrs. Spratt-Williams gave her some medicine she said would help Amy's milk dry up faster," Malloy said. "She drank it this morning, and now she's dead."

"How can you possibly think I killed her?" Mrs. Spratt-Williams asked. "It was that woman, Mrs. Walker. She did it!"

"Mrs. Walker?" Sarah echoed, totally confused.

But Malloy apparently understood. He just stared at Mrs. Spratt-Williams for a long moment, considering her. Then he said, "How did you know that Amy was with Mrs. Walker when she died?"

She opened her mouth but no sound came out. Her eyes were terrible.

"Dear heaven," Sarah said, shaking her head. "You killed Mrs. Van Orner, who was your only friend in the world, and then you killed Amy, and you were going to kill me. Who was next? Miss Yingling? She knew about you, too."

"No one would have believed her over me. I would have said she was the one who changed the names. They'd never take the word of a prostitute over a respectable woman."

She was right, of course. "How were you going to explain my death, though?"

"I was going to wait until you started to get groggy, then turn you out into the street. I would tell them you had some sherry and weren't yourself. Bad things happen in the streets to women who are intoxicated."

Malloy released her arm as if he could no longer stand to touch her.

"Abigail, I'm feeling faint," Mrs. Spratt-Williams said to the maid. "Could you get me some salts?"

The maid, whose hysteria had turned to shock, nodded and fled the room.

Sarah took a breath, realizing she felt a little faint herself and sank down into a chair. For just a moment, Malloy glanced at her. In that one second of inattention, Mrs. Spratt-Williams grabbed up her skirts and ran from the room.

Malloy cursed and started after her, but she pulled the door shut behind her, costing him precious seconds. He threw the door open and bolted out after her, racing to the stairs and down, to catch her before she reached the front door.

Sarah was right behind him, and she happened to glance up as Malloy ran down and saw Mrs. Spratt-Williams's figure disappearing down the upstairs hall.

"She's gone upstairs!" she called to Malloy and ran after her.

Just as she reached the top of the stairs, she heard a door slam.

The maid came running up the stairs, clutching a vial of smelling salts in one hand.

"Which one is her room?" Sarah asked the girl as Malloy came bounding up the stairs behind them, taking them two at a time.

The maid pointed at one of the closed doors.

Sarah strode over and tried the handle, but it was locked. "Mrs. Spratt-Williams," she called through the door. "It's no use trying to hide."

"Get out of the way," Malloy gasped. "I'll kick it down."

"No!" the maid cried. "Please wait! I'll get the key!"

She scurried away, leaving Sarah and Malloy staring at the locked door.

"Are you sure you didn't eat or drink anything?" he asked again.

"I'm positive, except for a sip of the tea. It tasted awful, so I just pretended to drink it, figuring she'd never notice if my cup was still full when I left."

"I think she would've noticed."

"Actually, she was so insistent, I had to tell her. She got very upset. That's how we ended up on the floor."

Malloy ran a hand over his face. "How does this keep happening?"

"What?"

"Nothing." He turned to the door. "Mrs. Spratt-Williams, you need to open the door, or I'm going to have to kick it in."

At Sarah's surprise, he shrugged, "It frightened the maid. I thought it might scare her into opening it."

But it didn't, and they had to wait until the maid came running back with a large ring of keys. After some fumbling, she found the right one and handed the ring to Malloy. He unlocked the door and shoved it open.

Malloy went first, and Sarah followed, leaving the maid out in the hallway, wringing her hands. Mrs. Spratt-Williams lay on her chaise. She turned her head to look at them when they entered the room but made no other move.

"I'm going to have to take you down to Police Headquarters," he told her.

"That won't be necessary," she said, her voice flat and defeated. "By the time you get me there, I'll be dead."

Sarah pushed past Malloy and went to her. Three empty

bottles of laudanum sat on the table beside the chaise. "Did you drink all of this?"

"Yes, three times as much as I gave Vivian and Amy and . . . and you. I'll be asleep in a few more moments, I think."

"Call a doctor," Malloy shouted at the maid. She darted away.

"I'll probably be dead before he gets here," she said calmly. She looked up at Sarah. "I thought I wanted to live. I thought if Harold were dead, people would forget what he'd done and everything would be like it was before. He was the first, you know. I think he was glad to go, though. He was so miserable. But people didn't forget, and they didn't forgive. Even though I was completely innocent, they kept punishing me." Tears flooded her eyes, but Sarah couldn't feel sorry for her.

Malloy shook his head in wonder. "Did you really kill Mrs. Van Orner just because she was going to tell the COS you gave them false names?"

"I couldn't let her take away my last remaining purpose for living," she said. Her eyes were growing heavy, her speech slurred.

"And Amy was going to blackmail you," Sarah said, watching her eyes close. "And she was afraid I would figure out what she'd done and tell the COS myself," she added to Malloy.

Malloy stared down at the sleeping woman in dismay. "Shouldn't you do something for her?"

"Why? So she can spend the rest of her life in prison?"

"Yes," he said. "She killed three people, and she tried to kill you."

This last, Sarah realized, was the real source of his outrage. Touched, she laid a hand on his arm. "I couldn't save her, no matter what I did. She took too much."

Mrs. Spratt-Williams was unconscious now, her breath slow and labored. Soon it would stop altogether.

"Let's wait downstairs," she said.

They did.

15

When Sarah finally got home that night, she was summoned to a birth. When she returned from that, she had some business to take care of, so several days passed before she had an opportunity to find out how Malloy had fared with Mr. Van Orner. He finally found her at home on Friday evening. They'd just put Catherine to bed. Sarah assumed he'd waited until late to call because she wouldn't want the child to overhear them talking about the case.

She, Maeve, and Malloy had no more than gotten settled around the kitchen table than a knock at the back door told them Mrs. Ellsworth had noted Malloy's arrival.

"Please excuse the lateness of the hour," she said, breathless from her rush to get there. "I just thought I'd save Mrs. Brandt the trouble of having to tell me the whole story again tomorrow. Mr. Malloy, how very nice to see you. How is that darling little boy of yours?"

Sarah noticed that Malloy covered his mouth to hide a smile. She invited her neighbor in, hurrying to shut the door against the cold night air, and in a few minutes, everyone had been served some coffee and the cookies Mrs. Ellsworth had helped the girls bake that afternoon.

Malloy told them about Amy's kidnapping and death at Mrs. Walker's house, then Sarah told them about her visit to Mrs. Spratt-Williams's house.

"Good heavens," Mrs. Ellsworth said. "I can't believe a woman like that could just start killing people for no good reason."

"Oh, she thought her reasons were very good," Sarah said. "I think she probably convinced herself that her husband was better off dead since his reputation had been ruined."

"She was better off with him dead, too," Malloy said. "Or at least she thought she'd be."

"But people still remembered what he'd done," Maeve concluded. "People are like that."

"Yes, they are," Mrs. Ellsworth said. "But Mrs. Van Orner wasn't. She'd remained faithful to her old friend in spite of everything."

Sarah shook her head in dismay. "The trouble with friendships like that, where one person is indebted to the other, is that the person who is indebted gets very tired of being grateful."

"Especially if she didn't feel like she did anything wrong in the first place," Maeve said.

"And Mrs. Spratt-Williams didn't. She thought it was unfair for people to punish her for what her husband had done."

Maeve nodded. "And then she saw a chance to make it up to Amy for what her husband had done to her family, and Mrs. Van Orner wouldn't let her."

Mrs. Ellsworth sniffed. "I can't blame Mrs. Van Orner for not wanting to help her husband's mistress."

"But it was mean of her to punish Mrs. Spratt-Williams by reporting what she'd done with the names," Maeve argued.

"I have to agree with Maeve," Sarah said. "I think I would've sent them false names, too. I even told Mrs. Spratt-Williams I agreed with her, but I don't think she believed me."

"That's the part that doesn't make sense to me, Mrs. Brandt," Mrs. Ellsworth said. "I don't understand why she tried to poison you."

"I've been trying to remember exactly how the conversation went that day. I think she must have been testing me, trying to find out what I knew and what I remembered. She didn't pour the tea until she was satisfied that I knew enough to be a danger to her."

"How did she manage to get the poison into your cup, though?" Mrs. Ellsworth asked.

"I remember thinking it odd that she had three of everything on the tray—three cups, three saucers, three spoons. I think she must have told the maid to set the tray for three people so she'd have an extra cup. The cups were stacked, and apparently, she'd put the laudanum in the bottom cup. I think—and this is only my guess—that if I'd satisfied her that I didn't know anything about her fight with Mrs. Van Orner, she would have poured my tea into the middle cup and saved the poison for . . . for whatever else she needed."

"But you didn't," Malloy said, not at all happy. "You had to tell her the truth."

"I didn't know she was the killer," she protested.

"At least you didn't drink the poison," Maeve reminded her. "But why not?"

"Just luck or perhaps divine providence. All I know is that the tea tasted awful. I didn't want to hurt her feelings by saying I didn't like it, so I just pretended to drink."

"God forbid you should hurt her feelings," Malloy grumbled.

"She got off too easy," Maeve said.

"Do you think dying was too easy?" Sarah asked.

Maeve made a face. "She chose to die. The people she killed didn't have any choice."

"Maeve's right," Mrs. Ellsworth said. "I think going to prison would have been a far worse fate."

"She probably wouldn't have gone to prison," Malloy said.

The women stared at him in surprise.

"Oh, because of the pigeonholing," Maeve remembered.

"But she didn't have a lot of money," Sarah reminded him. "She couldn't have bribed anyone."

Malloy shrugged. "She probably could've paid a lawyer and managed her bail. That's all she would need to do, and she could live out her life in her own house."

Mrs. Ellsworth sighed. "How unjust."

"So she punished herself worse than the law would have," Maeve realized.

Malloy gave her an approving smile. "Yes, she did."

Mrs. Ellsworth was still brooding over the lack of justice in the world, or at least in New York. "What about Mr. Van Orner? Did he believe Miss Yingling wasn't the killer?"

"It took some doing, but when I told him how Mrs. Spratt-Williams had killed herself after confessing to Mrs. Brandt, he finally came around."

"What about Miss Yingling?" Sarah asked.

"What about her?"

"What's she going to do now?"

"I don't know for sure, but when I left, Van Orner was begging her forgiveness and asking her to stay and help him raise the boy."

"He's keeping Amy's baby?" Sarah asked, very glad to hear it.

"He believes the boy is his son, so why wouldn't he?"

"But how will he explain his existence?" Mrs. Ellsworth asked.

Malloy shrugged one shoulder. "Oh, I'm sure he'll come up with a good story. People have been explaining inconvenient babies in all kinds of ways since . . . well, I guess since there've been babies."

Mrs. Ellsworth leaned across the table. "Mrs. Brandt, I think you should pay a visit to the Van Orner house to make sure that child is being well taken care of."

Sarah grinned. "And I'll be sure to let you know what I find out when I do."

"Tell them the good news," Maeve urged her. "About the women at the rescue house."

"Is someone taking over Mrs. Van Orner's work?" Mrs. Ellsworth asked hopefully.

"No, I'm sorry to say, or at least not right away. When I visited them today, no one had been to see them, and they were getting desperate. I convinced them to let me take them to the Daughters of Hope."

"What's the Daughters of Hope?" Mrs. Ellsworth asked.

"That's the new name for the Prodigal Son Mission. It's much more appropriate, don't you think?"

"Yes, I do! And did they welcome your guests?"

"Of course they did. The two women . . . they were just girls, really . . . will fit right in with the other girls living there, and Miss Biafore has found a new position."

"At the Mission?" Malloy asked in surprise.

"Yes, Mrs. Keller was very happy at the prospect of having an assistant to help manage the place. We won't be able to give Miss Biafore a salary at first, but she was just grateful for a safe place to live for the time being. I think I can convince the ladies who support the Mission to take care of her, though."

"I'm sure you can," Mrs. Ellsworth said. "I'm so very glad you were able to find a place for those poor women."

They sat in silence for a few minutes, absorbing the impact one woman had had on so many. Then Maeve asked, "Mr. Malloy, are you still mad at Mrs. Brandt?"

Malloy stiffened at the question and gave Maeve a glare that only made her grin.

"Why would you be angry with Mrs. Brandt?" Mrs. Ellsworth asked.

"Because she almost got herself killed," Maeve said. "*Again.* So, are you?"

"Yes, are you?" Sarah asked when Malloy didn't answer.

He turned to her, and she saw warring emotions in his dark eyes. The fear he'd felt and the pride in her courage. "No," he said, "not if she promises never to get involved in another murder."

Mrs. Ellsworth grinned. "That should be easy enough to do."

Sarah smiled at Malloy, absurdly glad to have him sitting at her kitchen table. "Yes," she said, "that should be easy enough to do."

Author's Note

As I have for many of my stories in the Gaslight Mysteries, I got the idea for this story while doing research for an earlier book. I found an interesting passage in a reference book about the New York Charity Organization Society (COS). They really did exist, and they built the United Charities Building to provide offices for the many charitable organizations that were created during this time of rising social consciousness. Mrs. Josephine Shaw Lowell, formerly a commissioner for the State Board of Charities, founded the COS in an effort to bring order and efficiency to the various charities because she found many of them to be "wasteful" and "encouraging pauperism and imposture." The quotes I attributed to her in the book are really hers and reflect an attitude toward charity that seems oddly uncharitable to us today. I couldn't resist incorporating these views into my story, even if I'm relatively certain they never motivated a murder in real life.

Please let me know if you enjoyed this book. I'd like to add you to my mailing list so I can let you know when the next book in the Gaslight Mysteries is released. You can reach me—and find out more about me and the series—on my website: www.victoriathompson.com.

MURDER ON FIFTH AVENUE

❋ *A Gaslight Mystery* ❋

Sarah Brandt's family is one of the oldest in New York City, and her father, Felix Decker, takes his position in society very seriously. He still refuses to resign himself to his daughter being involved with an Irish Catholic police detective. But when a member of his private club—the very exclusive Knickerbocker—is murdered, Decker forms an uneasy alliance with Detective Sergeant Frank Malloy to solve the crime as discreetly as possible. The stakes are higher than ever, because solving this crime could bring not only closure to the case, but Malloy the approval he seeks . . .

MURDER ON LEXINGTON AVENUE

✳ *A Gaslight Mystery* ✳

When an influential man in the deaf community is murdered, Detective Sergeant Frank Malloy is assigned the case, presumably because his own son attends the New York Institution for the Deaf and Dumb. Malloy suspects the murderer may be affiliated with his son's school—and reluctantly turns to midwife Sarah Brandt for assistance.

Finding herself in an unfamiliar world, Sarah must determine who is right and who is innocent before she and Malloy can ever hope to find the killer.

The Gaslight Mysteries are...

"Tantalizing."

—Catherine Coulter, #1 *New York Times* bestselling author

"Intriguing."

—Kate Kingsbury, author of *Decked with Folly*

penguin.com

From national bestselling author

VICTORIA THOMPSON

THE GASLIGHT MYSTERIES

*As a midwife in turn-of-the-century New York,
Sarah Brandt has seen pain and joy. Now she will work for
something more—a search for justice—in cases of murder
and mystery that only she can put to rest.*

MURDER ON ASTOR PLACE
MURDER ON ST. MARK'S PLACE
MURDER ON GRAMERCY PARK
MURDER ON WASHINGTON SQUARE
MURDER ON MULBERRY BEND
MURDER ON MARBLE ROW
MURDER ON LENOX HILL
MURDER IN LITTLE ITALY
MURDER IN CHINATOWN
MURDER ON BANK STREET
MURDER ON WAVERLY PLACE
MURDER ON LEXINGTON AVENUE
MURDER ON SISTERS' ROW

"Tantalizing."
—Catherine Coulter